IN A TRAITOR'S HANDS

❖

Annandale looked up from the low pile of blankets on which Abelard lay. In the weeks of captivity since their arrival, there had been no change in his condition. The King's eyes were closed, as usual, his breathing was shallow. The skin sagged from his cheekbones, and beneath the ragged garments he wore, his body was little more than bones and sinew covered with a leathery husk. She could feel his mind, however, and the never-ending torment in which he existed as his body and the last vestiges of his will fought Amanander's enchantment, and she did what she could to ease the misery. But her attempts were futile; nothing short of her own death could wrest Abelard from Amanander's control, and she knew that even were she to make such a sacrifice, the King would only die.

A wave of loathing swept over her, nausea so acute she felt as though she might vomit. *Hold fast, daughter.* The voice whispered through her mind, like a scent of roses in the midst of offal. She closed her eyes, concentrating on the voice. Hold fast? she wondered. For how long?

* * *

"ENGAGING AND POWERFUL."
—VOYA

ALSO BY ANNE KELLEHER BUSH

Daughter of Prophecy

Children of Enchantment

PUBLISHED BY
WARNER BOOKS

ANNE KELLEHER BUSH

THE MISBEGOTTEN *KING*

A Time Warner Company

WARNER BOOKS EDITION

Aspect® is a registered trademark of Warner Books, Inc.

Cover design by Don Puckey
Cover illustration by Thomas Canty

Warner Books, Inc.
1271 Avenue of the Americas
New York, NY 10020

Visit our Web site at
http://pathfinder.com/twep

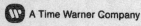 A Time Warner Company

Printed in the United States of America

First Printing: January, 1997

10 9 8 7 6 5 4 3 2 1

For Juilene Osborne-McKnight,
Christine Whittemore Papa and
Lorraine Stanton with love.
Some things can't be said with words.

Acknowledgements

Once again, special thanks are due to special people—Beal, Ms. Daae, Emerald Angel, Happy Angel, Shadowheart, Jemimah, Jackdotcalm, Skiperino, Vixen, Esua, Synkie, Isolde, Leaslyric, Dragonspawn, Precious too, Wildfire Di, and Picmaker—you all know who you are. Also, my long-suffering children, Katie, Jamie, Meg, and Libby, who have learned not to mind quite so much, Kathy Tomaszewski, who kept me on track, Don Maass and Betsy Mitchell for patience beyond belief, and finally, to Donny, who worked a bit of real magic on New Year's Eve.

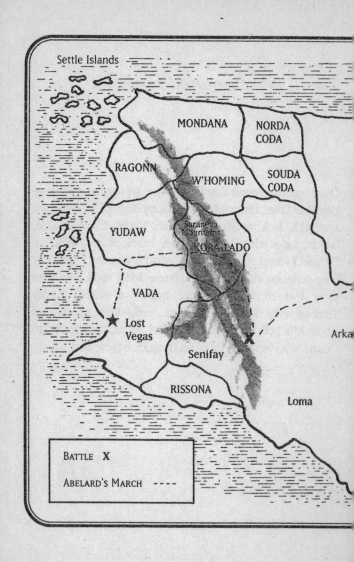

Settle Islands

MONDANA

NORDA CODA

RAGONN

W'HOMING

SOUDA CODA

YUDAW

Saraneva Mountains

KORA-LADO

VADA

★ Lost Vegas

Arka

Senifay

Loma

RISSONA

BATTLE **X**

ABELARD'S MARCH   - - - -

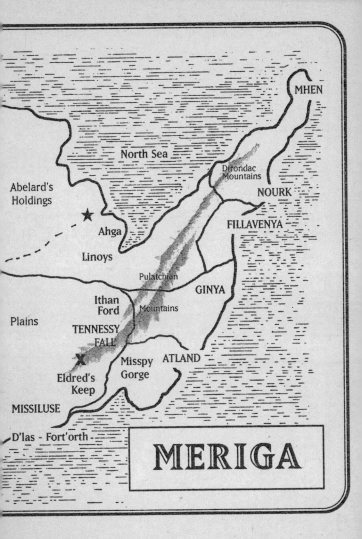

Prologue

The warriors of my people believe that words are only sounds which fall and fade into empty air, the weapons of the weak. I thought so, too, once. But I am old now, and I know better. For warriors die, in battle or in their beds, and only in the tales the Keepers tell do their deeds survive.

When I was young, my days were taken up with sword and bow, with lance and battle-ax and quarter-stave-weapons I wielded better than most boys. And for the other girls—the soft ones who spent their days learning to spin and sew, to cook and weave—and for the men and women we call the Keepers, those with wordskill, I had only scorn.

Did I know then, wild and unschooled child that I was, that in language there is more power than in all the weapons of men combined? Who could have convinced me, Deirdre M'Callaster, rebellious daughter of the Chief of all the Chiefs of the Settle Islands? I cared more for my father's title than any story men might tell of me.

It wasn't until *he* came to me, months after she had died—the woman who was his wife, the woman who should have been his Queen—that I began to understand.

He came, proud King of a prouder line than mine, and on his knees, his eyes empty of everything but grief, to me he poured out his pain. What choice did I have but to listen? I, too, had sworn to uphold the kingdom and the King unto death, and there was about his mouth the drawn, pinched look I have seen on the faces of the dying.

I tightened my fists and forced my face smooth, and I listened while the man I loved gave me the story of his passion for a woman as different from myself as sword from sheath. He had come to fulfill the bargain we had made between us, for he was a man of honor who always kept his word.

He had come to father me a son, but he could not—not in those long grief-haunted nights, when the only fire which burned between us was the one within the grate, the only wine which flowed were the flagons he drained one after another, until I thought my cellars would be emptied. And certainly not in those gray, rain-shrouded days, when he lay upon my bed, fully dressed, and slept, clutching my pillow to his chest like a little boy.

It was a full two weeks or more when the torrent of words finally ceased. He looked at me across the hearth, and for the first time, he seemed to remember who I was and why he was there. "I've talked all this time," he said.

I nodded, saying nothing. How could I answer the loss of a love so true, so deep?

"I'm sorry, Deirdre." He shook his head like a man waking suddenly from sleep. "I didn't mean to talk so much—I don't know what came over me."

I held up my hand. "The Tell is a sacred thing among my people, not given lightly. It is never refused."

"The Tell?" he frowned.

"Among my people, after someone dies, and one feels the need, it is the custom to go to one of those with word-skill, those we call the Keepers, and tell the story of that person's life. We call it the Tell. It is a sacred thing, for it is three times blessed—it honors the one who hears it, and the one who speaks it, as well as the one who died."

"You listened to all this—because you had to?"

"No." I glanced into the flames. "I am only a warrior, you know that. I was not trained to listen and remember. But when you came to me, you began to talk, and I could not refuse you."

He rocked back, drawing his knees up to his chin, and wrapped his arms around his legs. He rested his chin on his knees, and he looked no more than a child of ten or twelve. "You've never refused me anything, have you?"

In the firelight his eyes were darker than the ashes beneath the grate, and very steady, and I had to swallow hard in order to answer. "You are my King. As you reminded me once, there is an oath which binds us."

"An oath," he repeated. "And a bargain." He reached for me then, across the space that separated us, and this time, when he wrapped his arms around me and drew me close, there was nothing of the child in his touch.

Chapter One

⟨a·̣⟩

*Prill, 77th Year in the Reign of the Ridenau Kings
2749 Muten Old Calendar*

*I*t was the blood which Deirdre noticed first, the dark, liver-colored streaks which had dribbled down the face of the granite rock by the roadside and congealed in a muddy ditch into a thick, fly-speckled mess. The sight of it wrested her out of her mental rehearsal of the leave-taking speech she was planning to give her companions as soon as she found an opportune moment.

The warm, damp wind rustled the heap of rags lying on top of the rock, and all her instincts, honed by six years of ruling the most contentious men in Meriga, told her there was a body under the tattered fabric.

She reined her horse back and motioned to the tall man on her left who wore the insignia of the King's Guard on his olive drab tunic. "We'd better halt, Captain. I think there's a body on that rock."

Clearly startled, Brand raised his hand at once, and further down the line the sergeant of the company bellowed the order. Deirdre swung out of the saddle and handed her reins over to the bewildered standard bearer. "Careful with him, boy. He catches the smell of blood, he's likely to get skittish."

She ignored the standard bearer's nervous reply. Her

boots clicked across the smooth paved surface of the ancient highway, and the breeze lifted the few wisps of red-brown hair which had escaped the heavy coils of her braids. She adjusted her sword belt, and automatically felt for her dagger. The damp wind shifted, and over the hurrying clatter of Brand's following footfalls, she heard the horses whinny nervously as they caught the carrion stench.

"Wait, M'Callaster," Brand called, just as she touched the tip of one boot to the first rock.

She ignored him, too. Although Brand, unlike some of the men who served Prince Roderic, never forgot to address her correctly, he still had a tendency to behave like an old woman when it came to letting her go first into any situation he perceived as dangerous. As did Roderic, for that matter. She shoved the thought of Roderic aside. When he had left for Ahga, to await the birth of his hoped-for heir, she had told herself she would not dwell on his absence.

She tried instead to concentrate on the matter at hand: the campaign against the rebellious younger sons of the old Senador of Atland. Instead of returning with her men to the Settle Islands after the successful siege of Minnis Saul last summer, Deirdre had agreed to stay and aid Prince Roderic's struggle to guarantee the inheritance of Atland's oldest son and heir, Kye. So here she was on this muddy highway, which looped over the Pulatchian Mountains like a ragged ribbon, accompanied by Brand and a contingent of the Prince's Army, intent on rendezvousing with Kye by sunset at a garrison town still many miles away. But it seemed that no matter how hard

Deirdre tried to concentrate on plans to bring the rebellion to a speedy and successful conclusion, thoughts of Roderic had an annoying way of intruding when she least expected them.

She bit down on her lip as she reached for the pile of rags, searching with a gloved hand. It was a body all right. She tugged, and the thing slipped off the top of the rock, tumbling and sliding, to lie face-up like a rag doll, staring blindly at the lowering sky. She shoved a balled fist into her mouth and looked away. Despite the mutilations, the third eye, centered in the forehead above and between what remained of the other two, and the terracotta-colored skin made it clear that the creature had been a Muten.

Beside her, Brand stifled a gagging noise. "By the One," he managed at last. "What kind of monster did this?"

"It's—it was a Muten," she said. "Get Vere."

"Boy—" Brand spoke to the standard bearer, who was vainly trying to control both his own animal and Deirdre's, "call for Lord Vere. At once."

There was an immediate stir through the ranks as the boy slipped out of his saddle and ran down the column of men. Deirdre stared at the ruin at her feet. Something—someone—had seared the eyes from the Muten's head, wielding a pointed iron so deeply that the rubbery, grayish white matter of the brain lay revealed under the blackened flesh. Its mouth hung open, the jaw wrenched apart, and the remains of the tongue protruded from the jellied mass of clotting blood. The arms ended in bloodied stumps about three inches beneath the elbows. "Mother goddess," she muttered. No matter what anyone might think of the Mutens, who swarmed like vermin through the hills and hollows of the Pulatchian Mountains, none of them deserved to die like this.

She glanced up to see Vere striding forward, his long, green cloak billowing around his knees. She still did not quite understand Vere's role. She knew he was the second of all the missing King's illegitimate children, born to some Mayher's daughter from a village near Ahga when Abelard was no more than fifteen or sixteen. She knew that Vere had run away from Ahga years before, in his own youth, long before Abelard had married Roderic's mother. She knew that he had returned to the court last summer, and that it was common knowledge that he had lived among the Mutens. It was also common knowledge that Roderic relied upon Vere in his dealings with the Mutens. Once again, Roderic's face flashed before her, the familiar shock of fawn brown hair falling across his brow, lean cheeks and squared jaw rough with the faintest haze of beard. With a curse, she forced herself to think only of the situation at hand.

Without a word, Vere dropped to his knees, his cheeks pale behind the swirling tattoos—Muten markings—which were visible above his gray beard. Beads of sweat laced his forehead, despite the damp breeze. His hand rested briefly on the matted locks of blood-clotted hair, then he heaved a heavy sigh and rose to his feet. "Any others?"

"There's another one there—" Brand nodded at a body lying in a misshapen heap near another rock and pointed to another still, ragged form lying a little distance away. "At least one more there. You think the Pulatchian Highlanders did this?" He gripped his swordbelt with both hands and looked around, scanning the forest on either side of the road, his dark brows knit. Droplets of water off the trees gleamed silver in his steel-streaked hair. At forty-nine, Brand, the eldest of all of Abelard's children, was the Captain of the King's Guard, the commander of the elite corps of troops who were charged with the protection of the King's person, as well as the second-in-command of the Armies of the King. No other man in Meriga, save Roderic himself, wielded so much power, and Brand's loyalty to his father and his half-brother was absolute.

The men who dwelled in the Pulatchian Mountains and called themselves Highlanders hated the Muten Tribes and fought endless squabbles with them over the scarce patches of arable land in the mountains. If anyone was responsible for this breach of the peace, surely it was one of their factions. The thought that anyone could conceive of such a horrible killing made Deirdre, hardened as she was to the sights of battle, nauseated.

She glanced from one brother to the other and flung her brown-and-red battle-plaid over her shoulder impatiently. "We haven't the time to worry about who's responsible for this if we're to rendezvous with Atland's son at dusk. Leave a detail to bury these poor wretches."

Vere dragged the toe of a worn boot through the mud. "I'll stay. There're things which ought to be said over them. I'll see to that, then catch up."

Brand nodded and Deirdre shrugged. The first drops of rain stung her cheek. The warm wind blew harder, through the tangled mass of long gray locks on Vere's shoulder. As Brand turned on his heel, motioning for the sergeant, Vere tapped his brother on the shoulder. "I don't know why this happened, but I can tell you it wasn't the Highlanders who did this."

Brand frowned. "Why are you so certain?"

"What was done here was a parody—a travesty—of a secret ritual. This was done by other Mutens."

"You're sure?" Brand shot back. "If the Highlanders have violated the treaty, Roderic needs to know immediately."

Vere only nodded, hanging his head as though in shame. As Deirdre swung back into her saddle, she saw him admonish the soldiers to treat the body gently. Poor misfit Prince, she thought, not quite one of them, not quite one of us. Like me, she thought, not one of the men, not one of the women. Not that it made any difference now. She had fought and won her title six years ago, when she was barely twenty-two, and no man dared challenge her right to rule her father's estate, or to ride to war with the lords of the kingdom.

She flapped her reins and the horse trotted off down the road, eager to be away from the stench. "Why would anyone do something like that?" she asked Brand as he rode up.

"Who knows why the Mutens do anything? Just as long as it doesn't complicate things for us. This situation is bad enough already." His mouth was set and grim.

There wasn't much to smile about, thought Deirdre as the road dipped down into a slight valley, and the light rain spattered the black surface. Two and a half years ago, Abelard Ridenau had disappeared on a journey across the Arkan Plains. At the time, Roderic had been in the middle of his first command, the first Muten rebellion in more than ten years. Repeated searches across Arkan and Loma had proved fruitless. Abelard had simply vanished, leaving his eighteen-year-old heir to deal as best he could with a country smoldering under an uneasy peace.

Although Amanander, Roderic's traitor brother, had lain since the previous summer an unconscious prisoner in Ahga, there had been rumors that he showed signs of waking from his unnatural sleep, and Deirdre suspected it wasn't Roderic's concern for his wife and the impending birth alone that had prompted him to return to his capital more than a month ago. At least, she preferred to think it wasn't.

If that child were a son, thought Deirdre as she tightened her grip on the reins, Roderic would be released from his vow of fidelity to his wife and free to fulfill the bargain they had made between them—that in exchange for ten thousand of her men to be used in his struggle against Amanander to secure the throne of Meriga, he would attempt to give her a child. The Chiefs of the Settle Islands were so contentious Deirdre knew that only with the support of the throne would her son succeed her in relative peace.

Amanander lay helpless as a newborn in Ahga, no longer a threat, and while Roderic might always need extra troops, her side of the bargain had been fulfilled with the fall of the fortress of Minnis Saul last summer. She knew she couldn't expect Roderic to father a child when his attention was so taken up with the worst uprising in nearly twenty years, and she had decided it was better for all concerned if she went back to her own country to await him.

When they reached Grenvill garrison, she would leave her troops under the command of her second, Grefith. And between Brand and Vere and Atland's heir, Kye, who remained loyal to the Ridenau cause, and who would all continue to fight for peace in the South, Roderic had no need of her. She had fallen back into a half drowse when a shout went up from the troops riding just ahead. Brand half rose in his stirrups. "What is it?" he called, his voice terse and weary.

"Soldiers, Captain. Coming this way."

"Can you see their colors?" Deirdre craned her neck. The approaching horses were lathered, and they stumbled over the even roadway with the shambling gait of exhaustion.

"See there—" The scout pointed a long arm. "That blue, that green? That's Atland's colors—reversed. His heir comes to meet us."

Deirdre and Brand exchanged frowns. Brand held up his hand, and the company slowed to a halt. As the riders came closer, Deirdre saw that the men's uniforms were stained with mud, torn and filthy, and all of them bore bloody bandages. The leader, his head wrapped in a piece of linen so dirty it hardly qualified as a bandage, reined his horse just a few paces from where they had halted.

"Captain Brand?" His shoulders slumped in obvious relief, his mouth drooping. "Thank the One we met you. Grenvill garrison is no more."

* * *

In the light of the fitful fire, Deirdre watched the exhausted men accept bowls of stew from the hands of the cooks, dipping into them as though it were the first warm food they'd tasted in days. Which, she realized as she listened to their sorry tale, was exactly what it was.

Kye, the eldest son of the ancient Senador of Atland, held out his goblet as she lifted up the wineskin. "My thanks," he muttered, not quite looking at her. She was used to that reaction, although her lips twitched as she hid a smile.

She took a place next to Brand. Kye was not as tall as he had appeared in the saddle, for his torso was disproportionately longer than his legs, and his arms and legs were thin, while his chest looked as though it belonged to a man who did hard labor for a living. But though his body appeared to be constructed from spare parts, there was a weary spark of intelligence in his light brown eyes. The gash across his forehead was deep, and more than once he cradled his head in one hand, eyes shut.

Brand stared at a hide map, motioning his serving boy to hold the lamp first one way, then another. He wore a deep frown.

Deirdre looked down at the map, at the black double lines which marked the roads, the circles which marked the hills, and the truth leapt at her like an arrow. "Betrayed," she muttered. The ugly word dangled in the silence like a spider from a thread. She flung her thick braid over her shoulder and shifted on the low camp stool which was all that kept her out of the mud. She gave a soft snort and toyed with a loose thread in the sleeve of her tunic, meeting the stricken looks of the men with contempt. "Don't tell me the thought hadn't occurred to anyone else."

The men exchanged furtive glances, bulky shoulders shifting under heavy cloaks, for the wind whistled in the trees, and the night was cold. Spring in the Pulatchian Mountains was a long time coming.

Finally Kye raised his head and looked her in the eye for the first time since their meeting. "I can't believe that."

Brand said nothing, but the expression on his face did not change. Deirdre lowered her head and wondered why she wasted her time with these mainlanders, who refused to see treachery when it yanked them by the hair and stared them in the eyes. Then a vision of Roderic flashed before her, his gray-green gaze steady in the face of even the most calculated of risks. She swallowed hard and forced herself to speak calmly. "Do you think it was luck? Good fortune? How else could your brothers have known about our rendezvous at Grenvill garrison?" Impatiently, she shoved the map toward Kye, and the serving boy jumped. His lantern cast weird dancing shadows on the flimsy walls of the tent.

"They have scouts, as well—" Kye began, but stopped when he realized the route Deirdre traced.

She spread her hands flat on her knees, large hands, knuckles red and knotted, skin chapped and calloused as a man's, and stretched her long legs out to the side. "There's a traitor in your midst."

"You're saying one of my men—?" Kye threw back his cloak, pushing it away to reveal the hilt of the dagger.

Deirdre recognized the challenge and shook her head

in disgust. "No, lord, I am not. But someone—somewhere, between here and Atland garrison—gave the enemy your precise route. It was more than luck that put the equivalent of two armies between your men and ours." She raised her chin and met Brand's steady eyes. "What say you, Captain Brand?"

Brand nodded slowly. "I agree with you, M'Callaster. There is a traitor. But I'm afraid we have neither the time nor the resources to worry who he is. We have to plan what our next move will be. We can't afford to wait until Roderic returns."

"And when will that be?" Kye asked, a bitter twist on his mouth.

"As soon as his child is born," Brand answered. The shadows flickered across his face as the serving boy dipped the lamp. "Careful, boy." He looked up into the boy's exhausted face and shook his head. "Get to bed, boy. And you, Kye—we'll have time to talk of this in the morning. You look as if you'll fall asleep where you sit."

With a grunt, Kye got to his feet. "In the morning, then. I need to check on my wounded."

Deirdre nodded, and Brand set the lantern down in the middle of the low table. He picked up the flask of mead at his feet. "More?"

She nodded slowly, wetting her lips. This was as good an opportunity as she was likely to have, and it was better that Brand knew her intentions, before they met tomorrow. "I wanted to tell you, Captain," she began, her words tumbling out in a rush, "that I will be leaving within the next two weeks to return to my estate. I don't intend to withdraw my men. I will take only a squadron for an escort. The rest I will leave with you, under the command of my second, Grefith. I know he'll serve the Prince's cause as loyally as I."

"You're leaving?" He jolted upright and slammed the empty flask down. The cork flew out and landed in the fire, sending up a shower of sparks. "Why?"

The smoke stung her nostrils. "I have affairs of my own to tend, Captain. Not only Amanander lies sick in Ahga—Alexander is sick, as well. And without Alexander, there's no strong hand to balance the opposing interests in the North. I'm not there to unify the Chiefs. And while the lords of Mondana were certainly no threat when I left, there is no doubt in my mind that they will harry my people soon enough." She broke off, drawing her cloak closer across her shoulders as the damp air blew beneath the tent. "The winter's over—I can cross the Saranevas at the Koralado Pass. There's no need for me to stay."

She fixed her gaze on the fire and refused to look up. She heard the clatter as Brand's goblet fell on its side. "M'Callaster—Deirdre, surely you understand we need you. I need you. There's no one better at keeping hotheads cool, and keeping them off each other's throats. Roderic himself relies upon you, upon your judgment. What will I tell him?"

"The truth, as I shall," she lied, feeling a hot blush sweep up her cheeks.

He spread his hands and for a moment she felt sorry for him. Strong men always looked so helpless when at a loss. "M'Callaster, the spring campaign is barely underway—surely you could spare a month—two months?

You could reach the Saranevas long before next winter will close the pass—"

With a heavy sigh, Deirdre shifted once more and poured the dregs of the mead into her goblet. Her head ached, and not for the first time she wished that Roderic had not returned to Ahga. She thought with sudden longing of her lands in the Settle Islands, where the wild sea birds swooped over the craggy cliffs, where the sea pounded against the rocky shores and washed over the white beaches. "Captain, try to understand my position. According to the latest dispatches, it may be months before Alexander is recovered enough to return to his command of the garrison at Spogan. Without Alexander's presence—" Her explanation was cut off in midsentence as shouts broke the exhausted stillness of the camp.

With a curse, Brand was on his feet, sword already drawn. He was just about to grab the tent flap when it opened, bringing a gust of wind and Vere into the tent.

"Send for Roderic immediately," Vere said without greeting.

"Why?" asked Brand.

Vere acknowledged Deirdre's presence with a glance and a nod. "One of the Mutens back there on the road—he wasn't dead. He lived long enough to tell me that gravest danger is upon us."

"Us? Why? You said the Mutens did this—"

"Listen to me, man." Vere gripped Brand's sword arm and stared his eldest brother in the eye, his jutting hawk nose so similar to Brand's, they looked like twins in profile. "They had no mindskill—I haven't time to explain what that means. But you know that only the ruling families have the use of the secondary arms?" He paused just long enough for Brand to nod. "Before the last poor wretch died, he lived long enough to write one word." Vere fumbled in the pack at his waist and held out a crumpled piece of parchment. Together, Brand and Deirdre squinted over it in the dim light. Shaky black lines formed one word: FERAD.

Brand looked away with a curse. "We've got more important problems than the murder of a passel of Mutens, Vere. Kye's army was intercepted—Grenvill garrison destroyed. Deirdre informed me just before you came in that she's planning to leave—"

"Leave?" Vere frowned. He looked at her closely, and Deirdre felt the urge to squirm as those piercing eyes fell upon her. "Leave now? Why?"

"I can get over the Saranevas." She raised her chin, refusing to be intimidated by the probing gaze of the Ridenau sons. "I have concerns of my own, you know."

Brand swore beneath his breath. "I'll send a messenger out tonight, Vere. You add anything you wish." He glanced at Deirdre, disgust plain on his face. "And you, M'Callaster. If you've a message of your own for the Prince, I advise you to write it. But I can't believe you'd do this."

He strode out of the tent.

Deirdre glanced at Vere, who looked at her quizzically. "Why can't he believe I'd leave?"

"Because you haven't told him the truth."

Deirdre jerked around. "How do you know what I told him?"

Vere shrugged. "You gave him some story about the state of the Settle Islands. But I don't believe that's the real reason you want to go."

Deirdre tightened her jaw. "Then—"

"Let me tell you a story." Vere sat down before the fire and stretched out his hands over its heat. "Is there any food? I haven't eaten since dawn."

She rummaged through her pack and held out a piece of dried salted beef and a package of leathery dried apples.

He turned the food over in his hands, staring into the flames. "Many years ago, when I was young and lived in Ahga, I loved a woman." He tore at the beef and raised his eyes to hers as he chewed and swallowed.

A chill ran up her spine, for his words rang with the same authority as the tales of the Keepers of her people. What did Vere see with those shadowed eyes?

"She was the most beautiful woman I have ever seen," he continued, "and I am not the only one who thought so. Every man who saw her wanted her—every man who'd ever seen her would remember her. But she was more than beautiful—she was kind, and she knew more about Old Meriga than anyone I had ever met before. She talked to me as though what mattered to me mattered to her, too. No one else ever treated me like that. No one else so truly understood."

"What happened?" But Deirdre thought she could surmise the answer. This was a familiar story, after all.

"I was a boy—fifteen years old. She was a woman: ten, twelve years my senior, or more. And she belonged to my father, to the King. Everyone knew it, even though when I was there, she did not share his bed. So I ran away because I could not bear to see them together. But her image is burned into my memory—I have carried it with me wherever I've gone, all these years, and I only need shut my eyes to see her again."

Deirdre picked up a long stick, reached into the heart of the flames, and poked at the burning logs. The wood split with a hiss and a loud crack; the better, she thought, to cover the voice of such naked need. "Why are you telling me this?"

"Because the woman I loved was Nydia—the monster who saved us all from Amanander and his Magic last summer."

"The witch?" Deirdre whispered. The stick fell out of her hands into the fire.

"Yes." Vere looked back into the flames, his voice shaking with some suppressed emotion. "My father, Abelard, forced her to use the Magic for him—so that his Queen would conceive his son, Roderic. In consequence, Nydia became that horror. And from that day to this, I have wondered what my part in it was . . ."

"What makes you think you had a part?"

"Don't you understand, Deirdre? We are all part of the pattern. All our actions impact upon the whole. If you leave here, because you love Roderic—" He held up his hand as she opened her mouth to protest, and the words died on her tongue. "If you desert him, now, at the hour of his need, because that love imposes too high a price, is that love at all?"

Deirdre glanced down. Her worn, battle-scarred boots clung to the muscles of her thighs, hardened from long days spent on battlefields and in the saddle. The tunic she wore was patched and mended, as were the trousers beneath. Her knotted hands reminded her of other scars which marred the smooth muscles of her arms and legs, and the red, puckered line which was all that remained of her left breast. She was nothing like the woman Roderic loved.

And yet he had agreed to the terms she had offered him, to father her a son in exchange for her men, even though he had seen her naked body one rain-soaked night in the course of those agonizing negotiations made necessary by Amanander's mischief. Roderic's nobility clung like a second skin; he could no more pretend not to be a Prince than she could pretend to be the soft, delicate woman who was his wife. But even then, she had wanted him. Even then.

Deirdre raised her face to Vere and saw genuine sympathy in the deep lines of his weathered face, the look in his gentle eyes. "And if I stay?"

"I won't lie. If you stay, it will be hard. But look at what Roderic faces: Atland's sons and Missiluse in full rebellion, the lesser lords throughout the South likely to rise to their support. The Harleyriders will surely see this as an opportunity to advance into the central plains. And now—" Vere patted the pouch where he had slipped the crumpled parchment, "—now, there is clear evidence that Ferad himself has surfaced. He's finally made the move we've been waiting for. And he did not do it without much preparation—I promise you, right now, he holds all the cards. You know what the Magic can do. Brand scoffs, but he wasn't at Minnis last summer when

Nydia brought the siege to an end. You've seen the Magic work. Nydia's dead. Now there's no one who can use the Magic for Roderic. He needs every friend. Please, don't make a mistake you might have your whole life to regret."

Deirdre took a deep breath and got to her feet. "All right. I'll stay. But only until J'ly. I must be over the Saranevas by the first snow. Whatever I am, or am not, to Roderic, I am the M'Callaster to my people."

She pulled her plaid close, threw the end over her shoulder, and knew he watched her as she stalked away into the dark night.

Chapter Two

❧

The gray afternoon had faded completely into a dull twilight, and Roderic sighed surreptitiously, wondering whether to interrupt the First Lord of the Arkan Plains and call for someone to light the candles, or to wait for the inevitable summons to dinner to end Gredahl's long monologue. Roderic fidgeted in the hard seat, torn by the demands of cramped limbs and those of the Senator whose tired voice held him as much a prisoner as the rigid wooden back of the chair.

He glanced past Gredahl's hulking shape to the window, where the fog obscured everything but a glimpse of the winking torches in the guardhouses on the crushed rubble walls of Ahga. The rain pelted down the glass with grim monotony, wearying as Gredahl's voice. He wondered how his father had managed to control his restlessness, remembering all the hours Abelard had spent listening patiently to the ceaseless demands, petitions, and complaints of the Senators who comprised the Congress, as well as those of the lesser lords of the various holdings of the Ridenau estates, the merchants, the traders, and the farmers who made up most of the population of Meriga. No voice was ever denied the King's ear, no petitioner a chance of the King's justice.

He drew a deep breath, realizing abruptly that Gredahl had finished speaking and was looking at him curiously, waiting for a response. "Lord Prince?"

He shifted once more in the chair, stifled another sigh, and thought quickly of how to answer Gredahl, who had been his father's ally for more years than Roderic had been alive. "I understand your concerns about the Harleyriders—"

"Concerns? You call these concerns? More than a hundred men and women died last month on my border—an entire harvest was destroyed or taken. I do all I can, but by the One, Lord Prince, who are we to look to?"

"Lord Senador," Roderic began again, weighing each word, "in all honesty, I have not the men right now to increase the garrisons in Arkan—even the garrison at Dlas has been dangerously depleted. All I can assure you is that the troops at Ithan are alerted and ready."

He was glad he could not see Gredahl's face clearly in the gloom. The Senador's huge shoulders heaved like an earthshake, the long gray curls spilling over his furs like a flood tide. "You know what you condemn my people to, boy?"

Roderic fought the impulse to hang his head. The two years of his regency had taught him more about men and leadership than he had ever thought possible to learn. He spread his hands flat on the tabletop of smooth glass which protected the ancient maps flattened beneath it. "Lord Senador—" He stopped, wet his lips and began again. "I understand your fear. And while I don't discount what you say, I can assure you that the scouts report no more activity south of Loma than is usual in the spring, when the Harleys leave their winter camps." He drew a slow line down one ancient border. What he said was the truth. It might not be sufficient to allay the fears of the Arkan lords, who had lived with the threat of the Harleys for generations, but it was the truth. So far, there was no evidence at all that the Harleys planned to take advantage of the dangerously chaotic situation to the east.

"You listen to me, boy." The old Senador leaned forward over the table with a snort. "The last time your father's attention was diverted by a rebellion among the lords, the Harleys rose and ran all over the central Plains. It took years to push them out of Arkan, and more men than I care to remember died. The rivers ran red with their blood. It took more men than I can count to get the Kahn and his Riders out of Missiluse when that fool Eldred let them in. I'm old enough to be your grandfather, boy, and I've seen more battles than you've heard tell of. And I'm warning you that the whole country is on the brink of disaster. And what about your father, boy? Have you forgotten him?"

"No, my lord," Roderic answered quietly. "I have not. Why do you think I'm so sure of what I know about the Harleys? More men than I can count have combed Loma and Arkan for the last two years in search of my father." He saw the old Senador's eyes gleam. What little light there was reflected off the glass under his hands, and beneath it, the faded outlines of estates long vanished into history peered up at him, taunting him like silent accusing ghosts. If we can fade out of history, the old maps seemed to say, so can you. So can you. He moved his thumb, and a name caught his eye, raising the pale specter of hope.

New York. Nourk. Phillip. Dandified, fat, rich Phillip. Abelard's fourth son, whom he had married to the Senador of Nourk's daughter, hoping to bring the independent estate more firmly into the sphere of Ridenau control. Roderic took a deep breath. Two years ago, at the Convening which confirmed Roderic's regency, Philip had been less than eager to commit troops. And yet, Phillip was bound by the same Pledge of Allegiance all the Senadors swore, to uphold the kingdom and the King by any means at his disposal. Perhaps it was time to call him on it.

Roderic's gaze swept across the ancient map, glancing over territories vast and long forgotten. "Are you implying I've not spent enough men on the search for my father, Lord Senador?" He heard the bitter edge in his voice and forced himself to speak calmly. "But how many regiments do you expect me to send when they're needed elsewhere? How many shall I devote?" Roderic met the old man's eyes steadily, refusing to be intimidated. He was twenty-one on his next birthday, and he felt at least three times that old.

Without waiting for an answer, he pushed away from the table and paced to stare unseeing out the window, knowing Gredahl watched his every move. "I am sorry for your losses. But the numbers you give me are no greater than they have ever been—the borders of Arkan and Loma are dangerous places even at the best of times, you know that. I can give you no guarantees, Lord Senador. Not even my father could give you a guarantee when it came to the Harleyriders. But I will tell you this. My kinsman, Barran, my brother Brand's son, is in Dlas—commander of the garrison there. I will send a messenger to him tonight, warning him to watch the Harleys closely. If there are any signs that more than their usual raiding parties are approaching the border of Loma, he will alert my troops at Ithan. I will summon reserves from my brother in Nourk. Depending upon the number of his forces, I may be able to increase the garrisons. But more than that, Lord Gredahl, I cannot give."

Gredahl rose from the chair, his joints protesting audibly. "I mean you no disrespect, Lord Prince."

In the gloom, Roderic smiled. That was the closest thing to apology the old man was ever likely to offer. "You've been a good friend, Gredahl—I count on your influence in the Congress, even as my father did. I do not discount your concern. I will alert Obayana as well—between Ithan to the east, and Kora-lado to the west, if the Harleys invade Arkan, they will ride into a vise."

"And I will return to my people and prepare for war. It may never come, Lord Prince, but better to be prepared."

"As you say, Lord Senador." Roderic watched the old man haul himself heavily across the room, limping from the effect of wounds and age.

At the door Gredahl paused. "There is no word of the King?"

Roderic shook his head before he realized that in the faded light, the Senador might not be able to see the gesture. "No. It is as if the earth opened and swallowed him whole. There has been no sign of him in two years."

"Lord Prince," Gredahl began awkwardly.

Pity warred with respect for the old warrior as Roderic held up his hand. The Arkan lords were tough and proud and bent the knee to few, but they had always been utterly loyal to the king. "If I could give you more than those assurances, Gredahl, I would."

The old man's shoulders heaved once more, dark against the darker outline of the door. "As you say, Lord Prince." There was a rustle of clothing as the old man bowed his head, and then he was gone.

Roderic turned back to the window with another sigh. The gray weather did nothing to lift his mood. It was nearly time for dinner—through the glass he heard the muted orders of the guards upon the walls as the watch changed. He leaned his forehead against the cold glass, and for a moment, his shoulders sagged.

Oh, he had loyal supporters, all right—his brothers Brand and Alexander, Vere and Reginald at Atland garrison, Everard who governed the northern peninsula with a fair and even hand, the Senators of Kora-lado, Tennessy Fall, and Atland. And of course there was Deirdre of the Settle Islands, who even now, alone of all the Senators save Tennessy, was in the field. The thought of Deirdre made him smile. Alone among all the Senators, she had offered him troops when he needed them last summer, even if what she demanded in exchange was slightly unorthodox. But Deirdre herself was unorthodox—one could not apply ordinary standards to such a woman.

He wished he could send Alexander back to the garrison at Spogan before more time passed. But Alexander was not much better than he had been last summer. Roderic raised his head and stared at the flickering points of torchlight on the walls. Over the winter, Alex had seemed to improve, but lately—there was a sickly yellow cast to Alex's skin, and deep pockets under his eyes. His dark beard was streaked with gray. He was only thirty-five, but he had the appearance of a man near death. There was little chance that Alexander would be able to return to his garrison on the shores of the Western Sea this spring, and that left the contentious Chiefs and the lords of Mondana without a buffer.

And Amanander, his nemesis and Alexander's twin, lay in his unnatural sleep three stories above, just as he had for the last ten months, a latent, ever present reminder of the forces which threatened the regency.

Roderic flexed his cramped shoulders, massaged the back of his neck. His stomach rumbled, reminding him of the time. He would go to Annandale, and lay his head upon the round mound of her belly, and feel their child kick beneath the taut skin. Her time was almost here; the midwives said the child would be born any day. The thought of Annandale, her gentle smile, her healing touch, acted like a balm. Yes, she was what he needed. He would go to her, eat, and then speak to Phineas, who seemed to grow more frail with every passing day. But Phineas, old and lamed and blind though he might be, was still the King's Chief Councilor, the one man in Meriga whom Abelard had never failed to consult. Without Phineas's advice, Roderic knew he would never have held his father's throne for as long as he had. He was sure Phineas would approve of his decision to contact Phillip in Nourk.

In the corridor outside his rooms, he nearly collided with the servant who was coming to light the lamps. "I'm finished in there for the evening," he said to the startled man. "Go to Lord Phineas and tell him I'd like to speak with him after I've eaten with my lady."

The servant took off down the corridor. Roderic pushed against the door to his chambers. To his surprise, it was barred. With gritted teeth, he pounded for admittance. Finally, his eldest sister, Tavia, opened the door. She wore a short white kerchief over her head, and a large white apron, stained in places with what looked like blood. "What are you doing here? Why aren't you with Amanander? And why am I locked out of my own rooms?"

"Shhh, Roderic, you'll upset her."

"Annandale? What's wrong?" He tried to push past Tavia, to see through the outer chamber into the bedroom, but that door too was tightly closed.

"She's fine, Roderic. It's just time for the baby to come."

"Is she all right?" Through the door, he thought he heard a low groan, like an animal in pain. All the cares of his day vanished.

"She's fine—"

"How long has this been going on?"

"Since early morning—"

"And why wasn't I told? I want to see her."

"You've been busy all day—everything is fine. There's no need to bother you."

"Bother me?" He stared down at Tavia with all the disdain he could muster, and the sound came again. This time he pushed past her successfully.

"Roderic, we didn't think you—"

He paused with his hand on the door and looked at Tavia over his shoulder. "She is dearer than life to me."

In the bedroom, four or five women clustered around the bed looked up with shocked expressions at his entrance.

Roderic strode to the bedside. Annandale lifted her head. Her hair was matted and damp, her face pale, and beneath her eyes, dark smudges marred the delicate skin of her face. She was lying on her side, a pillow wedged between her thighs, her arms clenched around another. "Roderic?" Her voice was a harsh whisper through cracked lips.

"My love?" He knelt beside her, brushing the curls away from her forehead. "How is it with you?"

She managed a little smile. "As well as it can be, they say."

"How much longer?"

"I don't know." Her face contorted and she clenched the pillow as a spasm of pain gripped her. He tightened his hand on her arm and started as a twinge of pain, like an echo, filtered down his spine, flickering through his lower belly like a dying flame.

"There's nothing you can do for her, Roderic," said Tavia. "We are doing all we can."

He glared at his sister, who had drawn back into the tight circle of the other women. They were muttering amongst themselves. The pain shivering through his gut gave him an idea. He turned again to Annandale, who had rolled half over onto her back, and spoke in a low voice so only she could hear him. "We shared our desire when we made this child. Is it possible—?" He broke off, biting his lip as her face contorted once more, and she groped for his hand desperately. He twined his fingers in the tendrils of her hair, smoothing it off her damp face.

"You would help me bear this pain?" she whispered when she could.

"Is it possible?" he murmured close to her ear, so the others would not hear.

"You must accept it—totally and completely. Can you do that?"

"You know I would do anything for you."

She took a deep breath. "Get behind me. Help me sit up."

He positioned himself behind her, taking her weight against his chest, supporting her so that she half-reclined against him. The midwives eyed them suspiciously. She took his hands and guided them to the low swell of her belly. "Are you ready?" she murmured, close to his ear.

For answer, he hugged her tightly, and in the very pit of his abdomen, a great hand seemed to slowly clench into a great fist, then gave a shattering wrench. He gasped involuntarily at the depth of the pain.

"All right?" she whispered.

"That's what you've been feeling? All day?"

"Together, we can bear it."

An hour passed, and then another, as the great fist opened and closed with increasing intensity and sometimes wrenched two or three times before it eased. More than once, he had to bite his lips and hide his face in the heavy fall of her hair. Finally, he felt a pressure at the base of his spine, and Annandale grunted, shifting away so that he almost lost his grip.

The women hovered closer. "She needs to push, Lord Prince." They were all business now, having decided that since he was obviously immovable, he should be made to help in some way. "Move her here, over the edge."

Sweat stained his tunic and beaded his forehead as the two of them moved as one. The midwife gently placed Annandale's heels on the edge of the bed, so that her knees were bent, her legs wide and spread apart. The hard, driving pressure began to grow, and she twisted his arms, her nails digging into the flesh of his forearms. As though his own flesh responded to the sensation of the infant's passage, a growing weight burned between his legs as though it would split him in half. He stifled a moan and tried not to hug her too hard, peering over her shoulder. Annandale gave a final cry, and in a gush of clear fluid, the crown of the infant's head emerged. Almost at once, the pressure was gone.

"There, there, lady," crooned the midwife, kneeling between Annandale's thighs, "that's fine, easy now, no need to bear down. Let him come."

The shoulders turned of their own accord, and as he looked over Annandale's shoulder, he saw the squashed, grayish-blue face of the infant. The woman gently drew the baby out. The long cord which bound him to his mother was blue and pulsing. The baby waved his fists and the little mouth opened, and sounds, like a mewling kitten escaped. He turned blindly, sputtering.

"Is—is he all right?" Roderic wasn't quite sure what to think of the weird, gray-blue skin. The crown of the infant's head was covered with a little thatch of dark hair, and some white, creamy stuff covered most of the damp, little body. There was blood on his ears.

Annandale held out her arms, and the woman placed the squirming infant in them. Roderic was relieved to see the baby turning red.

"Oh, he's fine, Lord Prince. A bit small, but he'll grow. He'll pink up soon enough."

Annandale cradled the baby close, and then grimaced.

"What's wrong?" Roderic wrapped his arms over hers.

"Just the afterbirth, Lord Prince," answered the midwife. "Easy now, lady, this isn't like that head, you know. Ah—there." With a soft swish, the afterbirth slithered from between Annandale's legs and was caught by one of the waiting women. Another woman pressed a wad of linen between her legs.

"All right, Lord Prince," said the senior midwife, "lay her back against the pillows. Here, do you want to cut the cord?"

She handed him a pair of silver scissors. Roderic looked down at the baby, now eagerly sucking at a nipple which looked much too large to fit into the tiny mouth. Annandale nodded. "Go ahead, love."

Roderic bent and carefully snipped. The infant did not notice. He was as greedily attached to his mother as ever.

Annandale smiled up at him, her face radiant, and it did not seem possible that she had spent the last ten or twelve hours racked by such pain. His hand hovered over the child, hesitant. "Touch him, Roderic. You won't hurt him."

Tentatively, he placed three fingers over the baby's back. The child seemed impossibly small, his head no larger than Roderic's fist, his back smaller than the span of Roderic's five fingers. His legs looked like a frog's.

"What shall we call him?" Annandale asked.

Roderic brushed the soft down on the baby's head with the back of his hand. "I was thinking we should name him for the first of the Ridenau Kings. Rhodri. Rhodri Ridenau—my father's grandfather, who first restored the Estates of Meriga and made it whole."

Annandale smiled. "Rhodri Ridenau—I like it. What do you think, Tavvy?" She looked up at the woman hovering at Roderic's arm.

"It's a fine name. But you—" Tavia tapped Roderic firmly on the shoulder. "You *must* go. Send us all something to eat."

With a sheepish glance at his sister, Roderic picked up Annandale's hand and pressed a kiss into the palm. "Thank you."

"Thank you." She met his eyes with a look full of meaning. "Go, let them finish here. When he's been cleaned and dressed, you can hold him."

Roderic traced a finger over a tiny ear, loathe to leave the presence of such a new and beguiling being. The baby squirmed, turning his head against Annandale's breast, his skin reddening even as Roderic watched. Roderic bent to look at him more closely, and incredibly, the child opened his eyes and focused. Abelard's eyes looked out of the tiny face, and in that moment, Roderic understood why he would fight with his last breath to preserve his father's kingdom. Not for himself, not for his missing father, but for this fragile being, who had existed only moments before as anonymous lumps beneath his mother's belly, and now who lived and breathed and moved as independently as he. And with a pang of wonder, Roderic realized that when this infant was grown to manhood, and fathered children of his own, those children would live to see a time and a place he could never know. He had a sense of past and present and future, of the link from grandfather to father to son to generations yet unborn. He felt at once both humbled and exalted.

Roderic bent and kissed Annandale's mouth again. He had no words to express what he was feeling, but his eyes met hers, and he had the uncanny sense she understood. She nodded and closed her eyes, lying back against her pillows, her face suddenly white with exhaustion. "Rest, love," he murmured. At the door, he paused once more and looked at the bustling women. "Thank you all." He kissed Tavia's cheek. "I'm sorry I was rude."

She smiled, her wrinkled face crinkled around her faded blue eyes. "It is not every day an heir to Meriga is born."

He gripped her under the elbow and guided her to the antechamber. "How is Amanander? Has there been any other change?"

Tavia glanced into the bedroom and pulled the door shut. "No—not really."

"Not really? What do you mean by that?"

"This morning, before I was summoned here, Gartred

was allowed to see him—you know, her weekly visit—
and I could have sworn I saw him open his eyes and look
at her."

"He opens his eyes all the time." Roderic frowned.

"But this time—" Tavia broke off. "Perhaps it was a
trick of the light. It was so dark—we had candles lit well
into the morning."

"What do you think you saw?" Roderic asked gently,
aware that this sister hated Amanander with a passion
and lived for the day when he would answer for his
crimes before the Congress.

"I thought he looked at her as though he knew her. I
thought I saw recognition in his eyes."

Roderic tapped a finger on his chin, considering.
"Who's with him now?"

"Jaboa. She's been with him since—"

Roderic nodded. Jaboa, Brand's wife, was as trusted a
nurse as Tavia. She could well confirm or deny anything
that Tavia thought she might have seen. "Well. I'll have
the servants bring you all dinner. And I'll speak to Jaboa.
Perhaps she noticed some change, too. I'm going to see
Phineas, now. But I'll be back as soon as I can." He
leaned down and pecked another kiss on her plump
cheek.

If Amanander were to wake out of his unnatural sleep,
and stood trial before the Congress, it would without a
doubt contribute to a speedy end to the rebellion in
Missiluse. He went down the staircase to Phineas's
chambers with a light heart and an easier step.

Chapter Three

✎❀☙

$\mathcal{D}$own dark and winding corridors Amanander roamed, heels tapping, tapping, tapping on the faded wooden floor. He rounded corners, strode up and down dusty staircases, lost in a haphazard maze. He knew he searched, but why and for what he had forgotten, and that awareness gnawed as annoying as an itch.

Sometimes he thought he heard voices, a blurred buzz that rose and fell just at the periphery of his hearing. Sometimes he thought he heard his name, but each time he paused and tried to listen, the voices maddeningly faded.

Debris was piled in the corners, along the corridors, broken spears and swords which crumbled into dust when he touched them. Room after room was full of mismatched crockery, ragged clothes, and phantom chairs and beds and tables that vanished at his approach. He felt with frustrating certainty that someone searched for him, but where, or how to reach that person beyond the walls of this grim prison, he did not know.

And there was another, another he knew he ought to know, another so similar to himself that their thoughts sometimes intertwined. The random words meant nothing, for he could discern no sense in them. And there was a woman, too, or was there more than one—a woman with black hair and pale skin, who taunted him in language he did not understand as he restlessly roamed the corridors, who sometimes wore another face, a face of such unearthly ugliness he was tempted to shut his eyes until the apparition passed.

But that only lent strength to the apparition, and the only way he had discovered to make it go was to turn the full force of his will upon it, staring at it with every ounce of strength which he possessed, pouring it through his eyes. And when he did that, the vision vanished without a sound, leaving no trace.

He was getting better at it; if he caught a glimpse of it out of the corner of his eye, he could prevent it from manifesting entirely if he turned the full force of his glare upon it. It was good practice, he knew, for something that he used to know how to do and had forgotten.

There was no night or day within the shadowed walls, no candles burned to tell the passing of the hours, but Amanander knew that time, precious time, was passing, pouring out through his fingers like gold dust. Only his footsteps, echoing in the empty halls, lingering on the dusty air, gave him a measure of the hours and the days.

He counted his time in footsteps, and as the numbers grew, he knew that within the numbers were the secrets he'd forgotten. If only he could remember, he thought, just the very first, the very barest trace . . . but he wandered on and on, trapped within the labyrinth.

At the bottom of a crumbling staircase, he heard a

name—his name—spoken with such clarity, he scarcely recognized it.

AMANANDER.

He stopped. Nothing had changed. He touched a black-gloved hand to the wall of flaking stone, and the stone left a whitish smear across the leather. He curled his lip in automatic disgust and wiped it fastidiously on the inner hem of his black tunic. Then he paused. When had he put on the gloves?

AMANANDER.

The voice echoed again, louder, more insistent. Amanander looked up the staircase, then down the corridor over his shoulder. The voice seemed to be all around him, echoing off the dusty walls, again and again and again. He glanced down, realizing with a start that his boots were black and polished to a high gloss, and that he could see his own face looking back at him. He stared, jolted by the recognition of himself.

AMANANDER. This time there was the finest edge of pain in the intensity of the voice, as though he'd sliced his finger on a razor's edge. He looked up.

"Where are you?" It was the first time in weeks, months, years, since he'd heard his own voice, and it startled him, more than his reflection. The sound echoed and spun with a power all its own, cracking the walls of the corridor.

HERE.

A shower of fine powder fell from the ceiling, and he looked up, shocked to see a crack a handspan wide, and growing wider. He bolted up the steps, and the floor shuddered beneath his feet. At the top of the staircase, a figure robed in white stood waiting.

"We've got to get out of here," he said as he reached the top step.

The figure pointed to a room off the corridor.

"In there? You think we'll be safe in there?"

The figure inclined its head and stepped aside, allowing Amanander to go first.

The room was nothing like the dusty empty halls he had left. A fire burned in a highly polished grate. Beside the fire, two chairs, with high, cushioned backs, invited. Amanander sniffed. There was the scent of something cooking—roasting meat, the tang of herbs, bread baking—and suddenly saliva exploded in his mouth. Before the fire, a cushioned stool held a thin circlet of gold.

He turned to see the figure shut the door. "Who are you? Do I know you? Why have you brought me here?"

The figure swept the hood off his face, and in the firelight, three black eyes looked back at him with a feral gleam. "Lord Prince," said Ferad-lugz, "don't you know me?"

"Ferad." Pieces of memory came filtering back. This was his teacher, his tutor, his—his mind rejected the word *master*. Ferad was the one who'd taught him to use the Old Magic, who'd warned him against trying to use it before he was ready. "Where are we? What is this place?"

"I am here only in semblance. And you should know this place. It's your own mind."

Taken off guard, Amanander stumbled back a few paces. "My mind?"

"The witch Nydia sent you flying here, after the day

at Minnis, when the battle was lost. You don't remember? You will, in time."

"How are you here?" Amanander whispered. The fire made a crackling noise in the grate, and he whipped his head around. "This—all this—isn't real?"

"Real? You ask me what's real? Philosophers have argued for centuries over the meaning of what's real. Some would say that this is far more real than anything in the material world. But no, this place is not part of any physical reality as one normally defines it."

"The fire—it doesn't burn?"

Ferad waved his hand impatiently, and from the folds of his loose white garment, his secondary arms, tiny, useless appendages no larger than a human infant's, twitched involuntarily. "It burns because you believe it burns. I haven't time to explain all this."

"The hallway—the corridor—began to collapse when I heard your voice—why—?"

"Because once I got through to you, your madness began to collapse." Ferad advanced, eyes burning with that unnatural light, and Amanander took a step backward.

"I'm mad?"

"Unconscious. You've lain as though asleep for more than nine months. Much has changed in the world, little Prince, while you've lain oblivious. And unless you want the world to forget all about you, and go on about its business by itself, then I suggest you'd better come to your senses."

Amanander sank into one of the chairs. The flames reflected in the highly polished surface of his boots; the fabric was warm and rough beneath his palms. He touched the arms, and the wood was smooth and beautifully carved, and suddenly he recognized it. "This is my desk chair. From the garrison at Dlas."

"Was your desk chair. Another sits in your place."

"Who?" He sat bolt upright as Ferad took the chair opposite.

"Your brother Brand's son, Barran. Roderic sent him there."

"Roderic." He whispered the name, and the room seemed to resonate, the flames leap higher, the arms of the chair seemed to expand beneath his grasp. His eyes fell on the gold circlet. He shot a glance at Ferad and reached out to take the crown, seize it and put it on his head, and his hands passed through it as though it were hollow, a shell, a semblance, something which wasn't quite there. "What have you done with it?"

Ferad chuckled. "You haven't won it yet, my Prince."

Amanander leaned forward, suddenly conscious that he was much larger than the Muten. "It's mine. Give it to me."

"It isn't mine to give you," answered Ferad softly. "Don't you remember?"

Across the empty space, Amanander stared at Ferad as memory after memory fell into place, like the layers of an onion. The disappearance of his father, Abelard, Roderic's regency, the Muten revolt, Alexander's betrayal, the discovery of Nydia's daughter, the empath, Annandale, whose very nature was the key to the control of the Magic. In the depths of the dark, startling eyes, Amanander saw the past unfurl, his own core of memories restored. "My father?"

"I've kept him alive. He's with me, now."

"Where are you?"

"I've moved east of Dlas—into the Missiluse lowlands. My brotherhood has been on the move; we have successfully infiltrated the College of the Elders and annihilated at least fifteen of the oldest. And the most powerful."

"And Roderic?"

"Well within your reach. He's here, at Ahga. The empath has borne him a son."

"An heir." Amanander rose to his feet with a curse. "So much time has passed—I've lain here like a cripple—what can I do? Can we kill him?"

"Not so easily, my Prince. Do you think this trick is easy? I only broke through you because you were completely weak, defenseless. Your body is not what you remember. You're a wasted shell compared to what you once were. Even to get you out of the bed you lie in will require the Magic, and to get you out of Ahga and back to me—"

"Why should I come back to you?"

Ferad leaned against the chair. "Your impatience has cost you dearly, my Prince. I would have thought you'd have learned some lessons in all these months, but I see the time has been wasted. Allow me to instruct you. You have no power here. You can't even summon a jar to piss in. The moment you wake, Roderic will have you arrested, taken from this relatively comfortable room, and placed in a decidedly uncomfortable cell under heavy guard. And then he will call a Convening, and you will stand trial for the crimes of your sister Jesselyn's murder, the trouble in the Settle Islands, where you masqueraded so successfully as your twin, Alexander, and for inciting a rebellion against the throne." Ferad smiled as understanding at his predicament washed over Amanander's face. "Now you begin to see."

"What's your solution?"

"You will listen to me very carefully. And you will do exactly what I say."

The lone candle cast a gentle gleam across the room as Annandale gently disengaged the sleeping baby from her breast. A drop of milk seeped from the corner of the tiny mouth, and the child gave a deep satisfied sigh. She brushed a kiss on his round, pink cheek with the back of one finger, caressed the comical thatch of dark hair which stuck up in all directions from his head. The door opened and shut, and without looking up, she knew at once that Roderic had come. She raised her finger to her mouth in a warning.

Roderic halted just inside the door. "Is he asleep?"

She nodded, drew her nightrobe together, and rose. With a few quick strides, Roderic was beside her, gazing down at the infant in her arms with such tenderness it made her want to weep. She nestled her head in the hollow of his shoulder. He drew her chin up to his face, and bent to kiss her, when he saw her tears.

"Why do you weep?" he whispered.

She shook her head. She placed the baby in his cradle and picked up the candle. When she had shut the door behind them, he repeated the question.

"It's nothing—no reason." She brushed at her eyes.

"Just a silly thing—women get this way, you know, after childbirth."

"No," he said gravely, watching her closely, "I didn't know."

"Your expression when you looked at Rhodri—you looked as though you would fight a thousand men rather than let one hair of his be harmed."

"I would," he said, "for you both."

He reached for her, and she leaned into him, catching the flavor of his desire, his need. She nuzzled against him, savoring the closeness of his body, the warm masculine scent so different from the baby's. But there was something else, some sense of uneasiness, and she drew back, even as he pressed her closer against him, and she heard the unmistakable crinkle of parchment beneath his tunic.

"Is it too soon?" he murmured.

She pulled back, searching his eyes, so soft and green in the shadows, so different from Abelard's eyes, and wondered once more why no one had ever realized the total lack of resemblance between the King and his heir. "No." She reached up and drew his face down to hers. "Not at all. But what is wrong? Something is bothering you."

He gave her a rueful smile. "By the One, love, I will never have a secret from you, will I?" He sighed heavily and withdrew to sink into one of the chairs beside the hearth.

"What is it?" she asked again, as his disquiet wound itself about her like the tendrils of a clinging vine.

"A messenger came in from Brand just now. Things

are going badly in Atland. Old Kranak's younger sons destroyed Grenvill garrison. That was one of our more strategic outposts. Our men are cut off from supplies . . . they have little choice but to fall back into the Highlands and try to regroup. I need to find reinforcements. I know Phillip is likely to refuse—courteously, of course, and Everard is so far away. . . ." His voice trailed off.

She listened in growing dismay, watching the flames flicker over his narrow face. She felt the burden of his regency as a tangible thing. The charge the King had laid upon him was a weight that grew more heavy with each passing day. He sighed once more, and the sound reverberated deep in her chest.

"What else?"

He raised his head and met her eyes squarely, and from the recesses of his tunic he withdrew a scrap of paper. He held it out to her, and with trembling fingers she reached and took it. At once the impression of pain— torment beyond her comprehension—lanced through her body and she gasped, the paper fluttering from her grip.

"Annandale!" He was on his feet and beside her, his arms supporting as her knees weakened.

"Who-whoever wrote that died in great agony," she muttered, clutching his sleeve.

He shook his head. "I cannot say—"

"I can," she said.

"But Vere sent it—he found it on some poor wretch by the roadside, said Brand—and you know what it means."

Annandale stared at the shaky lines, the black script which snaked the lancets of pain into the very marrow of her bones. "Yes," she whispered. "I do."

He bent his head to gather her mouth to his, and she froze in his embrace as foreboding swept over and through her as though something had doused her with ice water. Momentarily the room seemed to darken, the shadows to grow and deepen, reaching from the corners with grasping tentacles. The candles guttered as though a chilling wind blew through the room.

"What is it?" He tilted her chin up, a puzzled expression on his face. "Sweet, what I can do about these things tonight has been done. Put it from your mind. But if it's too soon for you—"

"No." She twisted her hands in the fabric of his tunic, clutching him closer. "It's not that—it—" Her eyes darted around the room.

"What, then?" His gaze followed hers, every muscle suddenly tense. Beneath her hands she felt his heart begin to beat faster.

She hesitated. She wanted to say nothing was wrong, and yet she had the profoundest sense that something was more than wrong, something was out of synchrony. The air itself was too thick to breathe— "By the One," she whispered, as understanding dawned. "It's the Magic. Someone is using the Magic."

Without another word, she flung the door to the inner chamber wide and darted into the baby's room. The room was quiet, peaceful, the infant's breathing deep and even in the stillness. Instinct made her reach for him, cradle him close to her breast, and behind her, Roderic spoke from the doorway. "What can we do?"

She turned to face him, and her words were drowned out by a thunderous crack, and the whole building—all twenty-five stories—shuddered on its foundations. There was an enormous roaring screech as, on the opposite side of the wide inner ward, one of the five towers of Ahga sank into a massive heap of rubble. Over the rumbling crash, she heard the screams of men and animals. Roderic reached for them both and wrapped his arms around her, bracing himself in the doorway, shielding her with his own body. The baby stirred and whimpered in her frantic grip. Roderic pressed her head against his chest as the whole building heaved once more like an animal in its death throes, and then was still.

He rushed to the window. "By the One."

She peered outside. Although the darkness obscured the view, it appeared that one side of the stables had collapsed, folding in upon itself like a house of cards, an enormous pile of stones and tangled lines. In the wards below, the grooms and the men-at-arms called frantically, trying to rescue what horses they could before the fragile structure collapsed further.

Roderic turned to her. "I've got to get down there. Will you be all right here?"

"Roderic, this was Magic. Remember the backlash—there may be more to come. I think we would be better off in the hall."

A frantic servant knocked on the door of the outer chamber, "Lord Prince, Lord Prince. Please come—"

"Here I am, man, I'm here." He called out as he hugged her closer and pressed a quick kiss on her forehead. "Come, I'll see you safe to the hall."

The door opened and the servant peered into the room,

clearly frightened. "Lord Prince—Lord Prince. The Lady Tavia sends you this message. Amanander—"

Fear bolted through Annandale as Roderic looked up. "What about Amanander?"

"He's gone. Lady Gartred with him. The Lady Jaboa's dead. And Alexander—"

Annandale listened in horror, half certain of what the hapless servant would say before the words were out of his mouth.

"Alexander lies as Amanander did—in a sleep beyond our reach."

Chapter Four

The rising sun cast the courtyards into inky wells of debris and dark piles of haphazard stone. Roderic stared out the windows of the council chamber, watching the weary stonemasons scramble amidst the rubble at the direction of the captain of the engineers as they sought to stabilize what little remained of the northern tower. The clear light of morning revealed the extent of the disaster. Surely months would be required to undo the work of the previous night.

From his litter on the floor beside the council table, Phineas shifted against his pillows.

"Tavia was right," Roderic said softly, as he turned his back to the window and watched Phineas's sightless eyes roaming randomly beneath his papery lids. "I should have killed the bastard when I had the chance at Minnis last summer, instead of letting him live." The bitter taste in his mouth had nothing to do with the sleepless night he had just spent.

Once more, Roderic turned to the window and leaned against the glass, staring at the wreckage which filled the inner ward of Ahga Castle. Never again would the five towers of Ahga rise so proudly against the sky, her square bulk comforting and reassuring as the power of the Ridenau Kings.

"Roderic." Phineas's voice rasped gently behind him, and reluctantly Roderic turned to face the man his father had relied upon all the years of his reign. "This was not your fault."

"You don't know how much I wish I could believe you. The north tower's in ruins, and parts of the west may be damaged beyond repair. Every door was ripped off its hinges. In all the confusion, Amanander just walked right out." He could not hide the bitter edge of his words. He stalked to stand over the council table, the long plate glass reflecting rainbow prisms in the early morning light.

"My son—" began the old man, and stopped as someone rapped on the door.

"Yes?" Roderic raised his head, glad that the interruption had prevented the old man offering any more sympathy. This was his fault—he knew it as surely as he knew his own name. He had not learned to govern the whole of Meriga by shirking his responsibilities.

The door opened slowly, reluctantly, and a tired-looking servant let Annandale precede him into the room. "Lord Prince. Your lady-wife."

With a terse wave of his hand, Roderic sent the servant on his way. Annandale closed the door.

"Roderic, I must speak to you."

Phineas struggled to sit straighter at the sound of her soft voice, and Roderic noted the dark shadows beneath her eyes, the faint shadows of strain beside her mouth. This was the first time he had ever seen her look so utterly weary, and instantly he wondered what could have brought her to him at such an hour and at such a time.

"What's wrong? Are the children all right?"

"Oh, yes. Melisande slept through it all, and Rhodri is fine." She paused.

"Then go to bed, sweetheart. We can discuss whatever we must later."

"No, Roderic." Her voice was firm. She touched Phineas's shoulder, and the old man took her hand in his gnarled one and pressed it close. She raised her eyes to Roderic's. "We've seen to Jaboa's lying-out. A messenger should be sent to Brand at once. You must make sure to tell him she didn't suffer."

Roderic pressed his lips together. Jaboa's death raked his heart as cruelly as a lycat's claws. She had been the closest to a mother he had ever had, but he shook off the mind-numbing press of his grief. There was no time now to mourn. "It shall be done, lady. Is there anything else?'

"We must be ready, Roderic. There will be some repercussion to the Magic—somewhere, someone must be feeling the effect. You should be prepared for anything."

"What about us? Do you think it will strike here?"

She shrugged. "I have no way to know. That's part of what makes the Magic so terrible." She hesitated and bit her lip. "I have seen Alexander. Roderic, you must come and speak with him."

"Speak with him? Is he able to speak?"

She nodded, twisting her fingers in the fabric of her gown. "I was able to—to reach him. He's very weak, weaker than he should be, and in truth, I don't understand why. But you must come and hear what he has to say your-self, for what he says concerns not only Amanander—but the King as well."

"The King?" Roderic echoed, as Phineas gasped soft-ly. "What did he say about Dad?"

She shook her head tiredly. "It made no sense to me or to Tavia. Please, won't you come?"

For a long moment he stared at her. Finally he nodded. "Very well. You want me to come now? All right." Outside a gull shrieked and the shouts of the men rose above a dull crash. "I'll finish here with Phineas and meet you in his chambers."

Annandale patted Phineas's shoulder and nodded.

When she was gone, Roderic stared at the ancient maps of Old Meriga beneath the glass. "I had planned that Brand and the army should withdraw into the Highlands and await me there. But I think, in light of the current development, that a more strategic withdrawal is called for. I am going to order the troops to retire to Ithan Ford. What do you think?"

The old man stroked his chin. "You give ground in order to gain it. You do understand that Atland's heir might have a hard time understanding the necessity of a retreat."

"I understand that. The master engineers are assessing the damage. As soon as I have some idea of what must be done here, I will be off to Ithan as soon as possible."

Phineas knitted his fingers together. The rising sun cast a glow over the white linen and shone through the sparse wisps of hair which clung to the old man's scalp. In his youth, Phineas had sat at the King's right hand, had been the most powerful man in Meriga after the King himself. Even now, Phineas retained more than a vestige of that authority.

"Ithan Ford is a good choice. You are easily accessible to the Highlands . . . Atland's sons will hesitate to attack you there. But you must bind your allies into a strong coalition, Roderic. You can not afford to lose any more supporters."

"I know Amanander is going to strike, Phineas. The question is where."

"And when."

"Soon. *Where* is the more troublesome question. I cannot be in two places at once." He broke off and sighed. "I keep remembering what Nydia told me the day I found Annandale. She said there would be war in all four corners of the realm. So far, she's proven right."

Phineas drew a deep breath. "Be wary, Roderic. There are factions within the Congress—Abelard believed he could hold the lords in submission with the grip of an iron fist, but under the present circumstances—"

"That's the problem, isn't it?" Roderic placed his palms flat against the cold glass of the tabletop. "So I was thinking . . ."

"Yes?" prompted Phineas.

"I will call for a Convening at Ithan before I leave. Let the Senators remember what the threat of chaos feels like, in case any have forgotten. And let them see how easy it might be for their own sons to rise against them." He looked Phineas full in the face as though the old man could meet his eyes. "Atland, or Atland's heir, must bring a formal request for aid before the Congress, and I will only act if the Senadors consent. I have read the law, Phineas, the ancient law of Meriga. Only the Congress can declare war, especially against one of their own. Do you understand what I am trying to do, Phineas? You do agree with me, don't you, Phineas?" His resolution failed momentarily in the face of the old man's silence.

"Roderic," Phineas said faintly, "of course, I understand. How could I disagree with you?"

"I shall call all the Senadors—even Ragonn and Vada, and all the rest who rose against my father. I can't afford to let ill-feeling fester anywhere in this realm. My father may have ruled by the strength of his will, Phineas, but I must find something stronger and more enduring than the will of one man. Meriga must be ruled by the force of its laws."

"You will send for Owen Mortmain himself?" Phineas's voice was a shocked whisper.

"I must," answered Roderic. "I will send for them all, not the puppet administrators my father set over them. Nydia was right—in every corner of the realm there is the potential for disaster. The Settle Islands against Mondana—Vada and the Western lords against me—the South divided against itself—even here—" his hand swept over the northeastern peninsula "—Phillip's self-interest makes him a danger not only to me but to every other Senador in the region. What if the lesser lords in the Dirondac Mountains took it into their heads to invade Nourk? Could Everard stop them? Could I?"

Age-spotted skin stretched taut across Phineas's bony knuckles as he pressed his hands together. "Roderic." He paused, as if gathering his thoughts. "This may well be the better way, but it is not without danger of its own. Do you have any idea what it will mean to bring the entire Congress under one roof? The enmity between factions goes back centuries in some cases, to the Armageddon and before. I am not certain that all of them are farsighted enough to see that if one Senator's son challenges his father, all of them are vulnerable."

"This is not what my father would have done, is it, Phineas?" The ghost of a smile played at the corners of the old man's mouth, and Roderic cocked his head, puzzled. "What are you thinking, Phineas? Do you think Dad would be completely displeased?" Self-doubt gnawed like a toothache. Beside the memory of his father, he felt himself sorely lacking.

Phineas drew a deep breath and raised himself higher on his pillows. "I was fourteen years old when I swore my first Pledge of Allegiance to a Ridenau King, and ever since, I have sought to uphold that pledge by any means at my disposal. Abelard no longer reigns in Ahga. He may be King yet in name, Roderic, but you are the ruler of the realm. I will not waste my time thinking of what Abelard would have done, because it no longer matters. Since the day you were proclaimed Regent, the decisions which mattered to me were yours."

"Have I made the right decision, then?"

There was another long silence, broken only by the muted shouts of the workmen in the inner ward. "You have made a good decision, Roderic. I wish I could tell you if it were the right one. I can only make you aware of who your allies are, and who is not."

"Let me guess. Kora-lado, Tennessy Fall, Mondana, Arkan—"

"Take Gredahl with you, and make sure of his support on the journey. You will need the Arkan lords to hold the Harleys at your back. You don't want to fight a war on two flanks."

"Gredahl requested aid from the garrisons." Roderic suppressed a sigh.

"We must look to the north for reinforcements. Before you leave, letters must go to Everard and Phillip—it is time that your brothers bore their share of this war. And what of Reginald—what does Brand say of the garrison in Atland?"

Roderic withdrew the folded parchment from the inner pocket of his tunic and slowly smoothed it on the table. "He doesn't say."

"Nothing?" Phineas's voice rose to a sharp pitch and the old man's eyebrows arched. "No mention of Reginald at all? Why didn't he ride to the defense of Grenvill?"

Roderic shook his head slowly. "I don't know. I can't imagine. Grenvill is less than two days march. It should have been possible for Reginald to relieve the garrison, or at least attempt to, but Brand makes no mention of him at all." Slowly, Roderic reread his brother's dispatch, wondering as he did so how he was going to break the news to Brand of his wife's death. Abruptly his eyes flooded with tears. He choked back the emotions, trying to focus on the matter at hand, and from the very deepest recesses of his brain, some half-forgotten warning tolled like a distant bell. He sighed, hoping that when he spoke his voice was steady. "According to Brand, the army was intercepted between Grenvill and

Atland garrison. Reginald should have had a clear march."

Roderic raised his head and frowned. "Now that I think of it, this makes no sense. There are over five thousand men garrisoned at Atland. Reginald . . ." The words faded in his throat, and his eyes dropped once more to the parchment before him. Treachery. Brand said Deirdre had suggested that someone somehow had betrayed the cause of Atland's heir.

Brand, hard in the thick of things, had enough to contend with without looking for treachery. But he had thought enough of Deirdre's opinion to put it in the dispatch, and Roderic, who knew the terrain and the roads of Atland better than he cared to, saw at a distance what Brand could not.

"What are you thinking, Roderic?" Phineas's voice quavered unexpectedly.

"I am thinking of treachery," Roderic answered. "Deirdre—the M'Callaster—suspected treachery. Brand mentions it, but only in passing. I think . . ." Again he let his voice trail off, lost in thought, knowing that there was something about Reginald he ought to know.

Reginald, the youngest of Abelard's illegitimate sons, commander of the garrison in Atland for as long as Roderic could remember. An able enough soldier, but no diplomat—Phineas had sent Everard, another brother, south after the last Muten rebellion to ensure that Reginald's blunders did not break the tenuous peace. Would his own place in the birth order of Abelard's brood make him sympathetic to the demands of Atland's younger sons? And during the Muten rebellion, hadn't he noticed Reginald in Amanander's company more often than not? A thought which even then had struck him as odd, for Amanander was polished, fastidious, and Reginald reeked of old sweat, his stringy hair matted and greasy. If ever two brothers were direct opposites, surely it was Reginald and Amanander. But no alliance in the quest for power was unlikely, thought Roderic. "It's Reginald," he said, more to himself than to Phineas. "I should have seen this before. It was Alexander who warned me. All those months ago in the Settle Islands— he warned me to expect an attack upon Ithan. But it never came, and I forgot about Reginald. What made him wait, Phineas? What made him stay his hand?"

"If he allied himself with Amanander, while Amanander lay here in Ahga, perhaps he wasn't sure what to do. Reginald has always been an able enough soldier, but he lacks subtlety. He would have waited to see what happened next. But I suppose the lesser lords were able to persuade him to aid them in their fight against Kye." Phineas paused. "I think," he said, softly, "you had better leave for Ithan as soon as possible. This realm is like a house of cards—one tremor and the whole nation may collapse."

"Will you come with me, Phineas?" Roderic asked. He ran his hand over his jaw, feeling the rough haze of his beard. He felt like a boy barely old enough to shave, let alone a man old enough to govern a country.

There was another long pause, and finally Phineas spoke, his voice a thin quaver as though he held back some unnamed emotion. "Of course I will come. My son."

Chapter Five

Alexander lay against white linen pillows, his shock of graying hair outspread. His face had a sickly yellow cast; his lips were cracked and bloodless. His dark eyes seemed to peer at Roderic from miles away. He looked like a withered husk, from which all the vitality had been sucked by some loathsome parasite.

Tavia hovered in the doorway. Her white-streaked hair was twisted in a careless knot at the nape of her neck, her apron smudged with blood and dirt. She had spent most of the night tending the wounded in the great hall below. "Don't tax him too much," she cautioned, just before she shut the door, leaving the two brothers and Annandale alone.

"Alex." Roderic leaned over the sick man, searching the web-wrinkled face for a response.

Alexander turned his head slowly as Annandale bent low to whisper in his ear. "Tell Roderic, Alex. You must tell Roderic what you told me."

"What can you tell me of Aman, Alex? Where has he gone?"

"Death walks." His voice was less than a sigh. "On two legs. I see his face, and it is mine."

"Do you mean Aman, Alex? Where's he gone?"

"Beyond our reach. Far, far beyond us all."

"Do you know what he intends? Can you tell me what he will do?"

Suddenly, Alexander's eyes snapped open. His head righted against the pillow and his eyes stared up at a place on the far wall. A visible pulse pounded in his temples. "He grows like a worm in the bud—he will bring such a blight upon the land, and he smiles . . . oh, how he smiles to do it. Beneath the stone mountain, lies the King—where the dark is blacker than the night, colder than the grave." He drew a deep shuddering breath, staring across the room with such a look of utter horror and dismay, Roderic involuntarily glanced at the blank wall. "Oh, Aman," groaned Alexander. "Why don't you just let him die? Let him go—how can you hate Dad so much?"

At the word "Dad," Roderic gasped and grabbed Alexander by the shoulders. "Amanander does have Dad." Alexander sagged and nodded. A tear streaked down his wrinkled face. Roderic placed him gently back against his pillows, and looked at Annandale. "Oh, my love," he whispered. "What are we to do?"

Alexander's ragged breathing filled the room. Finally, Annandale bent over Alexander and picked up his withered hand. Her face softened with pity and she gently stroked his brow. "He's dying, Roderic."

"Can you save him?"

"I—I can try."

"Don't do anything to harm yourself." He caught her arm and gazed into her eyes with alarm.

"I won't." She pressed Alexander's hand between both of hers. "Alex."

Alexander stirred and groaned. "Lady." His laboring chest heaved with his effort to breathe.

Roderic glanced down, staring at the old man's claw held between Annandale's small hands. Before his eyes, the supple skin of her fingers cracked and dried, like a leaf withering in the glare of a merciless sun. Her nails shriveled and turned yellow. He did not dare look up at her face. The air seemed to shimmer, rippling with the faintest gleam of gossamer light, like spun strands of purest silver. And then, like the opening of a flower, her flesh plumped and pinkened, the nails grew straight and rosy once more. Roderic dared to look at Alexander's face.

His breathing deepened. He had fallen into a sound sleep.

Annandale sagged and Roderic caught her before she could topple over. Sweat tinged with blood rolled down her face. He cradled her against his chest and reached for a linen square. "By the One, what have you done? Are you all right?" He dabbed at the pale pink drops.

She nodded weakly. "He was very close to death— closer than I realized. It took more for me to heal him than I thought it would."

He pushed her hair away from her face, holding her close against him. "Oh, love, I don't want you to risk yourself that way—"

"Roderic."

Roderic looked up. Alexander's voice was stronger than he had heard it in a long time. He was sitting straight up.

"There isn't much time."

"Time for what, Alex?"

"To stop Amanander."

Roderic stared at his brother as Annandale nestled her head against his shoulder.

Alexander drew a deep breath. "You have my deepest thanks, lady. You saved my life."

From the shelter of Roderic's arms, Annandale nodded. "I think I understand how he got away, Roderic."

The two men stared at her. "How?" they asked, nearly in unison.

"Somehow, Amanander was able to use the Magic to link you to him." She wiped a shaking hand over her face and tried to straighten her shoulders. "He drew upon your—your self, in some way I cannot understand. That is what weakened you to the point of death. He will be able to do this again, and he may not need Alexander as his victim. He has always been able to control minds, at least in some limited, circumscribed way. But this—" She broke off and bit her lip, the shadows beneath her eyes dark smudges on her pale skin. "This seems to indicate that not only can he manipulate matter as well as human minds, he can—"

"He can drain a person of some part of their very selves," Alexander finished for her.

She nodded. "I-I don't know if I could do this again. If his hold on you had been any stronger—if he had taken any more than he did—I think it would have been beyond my ability to help."

"Can he do it again?" Roderic asked, more to himself than to Alexander or Annandale.

Alexander nodded slowly. "I think he can, Roderic.

There's a bond between us—even your lady can't break that. We are linked more closely than blood, he and I."

"I wish Vere were here." Roderic sighed. "When I go to Ithan—" Abruptly he pulled back and gazed into Annandale's dark blue eyes. "I think you must all come with me. You, the children, Tavia, Alex."

"You would move us all to Ithan?" Annandale sat up.

"I cannot risk leaving you here. Ferad and Amanander have proven they can reach into the very heart of Ahga itself. There's no place I could send you where you would be safe. I want Vere to talk to you, Alex. Perhaps there is some way to break this monstrous bond you share with Amanander. But we won't know that until you speak to him, and you, my lady, you and my heir must be protected. If I must keep you by my side always, then so be it."

"Rhodri is so young," she whispered.

"I know," he said. "But I swore to keep you safe."

She only pressed her lips together. Alexander coughed, and Roderic looked over at him.

"What's the situation at Ithan, Roderic?"

"Not good. It looks as though Reginald has allied with the lesser lords in the South. I know—you warned me months ago in the Settle Islands, but when Amanander was injured, Reginald must have decided to stay his hand. It looks as though he has thrown his allegiance in with them. I must consolidate our allies. And talk to Vere, now that Amanander has escaped.

"But there's another reason I need you to come, Alex. You have to help us find Dad. You said something, just now. The King lies beneath a mountain. Can you tell us anything else? Do you think you would know the mountain, if you saw it?"

Alexander spread his hands. "I'm not sure." A shadow crossed his face and he looked away. "I would sooner face an army single-handed than dwell upon those visions, Roderic. But if I must, I shall. I can tell you this . . . Dad is either dying, or he should be." He leaned upon the bed, shaking his head. "You know I will do whatever you wish."

"Roderic—" Annandale tugged at his arm. "It may be dangerous for Alex to come. Amanander has a—a way in, so to speak. If Alex comes closer to him, this—this may happen again."

Roderic looked from his wife to his brother and drew a deep breath. "Alex? What do you say?"

Alex met his eyes squarely. "In any of the dispatches, does Deirdre mention Brea?"

Roderic hesitated. Brea M'Callaster was Deirdre's younger sister, the woman Alexander had loved, and another victim of Amanander's charade when he had pretended to be his twin. "No, Alex. There's been no word of her—not since her daughter was born."

"His daughter," Alexander said through clenched teeth. He met Roderic's eyes squarely. "I'm coming with you. I'll do what I can to find Dad. I have a score to settle with Aman all my own. If going to Ithan brings us closer, so be it. Use me as bait, if you will. Amanander will find me a trap—with teeth."

Chapter Six

❧

Rain dripped from the overhanging branches of the trees and beaded on the tightly woven plaid of Deirdre's cloak like shimmering pearls. Mist swirled at her feet, and the dull thud of the hooves of her mount was curiously muffled. She glanced over her shoulder at the ragged line of men who trudged behind her mount. These trees, barely misted with the first faint green haze of spring, disturbed her—their misshapen trunks taunted her with memories of the twisted wreckage of the dead she had seen too many times in the last weeks. Just ahead of her, she caught a glimpse of Vere moving silently through the trees, his gray, tattered cloak blending into the surrounding terrain almost too perfectly. A Muten trick, she remembered, and immediately she scanned the area around the perimeter of her vision.

Her instincts told her to trust Vere, but her fear of betrayal made her wary. She hoped that by the end of the six days march which Vere had said would bring them to Ithan, they would find that Roderic had arrived as well. It was past time for planning. Kye and Brand and the main body of their forces were moving from the south. She could well imagine Kye's reaction to the news that they were to retire to Ithan. But she understood the necessity of the need to regroup. Vere was silent, worried about the situation more than he let on, but she knew he paced the perimeter of their campsites at night, knew he watched anxiously as he led them over the ancient roadway which wound across the foothills of the Pulatchian Highlands. Although there had been no more ghastly sights like the bodies she had found some weeks ago, she knew the incident was still in his mind.

She glanced up just in time to see Vere pause and hold up his hand in silent warning. Instantly she tensed, holding up her own hand and pulling at the reins so that her horse halted. She slipped out of the saddle, tightening her grip on the sword at her hip. Instinctively she drew a deep breath and choked. The air felt denser, thicker, as though suddenly it had changed to a liquid. She felt her lungs struggle to pull it in, and in that moment, out of the corner of her eye, she saw the trees on the periphery shudder as though something shook the trunks like sticks. Her eyes darted frantically from side to side, and beside her, the horse threw its head back, caught in the same struggle to breathe. She saw the tree closest vibrate as though some unseen force passed through it. With a jerk, something had been released, and she could breathe again. She took a deep breath and the trees on either side of the path burst into flames, like great burning torches.

With a shriek, she turned, and in that instant, a cloud of Mutens dropped from the trees, silent as the falling rain. A cry arose from the men, and she reacted instantly, pulling the sword from its sheath, and crouching as the first opponent jabbed a vicious side blow to her unprotected flank.

Behind her she could hear the sergeant try to rally the men into some semblance of order. The burning trees hemmed them in tightly, and the Mutens cut through the ranks as cleanly as a scythe through corn. Beneath the shouts of the frightened men, the screams of the wounded and the dying, the Mutens fought with silent, eerie precision.

Deirdre sliced her sword across a Muten's throat and it fell, blood fountaining across her in wide spray, blinding her temporarily as another sprang up in front. In the confusion she could see nothing but the red mist before her eyes, hear nothing but the hoarse shouts and high-pitched screams.

Her horse reared and neighed, hooves flailing, and out of the corner of her eye, she saw a razor spear whistle through the air, slicing through the animal's throat cleanly as butter. "No!" she cried, turning her back blindly, momentarily forgetting everything but the loss of the animal she had reared from childhood. And then Vere was there, swinging his quarter stave, knocking opponents off their feet, dodging blows with complicated twists and turns of his body. In the press of battle, he grabbed at her arm. "Come," he cried, "run."

"What?" she screamed back.

"We're outnumbered—there're more of them than you can imagine—this way—"

Deirdre glanced over her shoulder. The forest path was a mass of men and Mutens, white and gray shapes moving with deadly proficiency through the ranks of men.

"I can get you out—now."

The moment seemed to collapse, then expand, and the decision was made for her. To stay meant certain death. The furious flames hissed and snapped as the wet wood burned, leaping out with long tongues as though to snatch the hapless company. She cast a last desperate glance over her shoulder. Her men crumpled beneath the onslaught. She was less expendable than they.

She pulled her battle-plaid closer about her shoulders and nodded. Vere grasped her arm, and four white-garbed forms dropped in front of them. With one mighty stroke, Deirdre swung her sword and thrust simultaneously with her dagger as Vere slashed with his quarter stave. The Mutens fell, howling, into a burning tree. Vere grabbed her arm again and pulled her through the underbrush. They ran.

The stench of burning flesh, the cries of her abandoned men pursued them through the trees, the branches catching at her plaid like grasping hands. Finally, Vere paused, his breath coming in hard gasps.

She leaned against the black-ribbed trunk of an ancient tree, her own breathing ragged, her chest pounding. Her upper arm and her shoulder throbbed with a dull ache. She closed her eyes, seeing once again the mound of white forms writhing on the bodies of her men, like a thick mass of maggots. Bile rose in her throat, and she opened her eyes to see Vere staring into the distance, his gray hair blowing across his shoulders. "How did that happen?"

He turned to face her, the lines of his face etched deeply. "I don't know. I have never seen anything like that."

"You don't know . . ." she echoed. She gazed at Vere,

at the Muten dress he wore, the gray cloak held at his throat by an iron clasp of Muten make, at the faded Muten tattoos which swirled upon his thin cheeks. "You don't know."

With a motion so fast he didn't have time to flinch, she was on him, her dagger held to his throat. He stumbled back, taken completely by surprise, as she twisted her hands in the fabric of his tunic. She felt his body go limp beneath her as she pressed the edge of the weapon beneath his chin, the pain in her upper arm and shoulder entirely forgotten.

"Kill me if you wish, M'Callaster." His eyes were steady and dark in the shadowed light. "But I swear I had nothing to do with the ambush."

For a moment she hesitated, tightening her grip in the fabric of his tunic. She felt his body relax beneath her, and he moved only slightly, tilting his chin up in a gesture of submission. With a sigh, she let go and moved back, sheathing the dagger as she did so. "I'm sorry," she spoke over her shoulder. "I know there's a traitor—even if Brand refuses to believe me—and now—"

"I assure you that attack had nothing to do with either Atland or the traitor." Vere rose to his feet, brushing debris off his clothes. "It is as well that Roderic has called this Convening—Atland's sons had better give up this nonsense of rebellion, or there will be nothing for them to fight over."

"What do you mean?" Deirdre gathered her cloak around her, thankful that the heavy wool stayed dry despite the steady drip of the rain beneath the thick branches.

"Come, M'Callaster—with some luck, I can get us to Ithan. We may be able to travel more quickly—now." He paused, and his face was grim. "We have a few hours of daylight left. I know a place not far from here where we can spend the night."

"Tell me what the ambush means to you," she said as she hastened after him.

Vere paused and looked around, squinting through the trees. "This way. And not now. The forest may hide more secrets . . . and sharper ears than you might imagine may be listening."

Deirdre glanced over her shoulder. Nothing moved but the steady drip of the rain. A breeze made the leaves shiver on the branches. The forest was still. "Lead on."

Through the still and silent afternoon he led her, easing under branches, over underbrush, treading as carefully as a lycat in his boots of smooth leather. She followed as quietly as she could, cursing more than once the life she had spent in the saddle. As the light began to fade, Vere emerged into a clearing. "Here," he said, his voice low. "See there—we can shelter there for the night."

Over his shoulder, Deirdre saw the shell of an abandoned building. She looked down and abruptly realized they had been following the remains of an old road, heavy with undergrowth, the black surface nearly obscured by the forest around it, but the ghost of which had been sufficient for Vere to follow. A wind whined through the branches, and abruptly she shivered.

"There will be dry wood inside," Vere said, as if he had noticed her shudder. "Come, M'Callaster."

Silently he led her through the falling dark, into the crumbling shell of the building. With a dubious eye, she surveyed the crumbling mortar and stone blocks. Such sights were common all over Meriga. Vere fumbled in a corner and emerged carrying what looked like a clear-faced, shiny cylinder. He pressed a button on its side and abruptly light flooded the space. Deirdre jumped. "What's that?"

"Cold fire torch," he said shortly, as though he didn't want to be questioned further. "You should understand, M'Callaster, that there are things here you may not understand. It would be better if you kept your questions to a minimum . . . I would prefer not to lie."

"Why would you lie?"

"There are things here I am sworn not to reveal."

Another flick of the wrist, it seemed, and Vere had a fire burning in a battered grate. Curiously, in spite of herself, Deirdre watched him amongst the rubble. It occurred to her that the rubble was carefully placed; the whole place was artfully arranged so as to appear no more than what it appeared to be: an abandoned shell of an old building. As the flames flickered in the dark night, Deirdre ate the stew he handed her, forbearing to ask where he had gotten it. Finally, she set her bowl aside and winced as she straightened her arm.

"I'd better dress that wound for you, M'Callaster." Vere rummaged in one of the caches, and as she stripped off her tunic and her shirt, she could feel that he deliberately averted his eyes.

Silently he bandaged the wound, and she noticed detachedly that the wound was serious, that a razor spear had slashed nearly all the way to the bone. It would be a long time healing. But she saw, too, that his fingers trembled as they brushed her flesh, and she smiled to herself. Surprised, she felt an answering response in her belly.

"You saved my life," she said, watching him as he busied himself with the utensils.

"I did."

"Look at me."

Reluctantly, she thought, he raised his eyes to hers. The resemblance to Roderic was fleeting, she thought. There was nothing of the Prince in the narrow face, in the set of the eyes, or the long jutting nose.

"What happened back there?"

He dropped his eyes once more. Was it possible, she wondered, that any man could be more transparent than Vere?

"I don't give a damn about your Muten secrets, Vere. I just lost nearly three hundred men, and I have a right to know how they died. What happened back there wasn't natural and you know it. There's something gone terribly wrong that has nothing to do with human treachery. Now . . . are you going to answer my question?"

Vere took a deep breath. Even in the shadows the struggle was plain on his face. He sighed and slowly nodded. "You may not believe me if I tell you the truth."

"Try," she said dryly.

"Do you know what the old Magic is?"

"Old Magic?" She shrugged. The wind blew harder and she shivered. Her clothes were damp, and the falling dark had lowered the temperature. Vere held out a blanket. "The Keepers tell these tales . . . of men who could bend steel with their minds, who could shift the earth with a thought . . . but what have they to do with us?"

"You know what mathematics is . . . the study of numbers?"

She shrugged. "'Tis forbidden by the Church."

"Yes," he said, the flames leaping high as the wind blew through the low hanging of the branches of the tree overhead. "For good reason, I suppose. The old Magic is a series of mathematical equations which enable one to manipulate the fabric of the material world with the force of the human will."

Deirdre sucked in a deep breath, not certain she understood. "You mean that with the Magic a person can do anything he sets his mind to do?"

Vere nodded. "More or less. Did you feel how the air seemed to thicken before the trees burst into flame? That's one of the warning signs of the Magic about to manifest. It doesn't always happen, but—but often enough." He took another deep breath and stared moodily into the night. "But it isn't as it seems. For everything that one does—any changes one makes—there is always a price. Something else happens . . . something you can't control or predict."

Deirdre listened, digesting the information. "Then what was the price?"

Vere shook his head. "There is no way to know that. But someone—and I believe I know who—is becoming very bold in the use of the Magic—and is taking carefully calculated risks."

"Who?" Deirdre asked.

"The name will mean nothing to you. And I would rather not say it—there are too many variables at work here. It is impossible to say whether he or one of his minions is about—"

"You think there is someone near?" Instantly Deirdre

was alert. Her hand reached for her sword where it lay by her side, discarded.

Vere reached out and gripped her arm. "Relax, M'Callaster. No one is nearby. I only meant that this person has ways of listening—ways of finding things out. There is no doubt in my mind that the attack today was aimed at you."

"At me? What quarrel does a Muten have with me?"

Vere studied her face. "You are one of Roderic's allies."

"And what does this Muten want of Roderic?"

"His wife, for one thing."

A sudden gust of wind made the flames leap higher and Deirdre pulled her blanket tighter about her bare shoulders. Roderic's name triggered a vision of Roderic's face, and she gazed into the center of the fire.

She stared moodily into the black night. Vere crouched beside the fire, tending it. "Vere."

"M'Callaster?"

"You know my name's Deirdre." She tossed her thick braid over her shoulder. "I don't think I thanked you for saving my life."

He shrugged. "You saved mine."

She raised her brow, and he nodded. "It was your skill with that—" he pointed to the sword lying sheathed by her side "—that saved us." Suddenly he took a deep breath and looked at her. "I am glad you decided to stay."

She glanced pointedly around the surroundings and smiled ruefully. "I am not sure I feel the same way at the moment."

"You know what I mean." The intensity in his glance took her breath away.

"Yes." She nodded slowly. "I believe I do." For a moment they stared at each other, and she was suddenly conscious that the wind had died, that the only noises were the slow drip of the rain through the trees and the snap and hiss of the fire. To her astonishment color rose in his cheeks, staining the faded tattoos. "What are you thinking?"

He dropped his eyes and turned away, shaking his head, mumbling something indistinguishable.

A smile played at the corners of her mouth. "Shall I tell you what you are thinking?"

He looked up, suspicion narrowing the corners of his eyes.

"You're thinking that you're a man and I'm a woman—and that by the grace of the goddess we escaped with our lives today and the night is cold and you wonder if I am warm—" She paused, not letting her eyes stray from his face. "And if we would not be warmer together."

"M'Callaster—Deirdre—" he whispered. "I-I have—haven't—"

"Hush." She reached for him, cupping her hand around his chin, drawing her face close to his. "When there has been dying, there must be living. 'Tis the way of it, the Keepers say—the balance must be kept. 'Tis no surprise."

He made a little noise in his throat just as she pressed her mouth on his, and then his arms went around her, carefully, mindful of her wounds. As the flames leapt higher, they shuddered together in the orange light.

Chapter Seven

※⌒♪

*T*he stench from the poison pit burned his nostrils. Amanander curled his lip and turned his head, pulling his cloak closer against his face. A warm, damp wind shook the trees, heavy with oily droplets, and the sky overhead roiled with lowering clouds. He shifted in his saddle, less from impatience than from discomfort, and his companions paused in their deliberations, glancing at him over their shoulders. Their voices were barely audible, for they spoke in low guttural tones, their twisted speech falling in unfamiliar cadences upon his ear. Here and there he heard a word he understood, and again and again, he heard a name repeated: Jama.

Amanander flexed his hands. It had been three weeks since his escape from the confines of Ahga and his own mind, but his body was weak, his muscles wasted and diminished. It would take a long time for him to recuperate the strength which had been his, and he forced his shoulders square. But his mind—oh, that was another story. Through the process of sapping Alexander's energy, Amanander had felt himself renewed and replenished in a way he had never thought possible. Whatever force had been drained from his twin, it existed within

Amanander now, part of him and yet not part of him—a source of strength that allowed him to think with acute perceptions despite his weakened body.

He watched his tutor with a measuring stare. Ferad had raised the Magic to another level. That much was obvious. Amanander stared into the distance and considered the problem of how to make the knowledge his. He doubted Ferad would share the secret willingly.

"Are you in pain?" Gartred interrupted his thoughts, her voice a persistent whine as annoying as the beetles which swarmed through the campsites at night.

Amanander looked at the woman as though seeing her for the first time. The journey had been hard on her. Her hair was scraped back under her hood, and her eyes had dark shadows beneath them. Without the aid of her customary cosmetics, her skin was pasty. But her mind was as easily read as a child's primer, and he smiled slowly at her. She would make an excellent object for his experiments. "No." He slid his eyes away from her and fixed his gaze on Ferad. Deep within his mind, he was aware of some residual echo of Ferad's presence there. More out of idleness, he turned the focus of his thoughts inward, aimed upon that tenuous thread.

Amanander was surprised when Ferad turned as if in answer to a summons. An odd expression crossed the Muten's disfigured face, one almost of fear—definitely one of surprise. A ghost of a memory flitted through his mind. *Philosophers have argued for centuries over what is real—some would argue this is more real than the material world.* The words floated to the surface, twisting and beckoning like a ribbon of road at twilight, leading down to— To what? Amanander wondered. What was real—and what did that mean?

Before Amanander could continue to ponder this any longer, the whole group seemed to reach some kind of assent, for they grunted, and nodded, patched gray robes fluttering as the group dispersed.

A squat figure approached and reached for the bridle of Amanander's horse. "Come," the Muten grunted in its fractured accent. "Jama-taw awaits."

Amanander slid out of the saddle slowly, his lips narrowed from the concentration required to dismount without shaking.

"Let me help." Gartred offered her hand, and he rebuffed her with a look.

He would not have anyone's pity. Ferad's Magic had been sufficient to restore him to sanity, Alexander's borrowed vigor sufficient to restore his body to some semblance of its former self, but nothing but exercise could restore his withered limbs to what they had been before. Before. His mind shied away from the realization of what his impatience had cost. It was his own fault that he had taken Annandale, only to let her slip through his fingers. He should have ridden south with her, gone back to Dlas, risked capture rather than try to withstand the siege of Minnis. This time, this time, he vowed, he would move slowly, consider each action and its consequences before making the choice. He would not be thwarted again.

He favored Gartred with a smile. The hen simpered, her lashes fluttering grotesquely over her plump cheeks. Life in Ahga, even in her imprisonment, had been easy for Gartred. Where once she had been pleasantly rounded, her curves were now turning to fat. But she would suffice, he thought as he smiled at her over his shoulder. Oh, yes, she would suffice.

He followed the Muten off the beaten path, through the low hanging branches of the trees which dripped a silvery moss.

Beneath the hanging branches of a gnarled tree, another figure waited. Amanander slung his wet cloak over his shoulder and hooked his thumbs in his belt. He glanced at Ferad. "Well? We've wasted enough time."

The figure raised his head with slow dignity. Amanander looked down into the eyes of a Muten no older than seventeen or eighteen, who met Amanander's stare with a guileless innocence.

"Who the hell are you?"

The corners of Ferad's thin mouth lifted, and his secondary arms quivered. "My Prince, may I present Jamataw."

Amanander turned again to the boy before him. He was thin, this Jama. His hair was held away from his face by a leather circlet. The skin of his face was smooth, unmarked by the elaborate tribal tattoos which decorated the faces of every other Muten Amanander had ever seen. The absence of the tattoos, as well as his obvious youth, emphasized his human appearance, despite the third eye set in its wrinkled socket above and between the other two. Amanander shuddered inexplicably. There was something very disquieting in the youth's appearance. "I've met your father." He paused, remembering a day which seemed like a very long time ago. "And your brother."

The boy hissed. His voice was deeper than

Amanander expected, and he pronounced the unfamiliar words carefully, his lips slowly shaping each one around his accent. "You were there?"

Amanander nodded. "The day Roderic the Butcher forced your father's hand to peace? Yes." He wondered what the boy would say if he knew whose hand had forced Roderic's.

"You did nothing to stop him."

It was neither a question nor challenge, only a statement of fact, and Amanander looked harder at the boy before him on the ground. "There was nothing I could do to stop him." Amanander frowned. He did not like the idea of justifying his actions, past, present, or future, to this scrap of Muten flesh.

Jama's dark eyes did not waver. "But you are ready to do something now."

"Yes." Amanander met the boy's stare and wondered fleetingly if he might try just a hint of the Magic. No, he decided. Let the boy find out later just who—and what—he dealt with. "I claim the throne of Meriga."

"You are the heir of the Ridenau King."

Amanander glanced at Ferad and shrugged. Were they going to waste all day exchanging meaningless titles? "Would that your words carried weight in the Congress."

Ferad made a noise like a curse deep in his throat. "I brought you here for a reason, my Prince. Will you listen?"

Amanander glanced over his shoulder. He wanted nothing more than to be away from these creatures, who skulked on the edges of existence. His cousin Harland's castle was less than a day's ride away, and he longed for a hot bath, a soft bed, and peace in which to consider the implications of his newfound realizations about the Magic. But he remembered his vow to curb his impatience and so he nodded. "Of course."

"Will you sit?" The boy's voice scraped over his ear like gravel.

With a little grimace, Amanander sank down on the mossy ground a few paces from Jama. A rude clay cup was placed in his hands, and as he raised it hesitantly to his mouth, the green herbal scent made his mouth water unexpectedly. "Talk."

"My people have hidden in the hollows and the hills for generations. This you know, Prince of the Ridenaus. Your people have hunted us, killed us, starved us . . . but we have held on against all odds."

Amanander sipped from the cup. "What do you want of me that you acknowledge me to be the Prince of Meriga?"

"There is no poetry in your soul," whispered the boy. Fear flickered in his eyes as he glanced from Amanander to Ferad and back.

"None." Amanander drained the mug to the dregs.

"I offer you my men. In exchange for a homeland."

"You want a piece of Meriga?"

"A homeland . . . where we will not be beaten and starved and killed. Where we can grow old in peace and bear our children and raise them to adults. Is that so much to ask?"

"Why not go to Roderic? Even if he is the Butcher, he's the heir of Meriga. I am merely a dispossessed nobody."

"No," the boy's voice was soft. "He is not."

"What? What are you saying?"

Ferad leaned forward and his breath was soft on Amanander's neck. "Roderic is not the heir of Meriga, for he is not the son of the King."

"*What?*"

"Abelard forced his witch to use the Magic to aid his Queen to conceive," said Ferad. "And Roderic is indeed the son of the Queen. But not the son of the King."

"Who—?" Amanander paused as the answer reared up before him like a lycat on the hunt. "Phineas. A stablehand's son . . . my father left the throne of Meriga to the get of a stablehand's son?" He felt as though a claw of rage, black as obsidian and harder than granite, clutched his heart. He could scarcely breathe.

There was a silence, the only sound the steady call of the birds who hunted the swamps, calling back and forth. He raised his eyes to Ferad. "My father did this? To me?"

The Muten's three eyes stared back. "Do you think your father was above doing anything, if he thought it would secure his throne?"

Amanander gazed back. "No. But how do you know this? How are you so sure?"

Ferad shrugged. "As the King's condition has weakened—shall we say—it has become easier to breach the defenses of his will. I thought you would be particularly interested in that piece of information."

"Why didn't you tell me immediately?"

Ferad shrugged. "What use to us is this information?"

"What use?" Amanander echoed, his mind spinning through a thousand possibilities. He could confront the Congress. He could raise an army. He could challenge

Roderic before them all. In a burst of triumph, he saw himself ride into Ithan and demand to be heard. They would listen to him, the assembled Senadors, and Roderic would be set aside and the throne of Meriga handed to him—

"Prince," said Ferad softly, "we have no proof. If you go to Ithan and raise your voice against Roderic, what will it profit you? There is no one save Phineas himself who can corroborate this story, and I think that even Phineas's honor will allow him to lie under those circumstances. And you are the most wanted man in Meriga at this moment . . . who will entertain your story while you are sent to Ahga under heavy guard? No—confrontation is not the way. Surely you understand that. You must make alliances. And here is the offer of one."

"Where is my father?"

"Nearby, but very close to death. It is getting harder to keep him alive. Especially in such agony."

"I want him alive, Ferad."

"As you say, my Prince." The Muten leaned back and folded his hands beneath his robe. "But let us discuss that matter another time. What say you to an alliance?"

Amanander drew a deep breath, pressed his lips close together. His emotions were swirling, his thoughts a jumble of despair, anger, rage. How could Abelard have deliberately set him aside? What had he done to make his father hate him so? From the beginning Abelard had refused to name him heir, even when to do so would have meant that Abelard could have kept Nydia with him openly at Ahga rather than hiding her away in the wilds of the North Woods.

A thousand possibilities swirled through his mind, each one rejected almost as soon as it occurred to him. Not even Harland could hear this news—for how could he say he had come by it? Only the King, only Phineas— and Phineas's loyalty to the King and to his unacknowledged son was bound to be absolute. An emotion beyond rage surged through his spirit, fetid as the dark depths of the poison pit which smoked and stank just a few paces away.

And yet—in the midst of this anger, this hatred, some part of himself which seemed to stand apart, reminded him of the tremendous energy of the emotion he experienced. These emotions existed in every being, human or Muten. He stared up at the tree behind Jama, a vine snaking up its trunk to twine like a noose around the lower hanging branches. If such energy existed, surely it had enormous potential to be harnessed. And if he could learn to control this energy, focus it, use it, all of Meriga would be his for the asking. What would it matter then what he had promised these miserable Mutens?

He raised his head and met the eyes of the young Muten. In the inscrutable depths was no sympathy, no pity, only an even resolve. "I accept." He allowed his eyes to focus unblinking on the Muten who sat unmoving before him. "Aid me in this and all of the Estate of Nourk will be yours."

He saw surprise flicker in the Muten's eyes, and the impenetrable gaze registered shock. Nourk was a rich plum, defended by the mountains and the sea, a separate principality governed by his fat brother, Phillip, who never bestirred himself to either aid or hinder. Let him learn the cost of neutrality, thought Amanander. He looked at Ferad and rose, gathering the folds of his cloak around him. "Come." He gestured to his old tutor. "We ride to Harland of Missiluse."

"Where will we meet again, lord?" asked Jama as Amanander turned his back to stalk away.

"You will hear from me," replied Amanander. "Do nothing until you hear." The boy opened his mouth to protest, and Amanander glanced at Ferad. "Practice patience. Your people have waited five hundred years or more for a homeland. What's another month or two?"

"B-But, lord-" For the first time Jama sounded like he might be close to the age he looked. "We have already attacked. My men, aided by the Brotherhood, have destroyed three hundred of their troops."

Gartred gasped from her perch on the saddle. Amanander paused with his foot in the stirrup. He deliberately set his foot down and turned to face Jama. "You've done what?" He looked at Ferad. "You didn't tell me about this."

Ferad shrugged. "It seemed unnecessary. I didn't think—"

"No." Amanander narrowed his eyes. "That much is obvious. You counsel me to have patience. I suggest you hearken to your own advice." Jama had risen to his feet, but even standing, Amanander topped him by nearly a foot. "Did anyone survive this attack?"

"We—we don't know. But over a thousand of my warriors attacked a force of less than three hundred. I doubt anyone could have escaped."

Amanander frowned. "How old are you, boy?"

"Eighteen." Jama gasped as Amanander closed the distance between them and twisted the front of his tunic in his fist. The other Mutens growled and muttered, drawing in close, but Ferad held up his hand and they halted.

"Eighteen. Still have the taste of your mammy's milk on your tongue. You listen to me, boy. If you want this alliance, you will do as I say, when I say it, and not before." Amanander spoke with narrowed eyes and clenched jaw. He was gratified to see that flick of fear in Jama's eyes again. So the whelp was afraid of him. Good. Now, if only he could discover a way to turn that fear to his own uses. "How did the Brotherhood aid in this attack? Did they use Magic?" He bore down into the three dark eyes, unflinching.

"Yes," whispered Jama.

"You'd better pray that there were no survivors, or the hope of the Children will be short-lived. We don't want that upstart pretender to think that there's anything more afoot than he already suspects." He released Jama abruptly, and the youth stumbled back against the vine-covered trunk. "Is that clear?"

"Perfectly, Lord Prince."

He raked the whole company of Mutens with a look of utter contempt. "Fools," he muttered. "Your first order is to wipe out those who remain at the College."

"But—but, lord—"

Amanander leaned so close he could see the quivering lashes which rimmed the Muten's third eye. "The College of Elders is our greatest threat. You know they have ever counseled caution. They have stood in the way of your people claiming what is rightfully yours. They walk the path of peace, to the exclusion of all others. They prefer to hide their Magic when it could have been used to help you more times that you can begin to count. They blind and mutilate themselves, and the rest of you starve to death in your hovels."

Amanander stood back with a satisfied air at the horror he read in Jama's face. "Leave the humans to me. But sooner or later, especially now that you've attacked Roderic's forces using the Magic, Roderic is going to ally with the College, and we don't want that to happen. Do you know where the College is now?"

Jama bit his lip and gave a short shake of his head. "N-no, Lord Prince," he said sullenly.

"Then I suggest you find it. And quickly." He snapped his fingers at Ferad. "Come." He swung into the saddle and rode away without a backward glance.

Chapter Eight

❧

*T*he wide inner ward of Ithan Ford within the high walls of crushed rubble teemed with men, women, and horses, and makeshift shelters which housed children and small animals of every seeming description. As a young boy led his horse away, Roderic stripped off his gloves and turned to help Annandale from her saddle. "By the One," he muttered.

"What's all this, Roderic?" Annandale looked around with a mixture of interest and disbelief. Even on Appeals Days the inner wards of Ahga were never so crowded.

"Refugees," he said. Rumors of war were rampant. The Harleys were said to be poised to invade from the West, the Mutens were said to be on the move from the East. And with the lesser lords of the South in rebellion, the people were taking no chances. Around the great castle a city of tents and other temporary shelters had sprung up, a city which extended for miles around the perimeter of the outer defenses of Ithan. Roderic had noted wearily that the presence of the civilians would make the defense that much more difficult. And yet, he knew, who could blame them—the wretched people who scraped a living from the dust of the Arkan Plains or the hollows of the Pulatchian Mountains?

Within the walls of Ithan, supplies and provisions lay stacked in high piles along the walls, adding to the cramped chaos. Men in the uniforms of the King's Army, as well as the colors of the Senador of the Tennessy Fall, and the M'Callaster of the Settle Islands, interspersed with drably dressed servants, milled through the open space, their faces drawn and grim. Here and there a woman or a child scurried through the mass of men, intent upon some errand.

"Roderic!" Brand's familiar voice cut through the roar of the crowd with a definite authority. Roderic looked up to see the tall, broad-shouldered bulk of his brother moving through the crowd toward him with practiced ease. He extended his hand to Brand, who embraced him with a tight hug. "Thank the One you made it here." There were shadows beneath Brand's eyes, and deep lines extended from his nose to his chin. His face seemed to sag on his cheekbones. Despite his military bearing, Brand looked almost as old as Phineas.

"Brand?" Annandale's soft voice reached the men. Brand released Roderic and took the hand she held out to him. He brought it to his lips, and Roderic saw his eyes fill with sudden tears.

"Lady," he muttered, his voice rough in his throat.

"She didn't suffer, Brand."

Brand closed his eyes against the tears and breathed a long, shuddering sigh. "She was a good woman—the best wife a man could ask. She did not deserve to die that way."

"She was very dear to us all." Annandale gazed steadily into Brand's face, her small white hand wrapped around his scarred paw. As Roderic watched, a faint light, so subtle as to be unnoticeable except by those who knew what to look for, limned Brand's hand, and with a soft sigh, Brand nodded, the lines of his face relaxing momentarily.

"I know she's at peace, lady," he said as he released Annandale's hand. "I can believe that now."

With a sigh, and a shake of his head, as though he would shrug off his grief, he turned again to Roderic. "Which is more than I can say for the rest of us."

"Brand!" Alexander's voice preceded him. He hobbled through the crowd, one hand tightly gripping a wooden staff. As Roderic looked up, he saw the shock in Brand's eyes.

"Alex?" Brand whispered. "By the One—" He reached out to clasp his brother's free hand. "Are you—are you all right?"

Looking from brother to brother, Roderic realized just how sickly Alexander must appear to someone who had not seen him in months.

Alexander nodded and straightened his bent back with visible effort. "I am better, much better. You didn't think I would be content to chafe at home while you got all the glory, did you?" He grinned at Brand with something of his old humor. "I have business with Amanander of my own. Nothing would have held me at Ahga."

Brand sighed. "Unfortunately, Amanander is the least of our problems right now, Alex."

"I believe I may be able to assist in the search for Dad.

I think he's being held somewhere in these mountains to the south."

The look Brand shot his brother bordered on derision. "I mean our father no disrespect, Alex, nor you, but if we don't take some decisive action, and soon, we may lose the estates south of here."

Alexander flushed an ugly mottled scarlet. Annandale cleared her throat softly and Roderic took Brand's arm, guiding him away before he could say anything to upset Alex further. "What's the situation here?" With a little gesture, Roderic indicated the way through the crowd into the castle proper.

"Not good." Brand shook his head. "We lost a full regiment of Deirdre's men—they were ambushed by Mutens on their way here. Vere and Deirdre got away, but we can ill afford those losses." Brand stopped on the steps, hooked his thumbs in his swordbelt, and gazed over the ordered confusion in the ward. "There is so much to discuss and so little time to tell you all. The Senators have begun to arrive. Obayana is here, as well as Norda Coda and all the Arkan Lords. But Roderic—not one of the Western lords is come, nor has Phillip bestirred himself from behind his mountains. Kye is here to represent his father, and Ginya has sent his regrets. I can't blame him for thinking twice about venturing across the mountains."

"Missiluse?"

Brand shook his head. "Not yet. And to my mind, not at all."

Abruptly, Brand broke off and craned his head as sudden shouts announced another arrival. "Looks like someone else is here."

From the direction of the gates, there were commands among the guards, and the crowd parted to let through a mud-splattered man who stumbled across the courtyard with the shambling steps of exhaustion. "A messenger?" Roderic looked up and recognized the dark blue uniform of the kingdom messengers. Several soldiers pointed directly to him. The messenger crossed the cobbled courtyard, clutching a wooden tube in one gloved hand.

"Lord Prince?" The man raised a bearded face to the four standing on the steps.

Roderic beckoned. "I am he."

The messenger went down on his knee and held out the wooden tube. Roderic recognized the round wax seals. "Your brother Everard sends you greetings and begs you excuse his presence at this Convening. A matter of more pressing urgency has presented itself, and he begs you read this letter."

Roderic broke the seals, withdrew the parchment inside, and read the letter with growing alarm. With an anxiety that belied the square set of his shoulders, Roderic crumpled the parchment and stared at the messenger, who still knelt on one knee before him. "Are you sure of this?"

"My Lord Everard said to bring it to you with all haste, Lord Prince."

Roderic gazed into the messenger's exhausted face. Only the truth deserved such urgency. "Yes," he said slowly, turning the information over in his mind. "Go and get some food—the captain of the messengers will see to your needs."

"As you say, Lord Prince." The messenger bowed

with the stiffness of one who has spent many days in the saddle and disappeared into the crowd.

Roderic smoothed the parchment and read it once more in disbelief. How was it possible, he wondered, that so much could go wrong all at once? He handed it to Brand. "Read this. It's as well Phillip has chosen to stay in Nourk. Everard will need everything Phillip can give him."

Brand took the parchment and read it silently. "But will he give it?" His eyes met Roderic's, and Roderic knew both of them thought the same thing. Phillip's notorious reluctance to step outside the mountain borders of Nourk was rapidly becoming more than simply an annoyance. The Muten Tribes had launched another rebellion, this time one which extended well into the Dirondac Mountains. Everard, long trusted by the Muten Elders in the north, could only report that the situation had deteriorated into chaos. There would be no reinforcements from him.

Roderic slung his cloak over his shoulder and bit back a curse. "Summon a council meeting while I wash some of this stink off. I want Vere, the M'Callaster, Obayana, Arkan . . . and Phineas." Roderic gestured with his thumb to where the litter-bearers were helping Phineas out of the wagon and into his litter. "If he's up to it, after the journey."

"As you say, Lord Prince." Brand nodded grimly, without a trace of humor. "I know Deirdre is impatient to begin the campaign."

"Lord Prince!"

Roderic looked up. The doors of the central keep were

open. The Senador of the Tennessy Fall, a man some years younger than Brand, threaded his way across the crowded terrace, a silver welcoming goblet steaming in his hands.

"Forgive me for not greeting you before this, Lord Prince." Miles bowed and offered Roderic the cup.

Roderic took the cup, drank deeply of the spiced wine and passed it to Annandale. "Think nothing of it, Miles. I've little time for ceremony." He ran his hand over his chin. "It won't mean much to any of us if we can't untangle this coil."

Annandale spoke softly beside him as she passed the cup to Alexander. "I am very glad to see you again, Lord Senador."

An expression of near worship crossed the Senador's face as he gazed at her, and Roderic felt the familiar tingle of pride that his wife should be so beautiful. It was entirely possible, now that he had named his heir, that Annandale was free to seek her pleasure elsewhere. The thought of her taking another man pierced him like an arrow. He glanced down at her.

As if she heard the echo of his thoughts, she raised her face and gazed calmly into his eyes. Within the depths of cloudless blue, he read a wordless reassurance.

Miles babbled a welcome, sounding anything but the battle-hardened veteran he was, and with a little squeeze on Roderic's forearm, Annandale smiled. "I shall be glad to rest beneath your roof, indeed, Lord Senador, if you would be so kind as to show me where."

"Oh—oh, of course, lady. Forgive me, I didn't mean to keep you standing. Come, all of you."

Inside, the great hall of Ithan Ford was no less a scene of confusion than the inner ward. As Roderic slung his cloak off his shoulders and stripped his gloves off his hands, he gazed around the great hall. Like the hall of Ahga, Ithan clearly dated from before the Armageddon. Its high roof arched over great sweeps of glass. The fireplaces, which had been cut into the sides, were obviously more recent additions. As his gaze fell over the assembly, his eye was caught by a swirl of bright plaid, the fall of red-brown hair. A lanky form unfolded itself from a place by a hearth, and Deirdre moved with a lycat's grace to his side.

"Lord Prince." She rested her hand on the hilt of her dagger. Her face was pale with fatigue and he noticed her right arm was in a sling. She looked thinner than he remembered.

"Deirdre," he said softly. The sight of Deirdre, her feet firmly planted, her shoulders squared, brought a deep sense of relief. What was it about the woman, he wondered, that made him believe that no matter how awful the situation, he could prevail?

Deirdre nodded. "And this, your lady-wife?"

Suddenly he was aware of Annandale beside him. He glanced down, and she smiled up at him. Deirdre stood quietly, looking at the two of them with cool appraisal in her dark eyes, and suddenly he remembered the night she had come to him and offered her aid, the bargain they had made between them, and the dreams he'd had afterward. With the naming of his heir, he, too, was free to seek his pleasures elsewhere. But Deirdre, every bit as much a warrior as he, was not likely to insist he keep the promise now.

Annandale gazed at the woman, who swept her dark eyes over her as boldly as a man. There was an energy about the woman who stood before them, which leapt as eagerly as a fire in a dry hearth. Her huge hands, webbed with old scars, gripped the hilt of her dagger and her swordbelt with white-knuckled tension. Why tense? wondered Annandale. For in every line of the woman's raw-boned face she read loyalty. And then, she saw Deirdre's eyes fall upon Roderic. A rush of feeling swept over Annandale like a tide. She stifled a gasp. Why, she loves him, thought Annandale. With everything she has, she loves him.

Deirdre's eyes met hers, and in them Annandale read sorrow and love and a certain envy. Don't envy me, she wanted to cry. He may be mine for the moment, but that will change. Everything is going to change. But she bit the words back, and instead glanced at Roderic. His hand was tight upon her arm, and for the first time in weeks, she saw a genuine smile play across his face. The burden of his responsibility lightened, suddenly he looked young again, instead of a man twice his age. She's good for him, thought Annandale. She thought again of the final prophecy she had seen in her mother's dying moment. This woman who stood before them both, rawboned and vital, with strength emanating from every line, this woman was the woman who would help Roderic bear the sorrow of her death.

Tears filled her eyes, and she gripped Roderic's arm tighter. A sob choked her, and Roderic broke off in mid-sentence. "My love," he said, turning to look down at her, "what is it?"

She bit her lip and closed her eyes, knowing the color drained from her face.

"You're tired and here we stand. Forgive me, lady." He looked at Miles, who was talking to Alexander and Brand. "Take us to our rooms. My lady is still not recovered from the birth of our son—she needs to rest." His arm went around her, steadying her, pulling her close, and she nestled instinctively. "Come, sweet—" He nodded to the others. "We'll talk more later."

Immediately, Miles beckoned a broad-bosomed woman with white hair. "My First Lady, Lord Prince, Lady Princess. This is Norah. She will see you to your rooms. If there is anything you require, lady, say but the word."

Annandale nodded, and as Roderic gestured for her women, they were shepherded from the hall. Clucking, Lady Norah led them through the crowd, through the maze of corridors and up several flights of steps, to the set of rooms which was to be theirs. As she opened the door, Rhodri gave a high-pitched yell from his nursemaid's arms.

"Oh, the poor little one," crooned Norah. "Such a journey for such a little lamb. I'll send you more hot water, lady. There's fruit and bread and cheese—if you require anything at all, it will be my pleasure to provide it."

With a gentle squeeze upon her hand, Norah was gone. Roderic eased her through the door, motioning to her women to come and help remove the heavy cloak, the muddied traveling shoes.

When at last she was lying on the wide bed, the baby nestled, nursing in her arms, the fire snapping on the broad hearth, he sat beside her on the bed and touched her cheek.

She smiled. "I know."

"You *are* a witch, aren't you?"

"It doesn't require witchcraft to understand that you have work to do. I know you're itching to begin. Go on."

"Will you be all right?"

"I'll be fine."

He touched the baby's forehead with the tips of his fingers. "You two are the most precious things in the world to me, you know that, don't you?"

The child sighed in his sleep, and the nipple slipped from his mouth. She shifted her position and touched Roderic's cheek. "Of course I know that. Now. You have a throne to secure—for you and for him. Go."

When he was gone, she lay a little while, musing, drowsing. She knew her ladies came in, took the baby from her arms, and covered her with a blanket, and as she was slipping into deeper sleep, a knock on the door roused her.

"My lady?"

She raised her head from the pillows and blinked. The concerned face of one of her ladies peered around the corner. "Yes?"

"Forgive me, I would not disturb you, lady, but Lord Vere is here—he asks to speak with you on a matter of utmost urgency."

"With me?" Annandale raised herself to a half-sitting position.

"Yes, lady, he says it is most important that he speak with you—you and you alone."

"Very well—I'll see him. Come and help me dress."

When she had been restored to some semblance of order, her hair brushed, and her face washed, she entered the outer room to find Vere standing beside the fire, staring into the flames.

"Vere?"

He raised his eyes to hers, and a slow smile spread across his face, softening the harsh craggy contours of his face, making his mouth more vulnerable, his eyes kinder. He crossed the room in a few swift strides and was down on his knee before her, her hand pressed to his lips, before she could stop him.

"I'm glad to see you, too, Vere." She smiled.

"Lady." For a moment his shoulders sagged, and a wave of immense weariness washed over her.

"What is it, Vere? What's wrong?"

He shook his head, overcome by emotion, and she gently disentangled her hand. "Come sit, have some wine. Tell me what is wrong."

He took a long, shuddering breath and slowly rose to his feet, his bony shoulders gaunt beneath his worn, gray garments. She noticed how pale his face was beneath the faded tattoos. "Everything is wrong, lady. Everything."

"Yes. It seems that way."

She drew him to the chairs beside the fire, poured out a goblet of wine, and handed it to him. As he drank, she waited.

Finally he spoke. "I have just come from speaking to Alexander. He told me everything that happened—how you healed him of the hold Amanander had upon him—of the visions he has had while in Amanander's grip. Lady, I cannot tell you how this troubles me."

"Yes," she said. "I wondered if it were wise to bring him here, nearer to Amanander. But he insisted, and Roderic felt even Ahga was no longer safe."

"Roderic was right," Vere replied. "For it seems to me that Amanander, or Ferad, or both of them together, have discovered a new way to use the Magic—a way which may have no consequences at all."

Shocked, she raised her eyes and looked at him. "What do you mean?"

"On our way here, Deirdre—the M'Callaster—and I were attacked, set upon by Mutens. Magic was involved, and close to three hundred men died. Ferad, or Amanander, used the Magic to get out of Ahga. That's a lot of Magic to be used with such impunity. That suggests to me that they have either discovered a way to control the effects of the Magic, or for some reason, they are no longer worried about them." He paused, sipped his wine, and raised his eyes to her. "I've come to ask you to come with me."

"Go with you?" she echoed. "Where?"

"To the College of Elders. To my masters."

She sat back, profoundly shocked. Part of her rebelled instantly—the thought of another journey made her bones ache and her muscles sore just by thinking of it. Part of her was instantly curious. The mysterious College of the Elders—where the Muten knowledge of the old Meriga was kept, where the secrets of ancient Meriga were reality not legends. Where she would need not be afraid of the priests, of the superstitious waggle of tongues, where her ability would be cherished, prized, where she might find the same sort of acceptance as Vere.

"Why?"

He set the goblet down beside the fire. "The Elders need you. There is only one way to fight this Magic, and that's with Magic of our own. Ferad is back. His Brotherhood has infiltrated the College. Many of our highest professors were slain, the apprentices butchered. And this time he has found an ally—a Muten warrior named Jama-taw. Does that name mean anything to you?" Vere sighed. "He is one of the sons of old Ebram-taw, the one whom Roderic fought in the last rebellion. Old Ebram has never been the same, but this son of his has stepped into his father's place with a vengeance. He has made himself the leader of a highly trained, skilled force. Jama is still young—no more than eighteen or twenty at the most, and while his zeal may be an admirable thing, I have no doubt Ferad has found him easy to convince to use the Magic in his pursuit of his goals."

"What of Amanander?"

"I don't know what Amanander knows, or how he fits in with Ferad. What I do know is that we need you. We need to be able to use the Magic and we need to use it in safety. We need to be able to study it without fear of destroying the very land we walk on."

"But—"

"My lady, I would not ask this of you were the matter not of such importance. The fate of all Meriga—no, even the entire world—hangs in the balance. If Ferad and his minions are able to use the Magic as they please, imagine what will happen. Nothing will be able to stop them. Up to this point, the consequences of the Magic were so potentially devastating that no one, not even Ferad, would use it without dire need. But if there are no consequences, or if they can be controlled at will, what's to stop him from taking over the world? Who will stand against him?

"You know only the Elders possess enough of the knowledge of the Old Magic to fight Ferad, and only with your help can they use it without fear of the repercussions."

She glanced beyond his shoulder to the room where she knew the infant prince slept. "But, there's Rhodri—"

"Bring the baby with you if you must. It's the only way, lady, surely you see that."

She stood up, shaking her head, twisting her fingers in the fabric of her gown. Outside the courtyard still rang with shouted orders to the grooms and the wagon drivers as they continued to unload the supply wagons. "What is it that the Pr'fessors would have me do?"

"Only do willingly what Amanander would have forced you to do last summer. Lend your will to their endeavors—lady, without your help their hands are tied. Without, they dare not do anything. Your gift is rare and precious."

"I know that, Vere. But Roderic will never allow—"

"Roderic must be convinced. He's seen the Magic work . . . he knows its power. He'll do what he must, even if—"

"Even if it means risking my life and the life of his heir? Vere, surely you understand he will never agree to what you suggest."

"Do you agree, lady?"

"Vere, it isn't me—"

"But, lady, indeed it is. If you decide you want to do it, surely Roderic will be convinced."

For a long moment, Annandale stared helplessly at Vere. She knew he spoke the truth, but she doubted that Roderic would ever be brought to agree that she should leave the relative safety of Ithan Ford, take their son, and go traipsing with Vere into some unknown territory. "Where is this place?" she asked faintly.

"About a two-week trek, lady. If we go we will go quietly . . . I know the hills and hollows. We will take the old Muten trails, and no one, least of all Ferad, will expect that you or the child will have gone to the College."

"Doesn't Ferad know where the College is?"

"No." Vere shook his head and uncrossed his long legs. "The College was moved for safety's sake. No one knows now where it is . . . except me and a few others."

For another long moment, she stared at him. She knew the truth of his words. If only, she thought, if only she had her mother's gift and could see the future. But no, she realized, his future would hinge on her response. "I will agree to talk to Roderic. I will agree to lend my voice to yours. But Vere—I can hardly believe that he will agree with this. You know that as well as I."

He rose to his feet, unbending his long frame, his gray braids swinging down his back. "Roderic must be convinced, lady. And there is no stronger voice than yours in all the Congress. You know that as well as I."

She lifted her chin and stared out over the walls to the hills, where the green buds swelled under the lowering sky. Ithan resonated with tension like a coiled bow string.

She could feel it thrumming through her bones, the accumulated residue of the emotions of more than twenty thousand men and women. Roderic had sworn to keep her safe—what would he think of Vere's scheme? Madness, she knew, that's what he will think. And yet— The awesome power of the Magic, which had leveled one of the towers of Ahga and released Amanander from his unnatural sleep, was a force to be reckoned with. Surely her own personal safety was to be discounted if her presence at the College meant that the Muten masters of the Old Magic would be able to work the Magic as they needed.

She sighed heavily and turned back to Vere. "I promise nothing."

"Then there is no hope, lady. No hope at all. And if your son survives the attacks Ferad is sure to launch, there will be no realm left for him to inherit. I can promise you that."

With a brief bow, he crossed the room.

As he reached the door, she cried, "Wait."

He turned with his hand on the knob.

"I will go with you. I think it's dangerous, and I think Roderic will be hard to convince. But I believe a way can be found, and I will go with you. Not for my sake, but for his."

With a grim smile and another nod, Vere was gone.

Chapter Nine

"*I* thought to call a Convening, Phineas, not a council of war," Roderic murmured as the Senators filed into the small room which served Miles as a council chamber.

Phineas shrugged. "Those who do not come to speak at the Convening have no voice."

"No," said Roderic, "but they will have plenty to say if we do something they don't like."

Phineas cleared his throat, and Roderic turned to look at the Senators ranged around the long table. He nodded to each in turn. Too many were missing. Of all the Senators of the Congress, only Obayana of Kora-lado, Filem of Norda Coda, Gredahl of Arkan, Deirdre and Miles were present. Kye was there, of course, to represent Atland's interests. Vere, Alexander, and Brand filed in behind the others and took seats at the far end.

When everyone was seated, Roderic leaned upon the council table and indicated the large hide map of southern Meriga pinned upon it. "I will try to be as brief as possible. So far as we know, the situation is this. Gerik and Cort," here he nodded at Kye, "the younger sons of the Senator of Atland, have been joined by Harland of Missiluse, as well as the lessor lords of Ginya. In addition, the Muten Tribes have launched another rebellion, which encompasses not just the southern Tribes, but those as far north as the Dirondacs. That means we can expect nothing from Nourk or Everard, for they will have their hands full putting down the Muten rebels in their own estates.

"To complicate our own position, the Harleyriders are on the move across Loma and southern Arkan, and appear to be poised to take up a position just west of the border of Missiluse. As I am sure you all recall, Harland's father entertained close ties with the Harleyriders. It is entirely likely that the Harleyriders will ally with the southern rebels." He paused. The faces around the table grew grim as the implications of his words became clear.

"There's something else you're forgetting, Lord Prince," said Deirdre in a dangerously soft voice. As the lone woman in the room, her voice struck an incongruous note, and the rest of the men craned their necks to look at her. She met their stares evenly with no trace of discomfort.

"M'Callaster?"

"The treachery which destroyed Grenvill garrison. The fact that Reginald has yet to show his face."

"Are you saying that Reginald is the traitor?" Brand asked, his eyes narrowed.

Roderic nodded slowly. "I suppose I would prefer to forget Reginald. Alexander, tell us what Amanander told you in Ahga."

Alexander leaned forward, his discomfort plain on his face. "In Ahga—at the Convening when Roderic was acclaimed Regent of Meriga—Amanander told me that he intended to recruit Reginald to assist in the rebellion which was fomenting among the southern lords—that he intended to use Reginald to break the peace in Atland any way he could."

"By the One," swore Kye, biting back an oath beneath his breath. "You knew this that long ago and said nothing? Do you know how many of my men have died? Did you know this, Lord Prince?"

Roderic shook his head. "Not at the time, no. And by the time we were able to get down here, it was too late. The damage was done."

"So you knew this, too?" Brand shot upright.

"Alexander told me in the Settle Islands." Roderic looked his eldest brother in the eye. "And then we were faced by the siege of Minnis."

"Gentlemen." Phineas's voice cut through the tense atmosphere like a blade. "This country is in a grave crisis. It matters not who knew what when. The damage has been done. The garrison at Atland was lost to us the minute you rode away two years ago, Roderic. Reginald was ripe for the picking, and Amanander saw the opportunity and took it. Now is not the time for recriminations. Now is the time to decide what you will do."

Roderic looked around the room. Kye still looked angry and Brand looked disgusted, but at least they had been silenced. His eyes met the almond-shaped eyes of Obayana.

"How many troops can you field, Roderic?"

This was the question Roderic had been dreading. He drew a deep breath before replying. "Our lines are stretched thin. If I bring the garrisons up to what they should be, I will have no reserves."

Filem of Norda Coda raised his face to Roderic. "I can send you troops. It will take a while for them to arrive— but if I send a messenger back to my captain in Arberdeen today, you will have them in six to eight weeks."

"My thanks to you, Lord Senador."

Filem shrugged. He was a relatively young man, still in his thirties, but his face was so weather-beaten and scarred it was hard to guess his exact age. Life on the border was harsh. "I but honor my pledge, Lord Prince. If the King had not sent aid to me and my father, the Sascatch would have overwhelmed us long ago."

Roderic nodded slowly. This was the Meriga Abelard had envisioned, a system where each man could benefit in time of need. He gave silent thanks to the One that his father had honored his pledge-bonds so faithfully.

"Roderic, may I speak?" Vere stirred restlessly in his chair.

Roderic nodded, still mentally calculating how best to use the troops Filem offered.

Vere rose awkwardly. "We must not underestimate the Muten threat. Their sheer numbers—"

"But Lord Vere," interrupted Gredahl, "surely they lack supplies and equipment—"

"Not if they have joined forces with Missiluse, Reginald, and the southern rebels."

"Wait a minute," Gredahl said. "What makes you think they've joined with the rebel lords? What man of us would join with those—" He broke off, as Vere fixed him with a steady stare.

The old man flushed and Roderic knew Gredahl had remembered the stories and the rumors which were told about Vere's missing years away from the court—how he had run away at fifteen, disappearing for nearly thirty years, and had spent those years among the Mutens. He had only returned when news of Abelard's disappearance seemed to be connected to the interests of the Muten masters he still served.

"There's a piece you haven't mentioned, Roderic," said Vere softly. "Amanander."

"What about Amanander?" Kye looked at Roderic.

"Two weeks before we left to come here, Kye, Amanander escaped from Ahga. He did so with the aid of a Muten. It is not outside the realm of possibility that Amanander is drawing all these threads together—the lesser lords such as Kye's brothers and other malcontents, Missiluse, the Harleyriders, and the Mutens, into one force."

"That still doesn't answer the question," Filem said, as Gredahl nodded in agreement. "What man would join that pack of traitors, thieves, and dogs together?"

"A man," said Obayana softly in the sudden silence, "who will do anything if he believes it to be in his own best interests."

Like thunder from a distant storm, a low rumble went around the table. It was inconceivable that Amanander or Reginald or even the southern lords would join with the Mutens, and yet, Roderic knew that Obayana spoke the truth, especially when it came to Amanander. Nothing was beyond Amanander, if he believed it would further his own ends.

"So what you're suggesting," Kye leaned forward, the scar on his forehead an ugly red, "is that we should expect all these enemies to attack as one?"

"On different fronts, perhaps," replied Phineas. "But we should not be surprised if there is a coordination to the pattern of their moves against us."

"So what do you require of me, Roderic?" asked Obayana.

Roderic squared his shoulders. "Full complements of troops. As many supplies as you can muster. Your men, my lord, will be needed to reinforce the garrisons across the Arkan Plains against the Harley threat." Out of the corner of his eye, he noticed Gredahl nod with satisfaction. He suppressed a sigh. That answered Gredahl's problem, but how to reinforce his own dwindling supplies was going to be another matter.

Filem cleared his throat. "I can offer you little in the way of supplies, but Mondana sent me to say that he is sending you a wagon train of supplies. It may even have reached Ahga by now. He told me to tell you he has not forgotten the aid you gave when Koralane burned."

Roderic raised an eyebrow. The lords of Mondana had suffered greatly in the fire which had swept through the Forest of Koralane just a little over a year ago. Those supplies had to cost the depleted lords dearly. "I will send him a message tonight, with my thanks, Filem."

"Well, there's always Vada," said Brand. "We might not be able to compel Owen to send his men, but we can take his grain. And Reez of Rissona is good for a couple thousand men at least—there're more troops to shore up the garrisons in western Arkan."

Roderic nodded slowly. He had desperately hoped that it wouldn't be necessary to compel anyone to do anything, and yet, despite his invitations, it seemed that nothing was going to change.

"I say we do compel him," put in Kye. "Why should Mortmain and the rest of the Western lords sit behind the Saranevas and grow fat while we bear the brunt of this war?"

"Because as a practical matter, we cannot force him to send his men," replied Brand. "We barely have the numbers we need now. And there is another matter. If the West were to know how desperate the situation is here, they might be tempted to rise again."

Roderic stared at his brother. That was a possibility he had never even considered. Involuntarily his eyes went to Deirdre. Her face was unreadable, and he knew doubts concerning the recent treaties with Mondana gnawed at her.

"Brand is right about Rissona," said Obayana. "Old Ezram is still alive and he never leaves his estate anymore, but young Reez can be counted on."

Roderic drew a deep breath and frowned down at the hide map of Meriga on the table. "If we deploy your troops and Rissona's in Arkan, that will free the main body of the army to concentrate on the main threat. At this point, it looks as though we will have to rely on Everard and Phillip to hold the Northern Tribes in check." He raised his head and looked at Miles. "It seems, Lord Senador, that this war will be fought from Ithan." He cleared his throat. "Is it by your leave?"

Miles nodded. "You have my permission, Lord

Prince, to move whatever is required into Ithan. The Tennessy Fall stands with the throne of Meriga." He spread his hands.

Brand cocked his head, frowning at the map. "There's a weak link, Roderic. Do you see it?"

Roderic looked down at the map once more. The outpost garrisons were marked in circles, the larger ones with squares, and the largest of all with stars, all of them scattered across Meriga in a seemingly random pattern. "If we fortify the garrisons in Arkan—"

"It's Dlas, don't you see?" Brand stabbed a finger on the map. "Look—Missiluse is just to the east—the Harleyriders are going to go right through if what we think is true."

Roderic looked up quickly. There was another reason Brand was concerned. Barran, Brand's son, just a few years older than Roderic, was in command of the garrison.

"The garrison must be strengthened. Immediately." Brand folded his arms across his chest.

Roderic glanced at Phineas. Out of the corner of his eye he saw Deirdre raise an eyebrow questioningly. Brand was right. Even if one forgot that it was his son in potential danger, Brand was right. He nodded. "I think you're right, Brand. I will send out troops immediately to reinforce the garrison—you'll see that a messenger goes on ahead?"

Brand nodded, and a look of understanding passed between the two brothers. "All right. Now—" Roderic folded his arms over his chest. A knock on the door interrupted his thoughts. "Yes?"

The door opened and a servant peered timidly into the room. "I-I beg your pardon, Lord Senador, but the Lady Norah sent me to tell you the feast is ready. She would prefer you to come and eat it now."

Roderic glanced at Miles, who shook his head. "All right, we'll be right there. I'm sorry, Lord Prince."

Roderic smiled. "It's all right. I'd like to meet again later, after the food. I need a better idea of what our strengths are, and our weaknesses." The men got to their feet. Brand and Vere picked up Phineas's litter. As they filed out, Deirdre hung back. He smiled at her as he plucked at the edges of the hide map.

"What's wrong?" she asked.

He shrugged and shook his head. "I hoped this would be a true Convening, Deirdre. Instead—" He broke off and stared down at the map, reading the potential disaster in its faded lines and circles. He ran a hand through his hair. "Well. You've been wounded. Are you all right?" That this was the first time he had been alone with her in months ran through his mind, and abruptly he wondered why that mattered.

It was her turn to shrug. "'Tis nothing that won't heal."

"But that's your sword arm—will you be able—"

"Aye," she snapped.

Taken aback, they stared at each other. Roderic was suddenly conscious of the exact distance of the space between them, of the fire which smoldered in the depths of her eyes. He nodded slowly, fearing to risk offending her pride. "As you say, Deirdre. Forgive me, I didn't mean to doubt your ability."

"No," she said, looking away. "I know." She took a deep breath and tossed the end of her plaid over her shoulder. "The feast awaits, Lord Prince. If we don't go to eat it, I think we'll have battle with Lady Norah, and she's not one to cross. Shall we go?" She opened the door and stood aside, waiting for him to go first.

He caught a whiff of her scent, a blend of leather and soap and something indefinable that was uniquely her, as he walked past, and he wondered what words went unspoken between them.

Chapter Ten

❧

A full moon had risen above the walls, pale and flat as the eye of a dead fish, Deirdre noticed as she stepped onto the terrace. She stared moodily at the moon, plucking at the frayed edges of her plaid.

From the hall, music filtered out, and the song the harper sang seemed to speak to her:

> Farewell to fame and fortune
> Farewell to arms and strife
> I lay down all my weapons
> And offer up my life.
>
> For all my years of fighting
> And all the arts of war
> Are nothing if my lady
> Will love with me no more.
>
> And all my restless wanderings
> They never brought me home;
> If I cannot have my lady
> I'd rather die alone.

The melody faded into the night and the raucous sounds of feasting continued. Her head ached and her healing wounds itched and restlessness gnawed at a place deep inside. Her arm was stiff and sore, and she knew it would be many days before she would be able to wield any kind of weapon again. Roderic's concern had been justified. There had been no reason for her to snap at him like an untried girl in the presence of her first love.

The thought that she might not be able to fight troubled her. Roderic didn't need her lagging behind. At the thought of Roderic, a wave of longing swept over her and she tightened her broad hands around the rough stone of the low wall before her. She felt a sharp edge prick her hand, slicing through flesh, but she didn't care. She shut her eyes.

Honesty compelled her to admit that the sight of Roderic with his wife seared her to the very marrow of her bones. The Lady Annandale was more than everything she could never be: a woman more beautiful than any she had ever seen before, and those eyes—those sea-blue eyes that seemed to look through her, into the deepest places where Deirdre kept the secrets of her soul. Had the lady guessed, Deirdre wondered. Had she been able to see that Deirdre loved Roderic?

A sudden noise made Deirdre turn with heightened reflexes. Annandale stood on the threshold of the door, a slight figure with a white shawl held to her throat against the late spring chill.

"Lady Annandale!" Deirdre whispered in disbelief. It was as if her thoughts had called the lady here.

"M'Callaster," Annandale replied with grave courtesy.

She held out her hand. "The hall is hot—I came for a breath of air."

There was such sincere simplicity in those words, Deirdre relaxed in spite of herself. "Then join me, lady. If you don't mind my company."

Deirdre heard the soft intake of breath and the slap of her thin leather slippers on the rough surface of the stone as Annandale walked to stand beside her. Deirdre glanced down. The top of the other woman's head came to her shoulder. For a moment, Deirdre felt large and gawky, like an untrained colt. She shifted on her feet, wondering why the presence of this woman at once unnerved and soothed her.

"You're in pain."

The sound of Annandale's voice startled her almost as much as the words. It was not a question, it was a statement.

"Yes—no—'tis not so bad. 'Twill heal."

Annandale turned to face Deirdre, her head cocked to one side. "Roderic is lucky you are here."

Deirdre felt her cheeks grow warm. "Well," she said, gruffly. What did one say to the wife of the man one wished to bed? Such a thing had never happened to her before. The Settle Islanders made little fuss of such matters, and as the M'Callaster, it was understood that she had her pick of the men, as her father had had his pick of the women.

Annandale reached out and took Deirdre's hand, and Deirdre started and tried to pull back. But the other woman's grasp was firm, and in that very instant, a thin blue light flared between them at the point of contact.

She gasped at the sight of that supernatural light, unable to move or react. On the pale skin of Annandale's face, beads of sweat appeared over her lower lip and laced her forehead. Inexplicably, a red line blossomed through her shawl, staining the fine white wool. And as Deirdre watched, transfixed, the pain drained from her body like water through a sieve. A feeling of wholeness, of health, swept over and through her like a tide. Her knotted muscles relaxed, the thick scabs flaked away. She moved her arm and the motion was smooth, unencumbered. She stared in disbelief at Annandale.

The other woman opened her eyes, and for a moment the two women only gazed at each other. Then Deirdre spoke in a hoarse, breathless voice: "Lady, what did you do? How have you done this?"

Annandale looked down, her cheeks still pale, her face wet with sweat in the moonlight. "It is a gift I have. To heal."

Deirdre shook her head as though to clear it. "By the One, lady, what manner of woman are you?"

"I am," said Annandale with a little rueful smile, "what the priests consider a witch." She cocked her head and gazed up at Deirdre.

Does she expect me to cry for the priests? wondered Deirdre. "A witch? Lady, how could anyone think that you of all people—surely not—"

Annandale nodded. "A legacy of the Armageddon, I'm afraid. The Old Magic made me as surely as it made Meriga what it is today." She turned away to stare over the heavy balustrade at the walls before them.

"Old Magic," repeated Deirdre. A vision of the Muten

attack rose before her eyes, white forms moving like ghosts through the skeletal shapes of the trees, and involuntarily she shuddered, remembering the heat of the flames, the screams of her dying men. "I know it's real, lady."

"I know you do." Suddenly Annandale gripped her forearm with a hand not much larger than a child's. "I need your help."

"My help?" Deirdre echoed, beginning to understand why this woman unnerved her so. "How can I help you?"

"You must help me convince Roderic to let me go with Vere to the College of the Muten Elders. Please."

Deirdre stared down at her, uncomprehending. This whole conversation had a tinge of the absurd, the unbelievable. Here she stood on the crumbling terrace of this forsaken outpost castle, side by side with the wife of the man she loved, a woman who had just performed a miracle, speaking of Magic and Mutens—she shook her head to clear it. "Go with Vere where?"

Annandale sighed. "There is a place—they call it the College—where the Muten Elders study the Magic. And in order to learn as much about it as they can, they need me. Vere has offered to take me there, but Roderic will never agree—"

"As well he shouldn't, lady. Have you any idea how many enemies await beyond these walls? And Vere— Vere is a fine enough man, but he is no soldier. He wouldn't be able to protect you if you met any real trouble along the way. Where is this place you want to go?"

Annandale sighed again. "I don't know."

"Lady—" Deirdre broke off, wondering what she

could possibly say to convince this woman of the madness of her proposal. How did men ever deal with women like this?

"M'Callaster—Deirdre." In Annandale's voice was a ring of such quiet conviction, Deirdre looked up in spite of herself. "I know you love him."

At once her cheeks flushed painfully. "Lady, I—"

"I know you do. And I know he's quite taken with you, too, although he doesn't know it yet." There was a trace of amusement in her voice, and a touch of sadness, too, and suddenly Deirdre felt terribly guilty.

"It's not my intention—"

"Deirdre, listen to me." Annandale's face was pale in the moonlight, but her eyes glowed with an intensity that kept Deirdre's eyes focused upon her face. "I know you love him and I am glad. He needs you—he will need you—will need your strength, your courage, your spirit. The days ahead are dark, and as for me—" She stopped speaking and looked toward the horizon. "As for me—" Again she stopped. "We all have our parts to play. And mine—my most important part is done."

"He loves you," Deirdre whispered, still not quite comprehending what she heard.

"And I love him." Annandale looked up at Deirdre. "But sometimes love isn't enough, and sometimes love requires that we do things which the other person doesn't understand. I have a gift which will enable the ones with the right knowledge to use the Magic without fear of destroying the world and all we know.

"It isn't my choice to leave, but I can't remain here behind these walls, wrapped in some cocoon, while

Roderic and you and all the brave men fight a battle which but for me might well be lost. I've given Roderic his heir. But what use to him is an heir when his throne is so shaky? I cannot hide behind such courage as yours, when—"

"What would you have me do?"

"I will speak with Roderic myself, and if it becomes necessary, I might need you to add your voice to help me convince him."

"You will need an escort, lady. There is no way Roderic will ever let the two of you step one foot outside these walls alone."

"He needs you here."

Deirdre startled. Had the woman read her thoughts?

"But perhaps one or two of your most trusted men? He has come to rely upon your Islanders as he does no others."

"Only one or two?" Deirdre shook her head. "To protect the person he holds most dear? No, lady, surely—"

"I doubt that a full complement of men will be allowed to get close enough to the College to do any good."

There was a long pause as Deirdre cast a considering look at the woman who stood beside her. "That's why you've come to me, isn't it?"

"What do you mean?"

"You don't need my help if Roderic gives his consent. You need it in case he doesn't."

Annandale flushed and dropped her eyes. "You are indeed perceptive, M'Callaster."

"But why to me? Why did you come to me? All of these men have retainers—"

"But would any of them understand that sometimes a woman must play a larger part than sitting and waiting for the wounded?"

The arrow hit home. Deirdre stared at Annandale. In the depths of those blue eyes, she saw a will forged of pain and suffering beyond even her experience, and though Deirdre knew that Annandale was years younger, she suddenly felt as though she stood in the presence of something ageless. She took a deep breath. "Go to Roderic. And when he says no, come back to me."

"Thank you," whispered Annandale.

Deirdre glanced up at the bone-white moon. "No, lady . . ." Her words stopped Annandale at the door. "Thank you."

꩜

Chapter Eleven

She found Roderic by the window, staring out at the same moon as Deirdre, his face gaunt in the moonlight. He did not turn when he heard her step across the threshold.

"Roderic?"

"Yes." There was such resignation in his tone, her heart ached.

"Are you all right?"

He nodded, still looking out the window. "Just tired. I didn't get a nap." It was said without reproach, and she knew he only meant to tease, but his voice held a trace of bitterness, of weariness beyond his years. Was it possible, she wondered, that they were both but twenty-two?

He turned to face her, and in the wavering candlelight, he looked like a stranger. His face was lined, his mouth drawn tight and grim.

"This—situation—is bad, isn't it?"

"Yes. Potentially, it is worse than anything my father ever faced." He stripped off his shirt, and she saw the ripple of his muscles beneath the skin, and the scars which bore silent testimony to the battles he had fought. Only she could read the scars which lurked beneath his skin, the ones he bore upon his soul.

"Come, then, let's get to bed. The morning comes early, and—" Here she paused, wondering if this was the opening she needed. "I didn't get a nap, either."

"No?" he said, as he sat down on the edge of the bed. "I left word you were not to be disturbed."

She shrugged a little, her eyes fixed on the coverlet. "Vere came to talk to me."

"Vere? What did he want with you?" Roderic paused in the removal of a boot.

"He came to ask me to go with him to the College of the Muten Elders."

"Go with him?" Roderic gave a soft snort. "I hope you told him it was out of the question. I would sooner face the Muten hordes alone than allow you to leave the safety of these walls."

"Actually—" She came around to the other side of the bed and stood before him, wondering why she felt like a child asking permission. "I told him I would talk to you about it."

"Talk to me? What is there to talk about? I can't let you leave Ithan—do you have any idea how many enemies surround us? Harleyriders to the west, Mutens to the east, Atland's sons to the south, Amanander out there the One only knows where, still itching to get his hands on you, likely as not. Annandale, are you mad?"

"No," she said coolly. "I am not mad. And I wish you would at least listen."

Roderic heaved a sigh. "Listen to what? Madness? Lady, do you have any idea what we face?" He ran his hand through the shock of hair that fell across his forehead. "My lines are stretched to the limit and beyond. There are no reserves here. If Obayana and Rissona don't honor their pledge and deliver up some troops, and if supplies don't come from the Western lords, there is a very good possibility right now that Meriga will splinter.

"It looks to me that Amanander is putting together a cohesive force and the One be with us all if I am right. The connections are there—and you and I both know he would do anything, anything at all to win this throne. Including using the Magic." Roderic broke off and shook his head. "By the One, lady, you must be mad."

"Roderic, you haven't even listened to me."

"I heard you." He picked up a goblet of water on the bedside table and took a long drink.

"How dare you dismiss me like this?"

"Dismiss you?" He set the goblet down with a thud. "I am not dismissing you. You don't seem to have listened to me, either."

"I am well aware of the current situation. You only repeated what we both already know. What I have to tell you is crucial to the success of your campaign."

He sighed again. "How?"

"You know Amanander's going to use the Magic—he already has. How do you intend to fight that?"

He dropped his eyes. "I-I don't know."

"Your mind's been so full of strategy and logistics and men and animals and supplies that you forgot what started all this in the first place. Vere believes that Ferad or Amanander or both of them have discovered a new way to use the Magic, one without devastating repercussions. If Vere is correct, then both of them will be able to use the Magic where and when they please, and Deirdre's loss of three hundred men will seem like a grain of sand in a desert. You have no way to fight that, Roderic, and the Muten Elders are willing to help fight Ferad—"

"He told you that? Vere said that?"

"Well . . ." It was her turn to drop her eyes. "No . . ."

"What makes you think they will help me? You know what they think of me."

She twisted her fingers in the fabric of her gown. "You know they will do anything to fight Ferad. And with my help—they can use their Magic against him. At least it will keep the Magic from being directed at you."

"By the One." He rose and paced to the window, then back again. "How can you expect me to let you go out there—with Vere, of all people?" He gripped her by the shoulders and stared down into her eyes.

She met his gaze fearlessly, staring back with the full force of every ounce of will she possessed, and inexplicably, his face changed as a shadow clouded his eyes. He pushed away from her, dropping his hands by his sides, and she felt him recoil.

"Lady," he whispered. "Who are you?"

"What?" She looked back at him, puzzled, for he stared at her with an unreadable expression. The emotion which she sensed was clearly suspicion, under which was an inexplicable current of disgust. The sudden change confused her. "You know who I am."

"Who are you?" he repeated. "Your eyes—just now—who—who—" He grabbed the candle on the bedside table and held it up to her face, his eyes narrowed and suspicious. "Who was your father?"

"Why do you ask?"

"Answer the question."

"No—no man ever claimed me." She glanced sideways, wondering how to answer an impossible question.

"I know that. But you had a father—and I think you know who he was. Rumor says it was Phineas—but it wasn't Phineas, was it?"

"N-no," she choked out.

"Then who, lady? Who was your father?"

"My father—" She paused and gathered her courage like a cloak. "Was the King."

He glanced at the bed, horror plain on every line of his face. "By the One." His face drained of color and sweat beaded his forehead. His mouth worked and he looked as if he might vomit.

"No," she cried, reaching for him. "No, there is no blood between us. What we've done—it isn't wrong."

He paused, his breathing fast and shallow, his eyes wary as a hunted animal. "What are you saying?"

She gave a deep, sobbing breath. "You are not the son of the King, Roderic. There is no blood between us—we've done nothing wrong."

"What are you talking about? I am not the King's son?"

"You are the Queen's son, Roderic. Not the King's."

Disbelief twisted his face into something unrecognizable. "You lie. How is that possible?" He backed away from her, reaching for his shirt. "For two years and more now, I have fought to preserve this nation, I have held this realm together with little more than sweat and tears and the blood of my men. I have led men into battle and to their deaths in my name—the name of the rightful heir of Meriga—and now you say this isn't true? If I am not the son of the King, then who is? Amanander? I have spent these years fighting for something that isn't mine at all? Sent men to die for no good reason? You lie!"

He bolted from the room, grabbing his cloak and his tunic as he went. With a little sob, she sank onto the bed, staring after him as the candles guttered in his wake.

Roderic pounded down the shallow steps, her words reverberating through his tired brain. Not the King's son. Not the son of Abelard Ridenau. Not the rightful ruler of all Meriga. Not the King's son at all.

Through the hall he stormed, his boots clicking on the worn wooden floor. Out of the corner of his eye he saw Deirdre jolt upright by the fire, watching him with narrowed eyes as he stalked out of the hall. Through the quiet ward he stormed, past piles of supplies and equipment, past sentries who recognized him in the light of the flickering torches. He pushed open the door of the stables and the wooden frame quivered as horses nickered in their stalls. Sleepy stable boys peered from their nests of straw, but Roderic ignored them all.

He grabbed a saddle, went to the nearest stall, and threw it over the back of the horse, heedless of whose animal it was. The horse whickered and stamped as he led it out into the courtyard.

He leaped onto the horse's back and lashed at its side

with the reins. The animal jumped forward. At the gate, the sentries looked at him in disbelief.

"Open it, now."

"Lord—Lord Prince—?" The sentries clustered together, peering up at him in the wavering torchlight.

"Open it now, or you'll do double duty tomorrow."

They needed no more urging than that. They fumbled at the crossbar, raising it enough to let the heavy gates swing open to let him out, and without a backward glance, Roderic took off at a gallop.

Through the rows of tents and makeshift dwellings, he rode like one possessed, fleeing from a demon. The stallion's hooves echoed in the still night beneath the silent moon. Finally, breathless, the horse slowed of its own volition to a trot.

Not the King's son. The rhythmic gait of the horse's hooves pounded it over and over like a litany. Not the King's son. Who was he then? Nameless, fatherless, got when Abelard was away at war, most likely. What kind of woman had the Queen been? Abelard had never named another heir—both of them were bound by their vows—could she not have waited to take another man? What sort of man had caught the Queen's eye and made her forget the vows she had sworn to the King? Rage simmered through every conscious thought.

The horse's breath was a long white plume in the chilly night. The road wound down into a village, a little tavern at the crossroads. He tied the horse to the cross bar of the fence before the door and went inside. A lone barmaid was behind the bar, wiping the long wooden counter with a damp rag.

She looked up with fear on her face when she saw his disheveled appearance.

"Ale," he barked. He threw himself into a chair by the banked fire.

"Sir," she whispered, "we're closed for the night—it's late. All decent men are abed—"

With two long strides he was behind the bar, his arm around her. "What makes you think I'm a decent man?"

He released her and nodded at the row of kegs behind the bar. "Ale."

Reluctantly, she reached for a clay mug and slowly filled it with foamy ale. She set it on the bar before him and nodded. "There."

She raised her chin and stared him in the eyes. "Two coppers."

Something in the lift of her chin, the boldness with which she met his eyes, something about the aspect of her defiance, roused him, sparked the rage which simmered. "Two coppers," he repeated. "Two coppers."

She looked at him with fearful, questioning eyes. "Don't I know you?" she murmured. "Haven't I seen you?"

He saw fear leap into her eyes, and he twined his hand in her hair, jerking her to him again, and roughly he kissed her, bending her back over the bar so he could feel her round breasts strain against his chest as he pressed down upon her. She struggled, futilely, and he felt her soft thighs spread, as he thrust his knee between them. Someone would answer, he thought, someone would pay. The Queen had betrayed the King, and now, all these years later, Amanander was the rightful heir—any of the brothers had a better claim—Brand the oldest, Vere the runaway—Reginald the traitor—yes, someone would pay. He fumbled at the hem of her dress, pulling up her skirts as she fought, squirming like a child against his body.

She went limp beneath him, her hand on his chest. "Please," she whimpered, "are you not the Prince? The Prince of all Meriga? Isn't that who you are?"

At her words, he raised himself away from her, and his rage shriveled into shame. He closed his eyes. He was no Prince. His actions here had proved that. The woman lay utterly still beneath him. He heard the door open and close with a slam. A heavy hand come down on his shoulders, and a familiar voice shouted: "By the One, Roderic, have you gone mad completely?"

Chapter Twelve

❧

He turned to see Deirdre behind him. He released the girl and Deirdre swung at him with her right fist. She connected with the side of his head, and for a moment, his vision clouded. He shook his head to clear it, lowered his head, and she turned, grabbed his arm, and neatly flipped him over her shoulder. He found himself lying on the floor looking up at her, her dagger held to his throat.

"Now. Are you going to explain yourself and your shameful actions? Or shall I punish you the way we take care of men who're caught in such an act in the Islands?"

His breathing slowed. He could hear the snap and hiss of the low fire, the girl's ragged sobs. He could see the pulse which throbbed in Deirdre's throat.

"Is this the way the Prince of all Meriga behaves?"

He looked away, then, tears welling inexplicably in his eyes. "Let me up. I'll not touch the girl again, I swear it."

"Your word as the Prince of Meriga?"

He looked away, shutting his eyes tightly. "For all that that's worth . . . yes."

Deirdre backed off his chest, rose slowly to her feet. "You, girl. Are you all right?"

The girl nodded, wiping her tears with the rag.

"Get us some ale and something to eat . . . anything. I think we need to talk, Lord Prince." As the girl scurried to obey, Deirdre looked around for logs. She threw a couple on the fire and stirred it to new life. As the flames leapt higher, she looked back over her shoulder. "Get up."

He rose to his feet and slowly sank into a chair beside the hearth. "How did you find me?"

"You took my horse." She drew a deep breath. "For rape we take a man's balls. For horse thieving we take his head." She looked down at him, and then at the girl who gingerly sat trays of cheese and dried apples on the bar. "Go to bed, lass. We'll pay for this and be gone by morning."

Deirdre took the ale and the plate and set them on the table next to Roderic. "Now. Do you want to tell me what all this is about?"

"No."

"That's not the answer I was looking for. Care to try again?"

"No."

Deirdre plucked her dagger from its sheath and carefully began to slice thin pieces from the block of cheese. "Let me explain something to you. I have you in rape and horse theft. I could throw this dagger at you, and kill you, and be well within my rights to do it. Now, I probably won't do that, you see, since it would do nothing for the country were I to kill the Prince of Meriga—"

"Stop it!"

She stared. "Stop what?"

"That's not who I am."

"What are you talking about? Roderic, have you gone daft with it all?"

He leaned forward, into the light of the leaping flames, his face set and grim, feeling infinitely older than his years. "Listen to me. And then tell me how I should feel. Tonight I learned that I am not the son of the King. I am not a Prince of Meriga. I have no right to either the name of Ridenau, nor the title of Regent."

It was Deirdre's turn to sit back and stare. "What are you talking about?"

"Ask Annandale. Ask my wife. She'll tell you. *She's* the daughter of the King she said—I'm but the son of the Queen. Not the King. Get of a groom for all I know . . . a scullion . . . a musician who caught the lady's eyes while the King was off at war . . ." His voice trailed off as he stared into the flames.

"Listen to what you just said," Deirdre whispered.

He shook his head tiredly. "What?"

"If she is the daughter of the King, and you are the son of the Queen—Roderic, do you think your marriage happened by accident?"

With a start Roderic stared at Deirdre. "The letter."

"What letter?"

"My father left me a letter—wrote it the day I—we both—Annandale and I were born. He wanted me to marry her—but he never said why—"

"Maybe he never wanted you to know."

"Never wanted me to know I wasn't his son?"

Deirdre shrugged. "Did he ever treat you as if you weren't? Ever by deed or word indicate that you were anything less than the son of his body?"

"No." Roderic stared into the fire.

"Or maybe—" Deirdre leaned forward. "Maybe he never wanted anyone else to know either."

Roderic slid his eyes over to her face. She raised one brow and stared at him. "But why? My father—the King had—has many sons. Why would he make me heir if he knew I wasn't really his?"

"Have you any idea who fathered you upon the Queen?"

Roderic drew a deep breath and sighed. "Annandale said no blood—no ties between us—so that would mean someone . . . anyone . . ."

"No." Deirdre shook her head. "This was planned. There was no accident to it. The Queen knew—but she's dead. The King knew—but he's gone. Annandale—would she know?"

"She might. Her mother would have known . . . if this was a plan."

"Her mother? Nydia? She's dead, too.

"Then there's only one person left who really knows what happened. And that's the man who fathered you."

"If he's still alive."

"Go to your lady and ask her, Roderic. It's the only chance you have to make peace with this. You may not be the son of the King's body, but you are the Prince of Meriga, and there is no way this country will hold together unless you assume the command the King left you. You can't fall apart like this—none of us can afford for you to do that. Do you understand what I am telling you?"

He dropped his eyes and stared at the backs of his hands, at the scars and nicks which crisscrossed the skin like the pattern of Deirdre's plaid. "Do you understand at all how I feel?"

She sat back, her arms folded across her chest. "In a land where a man's whole identity is based upon his clan, his chief, his father—yes. Of course I know how you must feel. But you must put that aside. We have a kingdom to keep—for your son."

Rhodri. The thought of the infant brought him back. Those eyes, so like Abelard's, so like Annandale's . . . now he understood, he thought. Now he realized what it was about her that had seemed so familiar to him at first. It was her resemblance to his father. "Her eyes," he muttered.

"What?" asked Deirdre sharply.

"It was her eyes that made me realize who she was," he said. "She came to me tonight and wanted to leave Ithan, to go with Vere—"

"I think you should let her go."

"Let her go?"

Deirdre nodded. "She has another place in this, Roderic. There is more to this tale than you or I understand. I'll take her myself. But go on—"

"She looked at me with such determination—the expression was his when he had his mind made up—that's how I knew. No one ever looked quite like my fath—like the King when he was angry."

"You have to stop that."

"Stop what?"

"Correcting yourself. He was—is—your father. If he's ever found he'll tell you that himself, I have no doubt. But for now—" She uncrossed her long legs and got to her feet, feeling in her pouch. She pulled out a gold coin, and laid it on the bar. "That should be sufficient payment for the trouble which you caused."

"No—" He picked up the gold piece and handed it back to her. "They can't spend that here. We'll leave this, instead." From a pocket, he pulled out three silver pennies. "It's not quite the equivalent, but it will go further." He picked up a last piece of cheese. "And thank you. Once again."

She gave him a wry smile as she slung her plaid over her shoulder, adjusting her swordbelt at her hip.

He narrowed his eyes at the ease with which she moved, and suddenly he realized that her arm was no longer in a sling. "Deirdre—your arm. You aren't—your wound—"

"Your wife." She met his eyes. "Consider my promise to escort her my payment of the debt I owe to her."

Dawn was a pale pink streak across the eastern sky as Roderic and Deirdre cantered across the drawbridge, into the inner ward of Ithan Ford. The sleepy sentries stared at them in disbelief. He tossed the reins of his mount to a yawning stable boy, and with a last nod, he took off up the steps to his chambers. He saw her wink out of the corner of his eye.

In the doorway of his bedroom, he paused. Annandale lay across the rumpled bed, her arms wrapped around her pillow. He shut the door and bolted it. The floor creaked beneath his weight as he walked to the bed, and instantly she sprang awake. "Roderic."

"Forgive me, lady," he said as he knelt beside the bed. "I was wrong."

"I'm sorry, too. I should not have told you so abruptly, but I could not let you think—you thought we were brother and sister. I saw it in your face."

"It's hard for me to believe what you tell me."

"Sometimes it doesn't matter what we believe."

"Yes." He laughed bitterly. "Do you know Phineas said something like that to me, once? On the night I brought you to Minnis, and he told me my father—" He stumbled over the word. "When he told me the King wanted me to marry you." He paused, searching her face, and she looked at him so lovingly he wanted to weep. "I nearly did a terrible thing last night."

She gave a great sigh and held out her hand. "Oh, Roderic."

He buried his head in the crumpled fabric of her skirts. The early light gave her skin a pale grayish cast; for the first time since he had ever known her, she looked old, tired, as worn as he. A dull ache spread a low throb from the base of his skull to his temples. The intense rage was gone, and he was only tired beyond endurance. He sat down heavily in a chair beside the bed. "You had better begin at the beginning."

She nodded gravely. Her gaze went to the window and then back to him. "It began in the twelfth year of your father's reign. On his way to Ahga, he rode through a little town where there was about to be a public execution. The crime was witchcraft and the condemned woman was my mother. The King stopped the execution. He ordered them to take her off the stake, and when they pulled the hood off her face, he—"

"Everyone says your mother was beautiful."

"Do you think I am beautiful?"

"What does that have to do with it?"

"Do you?"

"You know I do."

"When she was young—before everything—she was even more beautiful than I. When Abelard saw her, he took her away with him. He used her gift, you see. When the village priest, the one who wanted to burn her, was made the Bishop of Ahga, he took her away to the North Woods, and there—"

"That's why he built Minnis."

"Yes. He meant to keep her safe, you see, at least as safe as he could make her. In the beginning, when the Bishop first came to Ahga, she had a great deal of power because she allied herself with Agara, Abelard's mother. And the King had married your mother, ending Mortmain's Rebellion and consolidating the realm."

"Hadn't he sworn a vow of fidelity to her, to the Queen?"

"Of course. But Abelard didn't love her. He treated her shamefully. She didn't want to marry him, I don't think. He forced her, as he forced everyone around him, to do his will. And it was that marriage that brought all the trouble about.

"You know my mother could see the future. There were certain limitations to her power. She couldn't see her own future, and she couldn't see past a choice. But once a choice was made, she could see what the outcome of the choice would be."

He frowned, trying to understand.

"Think of it this way. Imagine you stand at the highest tower of Ahga. From there you can see all the markets and all the roads leading to them. Suppose you see a farmer, leading his stock to slaughter. From where you are, you can see not only the farmer, but where he is going. You, in effect, see his future."

She paused. When Roderic nodded, she continued. "Now, suppose, there is an overturned cart around a corner. The way is blocked. You know that, and you know the farmer will have to turn around and make a decision to go another way, but he doesn't know that until he gets there, and you have no way of knowing what way he will decide to go once he does."

"So your mother saw the future as a series of possibilities?"

"Yes. Her ability could not interfere with anyone's will to decide for themselves, however. When you stood before her in her tower, she showed you what would have happened if you had left without me. Once you agreed to take me with you, the vision in the flames would have been different. But, as you have seen, some of what she showed you has already come to pass."

"So she used this ability to help my fa—the King?"

"She swore a pledge of allegiance to him, her foresight, in exchange for his protection. She was, according to the definition of the priests, most definitely a witch."

He nodded and she continued, "Shortly after she came to Ahga, Owen Mortmain and the other Western lords rebelled. Abelard forced Owen to give him his daughter. He threatened to rape her, and then let his men use her, if Owen did not agree."

Roderic flinched. "Go on."

"So Abelard married Melisande. But he didn't ask my mother before he did it, and Melisande turned out to be barren. After it was done, my mother told him the outcome. No son of his would ever reign in Ahga, she said."

The words shivered down his spine with the weight of prophecy. "Why not?"

"By that time, Abelard had seven sons. Agara, his mother, had a clear favorite, Amanander. But Abelard feared that a son born outside of a lawful marriage would give the Congress an excuse to dissolve the kingdom. And so it became critical to Abelard that his Queen have a son."

"My mother was a pawn."

Annandale nodded sadly. "He went to my mother and demanded she use the Magic to help him. She had sworn to uphold the Kingdom by any means at her disposal. By her own oath, he compelled her to use the Magic. And so, in the twentieth year of his reign, two children were conceived. One was you—the other was me."

"Who, then, is my father?"

"Phineas."

"Phineas?"

"Yes. He was the Captain of the King's Guard."

He stared back at her, memories of the old man rushing through his mind. For as long as he could remember, Phineas had been an invalid, honored and revered, but an invalid nonetheless, helpless, crippled, blind. But who else had answered his questions so patiently, who else had explained strategies more readily than even his tutors, who else had taught him to play chess, over the longest and dullest of the winter evenings? Who had never turned him away, always listened, never interrupted, always responded with interest, with kindness, with advice?

He rocked back on his heels, remembering a thousand times when others had been too busy, when the King had been away, when a servant had come looking for him, with the request that Lord Phineas desired the presence of the young Prince. And how much he had looked forward to the chats with Phineas beside the hearths, how often he had listened, entranced, to the old man's tales. How eagerly he had gone.

He thrust the memories aside. "Why did your mother change? What made her become the monster she was at the end?"

"Because she used the Magic, Roderic. All four of them were subject to it. Your mother died giving birth to you, Phineas was wounded, lamed and blind. My mother became the creature you saw. And Abelard—it was by his will that the Magic was used. I don't like to think about what might be happening to him. But you see, Roderic, if Amanander truly has discovered a way to use the Magic without the consequences—"

"Yes. I understand." He knitted his fingers together. "Deirdre says she will take you there herself, so that I need have no fear for your safety. How long have you known this? Have you always known?"

"No." She shook her head. "Not always. Shortly before we met, you and I, the King came riding through the woods. His horse injured, killed, and he was hurt. I was watching, you see, and my mother came—told me to heal him, that it was time he learned who I was. and so I did."

"You met the King then?"

"The first and only time."

"And he knew you were his daughter?"

"My mother told him who I was." She twisted her hands in her gown.

He reached up and brushed the curls which tumbled over her shoulders off her cheeks. "What did you think of him?"

She smiled a little sadly. "I was afraid of him. He didn't look as though he would be an easy man to love."

Roderic nodded, his hands straying to her shoulders. "Neither am I," he whispered.

At that, she drew him close, to nestle his head against her breasts. "None of us are," she murmured. "None of us are."

"I don't want you to go."

She pulled away and turned his chin up to hers. "Nor do I . . . but I think I must."

"What about Rhodri?"

She drew a deep, shuddering breath. "He must stay here. He will be safer here, and though the One forbid anything should happen to us on the way, an infant will only be a danger—to the entire party."

He gazed into her eyes. He had not realized before the depth of her commitment to see that the kingdom was preserved. Tears gathered on her lashes, clung like pearls, and as the first spilled over and trailed down her cheek, he gathered her in his arms and held her tightly, as though for the last time. There were no more words between them.

Chapter Thirteen

*O*n an early morning in that cold June, Roderic watched from the steps of the entrance of Ithan's keep as the little party prepared to leave the sheltering walls of the fortress. He held tightly to Annandale's hands, loathe to let her go. "Promise me you'll do nothing foolish, lady—"

"Bah!" Deirdre cut him off with a snort. "Is the lady in the habit of foolishness?" The early morning light glinted off the short sword strapped to her thigh, the polished brass of her bridle. At her shoulder, an intricate pin held her brown-and-red battle-plaid securely in place. Roderic gazed up into her square-jawed, strong-featured face and was not comforted.

"Swear to me, M'Callaster—"

"I've already sworn to you, Prince. 'Tis not the time for oaths. Today's the time to act." Deirdre's horse pawed impatiently, as though some of his mistress's own impatience was communicated to him through the saddle.

With a heavy sigh, Roderic looked again at Annandale. Her dark blue cloak was pulled high against her throat, her hair was bound in a plain white coif. Her hood was pulled low, and from the shadows of her hood,

he could see her eyes, that same extraordinary blue
remembered as his father's—the same as his son's—ar
a lump rose in his throat. "Be well, lady."

She leaned down in her saddle and brushed her glove
fingers against his cheek. "And you, my love."

Beside her, Deirdre wheeled her horse, her han
raised, her voice shouting the first commands to th
guards who were to accompany Vere and Annandale.

"Vere," said Roderic, looking over at his brothe
where he sat calmly upon a gray gelding, "she is m
life."

Vere's eyes flickered over him, up and down, and h
nodded. "I shall see her safely to the College, Roderic."

Roderic nodded and cast one last look at the dozen c
so riders who clustered by the gates. Deirdre had hanc
picked the very best of her men. He recognized all c
them by sight, at least, except for one, who he notice
was heavily cloaked. The rider seemed to be the mos
impatient of the lot to be off. He narrowed his eyes an
then glanced at Deirdre. She knew what she was doing
To question her choices in front of her men would b
most unseemly.

With a final nod, he stepped back. He waved his han
at the guards by the gates, and the heavy gates swung
open, with a low groan of ancient hinges. He watched th
little party ride across the drawbridge, down to th
ancient highway. They turned their horses east and the
were gone from his view.

He hooked his thumbs in his belt. A servan
approached. "Yes?"

"Lord Phineas requests a word with you, Lorc

Prince, before the meeting this morning." The servant bowed.

"Very well." He hooked his thumbs in his swordbelt and climbed the low steps. It was time to talk to Phineas.

He found Phineas waiting in what he had come to think of as the council room. He cleared his throat in the open doorway. "You wanted to speak to me, Phineas?"

The old man nodded, his sightless eyes turning in the direction of Roderic's voice. "Has she gone?" His voice had an unfamiliar quaver.

"Yes." Roderic drew a deep breath and stepped into the room, closing the door behind him. "I want to talk to you. Before she left, Annandale told me the truth."

"The truth?"

"About my birth—about her birth. I am not really the true heir of Meriga, am I?"

"No, Roderic!" Phineas pushed at the arms of his litter as though he would leap to his feet. "Never doubt that. You are indeed the Prince of Meriga. You were born for no other reason."

"Do you deny you are my father?"

Phineas seemed to grope for words. "This much is true. It was my seed which grew in the Queen's womb. But you were conceived for one purpose, and one purpose alone. And that was to reign in Ahga after Abelard was gone. You were born to be King."

"It was that prophecy of Nydia's. And you let him use you—he used my mother—Nydia. How could you agree? Didn't you know there were bound to be consequences? Didn't anyone explain how the Magic worked?"

"Oh." Phineas ran a hand over his chin. "Yes. I knew—I knew there would be repercussions. What happened to me didn't matter. I was sworn to uphold the kingdom—in nearly thirty years I had never violated that oath. At the time Abelard came to me, I couldn't see any other way." He took a deep breath and sighed.

"So—" Roderic sat down in a chair near the litter. "So you've been maimed, blinded—all in the name of loyalty?"

Phineas gave a bitter laugh. "You think this is hard to bear? I would have borne twice this and more if I could have saved your mother—saved Nydia. I lost both the woman I loved and the woman I should have loved, Roderic. That is what made these years so empty."

"What do you mean? You loved my mother?"

"As much as any man can love a woman, I think. She was an extraordinary woman—Melisande Mortmain. She deserved much better than she got. The four of us gave Meriga an heir, Roderic, but the price we paid was dear."

"What do you mean, the woman you should have loved?"

Phineas was silent. "Life is a series of choices, Roderic. I cannot deny that Nydia stirred my blood. She was the most beautiful woman I have ever seen—to this day her memory haunts my dreams. And sometimes—" He laughed again, that same harsh, sound that seemed torn from his throat. "Sometimes I think if it had been me who loved her—instead of Abelard—that things may have turned out so much differently than they did."

"You chose not to love her?'

"I knew the King wanted her. She was so vulnerable, Roderic, so achingly vulnerable. She had this knowledge, and this ability which would have damned her to the stake, and did—twice. But Abelard wanted her, and I—" He paused. "I was not in the habit of competing with my King."

"Would she have loved you?"

Phineas shrugged and shook his head. "Who knows? Perhaps it is only an old man's wishful fancy. But I was young once, tall, strong, not unpleasant of face. The Queen loved me.

"Nydia and the King—well, it seemed clear to me from the day we found her in that forsaken little village that she would be his. And I fell in love with your mother almost from the first day I met her in her father's estate when I was held prisoner there."

"But, why then did Dad marry her? Didn't you tell him how you felt?"

"Abelard married Melisande to consolidate the kingdom. He knew. It didn't matter to him how we felt."

"But then—didn't she swear fidelity to him?"

"Of course. It was a foolish, forbidden love."

"What did you do?"

"Tried to forget at first. Stayed away from Ahga for more than seven years. Oh, it was easy to stay away, believe me. Those were the years the Harleyriders invaded Arkan. But then, after the danger had passed, and the Harleys were pushed back into the deep deserts south of Dlas, he came to me. He had a scheme to circumvent the prophecy. And all it required of me was to spend one night in the arms of the woman I had loved for nearly ten years." He turned his head to Roderic. "What would you have done?"

Unbidden, an image of Annandale rose before him. "Yes," he said. "I understand."

"It seemed an easy thing at the time. How could I know it was to cost her life? I had no idea the Magic could exact so harsh a price."

"But—but why, Phineas? Why did Dad—why did the King use you so?"

"Don't you understand? It was Abelard's answer to Nydia's prophecy. Do you think Abelard was a man to accept fate's decree?"

"But, Phineas, my whole life is a lie. For I am not the son of the King. Brand, Everard, Vere—even Amanander has a better claim than I." Roderic rose to his feet and paced to the window, where he could see the cold breeze whipping at the dresses of the wash maids hanging out the laundry.

"You must not believe that, Roderic. All save Amanander and Alexander are the sons of common women—Abelard knew that the Congress would divide into factions over any of the others."

"Well, what of Amanander and Alexander? Why did Dad refuse to name either of them?"

"Amanander is the eldest. His mother was a noblewoman, related by some loose connection to Abelard's mother. But Rabica Onrada was not an ideal candidate. The reasons aren't important now, Roderic. All that matters is that you are the acknowledged heir, the acclaimed

Regent. Whether or not Amanander is the son of Abelard—"

"Don't you think it might matter to me?" Roderic interrupted. "All this time I have held this regency in the name of my father—and now I learn he isn't my father after all."

"Roderic." Phineas turned his face to him, and Roderic had the uncanny feeling that the old man could see him. "Do you really believe that? Did Abelard ever, by word or deed or look, ever treat you as anything less than the acknowledged heir of his body, and of Meriga?"

For a long moment, Roderic stared at Phineas. "No," he said at last. "I would never have known."

"And neither does anyone else."

"I only wonder now if I have the right, Phineas. Because the King willed it so, does that make it so?" Roderic looked at Phineas, his voice soft.

Phineas drew a long, shuddering breath, and Roderic wondered what nerve he had touched. "In the present circumstances, Roderic, it does indeed. Do you believe that Amanander would be the better King?"

Roderic stared once more out the window, remembering the cold, black look of his brother's stare. "No," he said finally.

"Then whether you believe it or not, you are the Prince of Meriga. And the charge laid upon you by the King is yours. Would you abandon this nation to Amanander?"

Roderic looked at the old man. "So I have no choice?"

Phineas sighed. "A long time ago, someone told me there is always a choice. You can choose to renounce

Abelard's will. You can even choose to run away. You can choose to fight Amanander and then, in the end, give the crown to Alexander, for example, or Brand or Everard or even Vere, if that is your wish. But, Roderic, remember this. Whatever you choose, you must believe that what you do is right, that the ultimate result will be for the good of whatever you hope to achieve. A leader may not know the answers, a leader may not know the outcome, but a leader always has faith. If you lose your faith in yourself, and in your ability to lead this nation, we are already lost."

Roderic stared at the old man. *Faith shall finish what hope begins.* The ancient motto of the Ridenau family ran through is mind. What hope had stirred in Abelard's breast that he had set in motion such a set of complicated events? And he had a stake in the future, too. Rhodri was his son. He remembered how he had felt on the day Rhodri was born. The past hadn't mattered then . . . only the future. He drew a deep breath as someone knocked on the door. "Come," he said.

Brand strode into the room and hard at his heels came Kye, followed by Grefith, Deirdre's second-in-command. "Roderic," Brand began, "the scouts we sent east and south have returned."

Roderic squared his shoulders. "Bring them in," he said without hesitation. "Call for the captains of the regiments. I shall review the troops this afternoon. We will begin to keep our enemies too busy to notice travelers." He glanced at Phineas. The habit of command—how easily he assumed it now. Was it really only a question of faith?

Behind Brand the captains of the divisions filed into the room. The men spoke with quiet voices, looking to him again and again as they talked amongst themselves. He sighed softly as he took his place at the head of the table.

There was a stir at the door and six travel-stained men entered.

"The scouts, Lord Prince," said Brand, taking his seat at Roderic's right.

Roderic nodded as the scouts bowed. "Come in, gentlemen. Sit down and tell us everything you can."

Less than a mile out of Ithan, the road forked north and west. At the crossroads, Deirdre paused, reining in her stallion as she turned to Vere to confirm the direction. Out of the corner of her eye, she caught a glimpse of the cloaked rider who had been careful to stay on the periphery of the group as they had ridden out of Ithan. She frowned, quickly counting heads. She wasn't mistaken at all. There was an extra man. "You there—" She guided her mount over. "Who are you?"

The rider swept his cloak off his head. "M'Callaster," said Alexander with grave courtesy. "I beg leave to accompany you."

Deirdre stared. Around her the men muttered to themselves. Vere jerked so hard at his reins that his animal whinnied a protest. Annandale broke the shocked silence. "Alex? But why?"

He looked across the men, mute appeal on his face. "I think I can find the King. If Vere will guide me, after he sees you safely to the College."

Deirdre glanced at Vere. Vere hesitated. "You think you know where Dad is, Alex?"

"I think I can find him with your help. Please. Roderic has enough on his mind. Dad's running out of time."

"How do you know this?" Deirdre narrowed her eyes, pinning Alexander with a stare her men recognized with a shudder.

Alexander looked from Annandale to Vere to Deirdre. "You wouldn't believe me if I told you."

The riders muttered and Deirdre swore beneath her breath, thinking fast. Now was not the time for such a discussion. She cast a quick glance over her shoulder. It would be a simple enough thing to return to Ithan, to force Alexander to stay and wait until Roderic could address the situation. And yet— She looked from Vere to Annandale to Alexander and made a decision based on intuition alone. "I have a duty to see this lady to the College of the Muten Elders. If you wish to accompany us, so be it, Alexander. Once the lady is safe, then you and Vere are free to decide where you wish to go." She looked at Vere. "Does that suit you?"

Vere nodded slowly. "Alex, we have to talk about this. You know that."

"Then the journey will give us the time we need." Alexander pulled his hood over his head with a satisfied nod.

Deirdre looked at the brothers and shook her head once more, swearing softly. Damn this tangled mainlander coil. She flapped at her reins. There was no more time to waste. "Well, Vere? Which way?"

Slowly, Vere turned to her, his face wearing a puckered frown. "That way, M'Callaster."

With another curse, Deirdre put the spurs to her horse, wondering why she had not had sense to stay home with the cows and the gulls.

Chapter Fourteen

❧

The wind whined across the cliffs, bringing no hint of summer warmth, no promise of the sun. Only a damp rain spattered fitful drops across Amanander's face, and low clouds scudded across the midday sky. He glanced at his cousin, Harland, with undisguised contempt. "They're late."

"Aman, they'll be here." Harland's voice had the slightest pleading edge, and Amanander smiled grimly to himself.

How was it possible, Amanander thought, for any man to be such an idealist? Harland had been less than three years old the day his father died so horribly at Ferad's hands, but he seemed to have absorbed his father's idealism with his mother's milk. Of course, Harland had no idea of the role Ferad had played in his father's death, and Amanander, who had witnessed the whole event, had never seen the need to tell him.

Amanander glanced sideways at the younger man, who sat poised and eager in the saddle beside him. The less Harland knew, the better. Now they waited on top of the rocky promontory, on the edge of the no-man's land which was the border of Loma, for the leader of the Harleyriders.

The wind blew more rain in his face. Up her
exposed, there was no shelter, but curiously, Amanand
was not bothered.

The equations of the Magic flitted through his min
as they did constantly these days, while he turned the
over and over in his brain, endlessly toying with them
He had delved a little into Harland's mind, loathe to g
too deep lest Ferad notice. There were already a fe
signs that his old tutor distrusted him. More than onc
he had felt a whisper of Ferad's presence in his min
Lately he realized that the intricacies of the Magi
could be used to shield his mind from Ferad's probing
And there was always Gartred. He had but to touch h
mind and Ferad withdrew, leaving the unmistakabl
trace of contempt.

It was that contempt Amanander had seized upon i
his initial experiments with emotion and its effects upo
the Magic. Directed upon Gartred, the hen responded a
he expected. But then he had realized that she had alway
been more or less in his thrall. He was eager to try hi
newfound knowledge on someone of greater mettle. H
looked at Harland with speculative interest.

Just then, Harland reached over and grasped his fore
arm. "Look there." He pointed. "I told you they woul
come."

Amanander followed the line of Harland's finge
Across the desert floor, a dozen dark shapes on shaggy
short-legged ponies emerged from the entrance of th
canyon opposite.

"Come on." Harland tugged at the reins, and wheele
the animal around. Amanander took one last look at th

dozen riders trotting across the valley. His gaze swept up and down over the heights opposite.

"Just how well do you think you know this Kahn, Harry?"

"You know my father and his shared the same dream," Harland replied. "I have known him all my life."

Amanander swept his arm to the surrounding hills. "If we go down there, we are vulnerable to anything they have placed in the hills. Let them come to us."

Harland stared. "That's an act of distrust."

Amanander met his cousin's gaze. "So?"

"Aman, I have explained to you and explained to you. We can't treat these people like enemies if we want to make them our friends—"

"Spare me the nursery lectures, Harry. If you want to risk your neck by going down to meet them, go on. I will wait here—you bring them to me."

"Aman!"

The two men stared at each other. Amanander considered using the Magic. Finally Harland dropped his eyes. "I-I will go down and see."

"Good." Amanander nodded his satisfaction and watched his cousin pick his way down the rock-strewn path. He pursed his lips. In any battle of wills, Harland was sure to be the loser. No wonder Abelard had treated Eldred, the father, with such contempt.

He had Abelard's will, Abelard's determination. In that, he was clearly his father's son. He knew that as surely as he knew now that he was the true heir of Meriga. And why he was successful at using the Magic— it was the force of his will which fueled the fire within.

A man like Harland might not have difficulty graspin the concepts of the Magic, but he might well have diff culty imposing his will. He intended to use that mettle bring about the destruction of every ideal his father ha ever cherished. And the best part of all was that Abelar would watch. He chuckled softly, thinking of Abelard red-rimmed eyes in his tortured face. There was nothin of the King about him now. Strange how low one coul sink when stripped of every vestige of dignity, ever basic human need.

He watched thoughtfully as the trail dipped down an Harland disappeared from view. It was easy to contro the minds of men like Harland, but the energy require was enormous, draining. He remembered how Ferad ha achieved a link to Alexander, enabling him to drain from his twin the energy needed to restore himself to relativ health. That link had been relatively easy to forge and to maintain, until that witch of Roderic's had interfered. I only there was a way to feed off the life force of anyone he wished. The answer seemed to hover just outside the range of his perceptions, but he was certain emotion wa the key. Harland's high-minded ideals were a bit to lofty, a bit too ephemeral. But it was a matter to which he intended to give a great deal of thought.

His attention was diverted as he saw the riders pull up short at the bottom of the hill and heard Harland's wel coming shout. He peered over the edge, taking in the view of the men below.

There were exactly a dozen of them, all clothed in black leathers, intricate chains bound over their chests, necks, and upper arms. Their hair was long and dirty, hanging in greasy locks down their backs. Water was sacred to the Harleyriders. So sacred they refused to waste it for bathing. They bragged that at puberty they were sewn into their leather skins and never removed them. His flesh crawled at the thought of being in the company of such unwashed vermin. He refused to apply the word *men* to them. Even dogs kept clean.

He watched as Harland gestured upward, and the eyes of the riders followed. Amanander gazed down calmly into the dark eyes and dirt-caked faces of his father's mortal enemies. Strange bedfellows, Dad, he thought, and then chuckled to himself. Well, maybe not so strange at all. The Harleys had roamed for centuries unchecked across the Arkan Plains, until the Ridenau Kings had risen to power and made Meriga a nation once again. He would turn the ancient enmity to his own advantage.

He nodded with grim satisfaction as the leader, at least the one he took to be the leader, gestured for his companions to follow. Harland turned his horse and started back up the path. "Very good, cousin," he mused. "Very good."

He waited until Harland emerged from the path and gave him a tight-lipped smile. "I knew you could make them see it my way."

"Just be careful, Aman," Harland hissed. "You've got tigers by the tail here. These men must be treated with all respect, or all the groundwork I have lain will come to naught."

Amanander slid his dark eyes over Harland, smelling the rank, greasy odor which clung to his cousin like the stench of the poison pits. "Let's hope they are as strong as their stench."

The odor hit him even before they emerged from the path onto the top of the cliff. He choked, his stomach heaving, and tried not to gag. He looked at Harland, wondering how his cousin could have stood the stench up close.

He narrowed his eyes and bit hard on his lip until the pain took the nausea away. He focused on the large figure riding closer, his shaggy mount sure-footed and steady across the rock strewn path.

He squared his shoulders and resisted the urge to cover his mouth and nose with his cloak. It wouldn't do much good, anyway, he knew.

The Harleys came closer, and Amanander saw the dirt-caked skin, the hard bright eyes in the filthy faces. He met their gazes unblinking.

About ten paces from where he sat, the company halted. "Kahn," said Harland, his voice higher-pitched than normal, "may I present to you my cousin, Amanander."

The Kahn did not reply immediately. He looked Amanander up and down, and in his eyes, Amanander saw the same kind of scorn he recognized. We don't have to bed each other, he thought. Amanander did not flinch beneath the scrutiny.

Amanander inclined his head in the fraction of a bow. "Kahn."

"Lord." The rider stared at him for a few beats longer, then gestured over his shoulder. "My woman. Mamma-Doc."

Amanander looked past the rider, to the figure who

pushed her pony forward. She was heavyset, with broad shoulders. Her enormous breasts splayed out from either side of the leather vest she wore. She seemed only marginally cleaner than her man. It was hard to tell what color her eyes might be, for her long, tangled hair hung low over her brow. He noted she wore no chains and carried no weapons. He nodded shortly.

"We have come," said the Kahn simply, and folded his thick arms over his massive chest.

Harland glanced at Amanander. Amanander drew a quick breath. "I seek to claim my father's inheritance. Help me regain it, and the Arkan Plains are no longer under the protection of the Ridenaus."

A stir went through the ranks, but the Kahn himself did not move.

His eyes flickered over Harland and then back to Amanander. "What are you saying?"

"That when I am in my father's seat in Ahga, I will not forget the debt, and the Arkan Lords who support my upstart brother—" Amanander tripped over the word *brother*. "There shall be no more aid from Ahga for them."

"I told you he thought as I, Kahn," said Harland eagerly. "I told you he believed that Meriga was big enough for everyone to live peacefully."

Amanander fought the urge to laugh. The look in the Kahn's eyes surely matched his own. He looked up as Mamma-Doc cleared her throat.

"Fine words," she said. "What else can you give us besides promises? We send our men to fight for you . . . we could end up dead . . . with nothing."

"Mamma-Doc," said Harland, with as much respect as he might have used to a lady of the court, "we have been friends, our people and yours, for as long and longer than I can remember. You have ever had friends in Missiluse. Would we turn against you?"

Amanander watched the woman's face closely. Her tension resonated through her like a plucked harpstring, palpable as a sound to his mind. With narrowed eyes, he allowed his mind to delve the first of the equations of the Magic. Harland's voice went on, making promises, sweet as honey, liquid as wine. Quickly as the arrow's flight, Amanander delved deeper into the Magic. He sought the woman's eyes, searching for an opening, feeling the emotion tangible as a thread leading him in.

A thousand images swam before his eyes: dark nights, white hot days beneath a merciless sun, the tang of the mare's milk, the rank odor of the dung fires, the sounds of the chains around the Kahn's neck as he bent over her to couple.

And then he was inside, deeper, in the place of all her secret hopes and fears, an open book laid before him as easy to read as a child's scrawl. Say yes, he murmured.

"Man," the woman murmured, using the title of respect among her people, interrupting Harland's awkward stammerings. "Yes."

"What do you say, woman?" The Kahn turned and stared at her.

"Say yes—accept his offer. I have a vision about this one."

The Kahn stared. "What—what do you see?"

"A vision of land, stretching out to the sky from east to

west, and horses, more than we can count between us . . ." Her voice trailed off as Amanander gently withdrew. No sense in damaging the hen. If she had this kind of influence over the Kahn, she was too valuable to be wasted.

A ripple went through the riders; they leaned their heads together and muttered. Mamma-Doc was a seer, a wise-woman known for her visions. She sat at the Kahn's right hand and guided his decisions. If she had said to do this, then it should be done.

The Kahn narrowed his eyes at Amanander, and Amanander wanted to laugh. The war between his own instincts and the timeworn lessons of his woman was so clear upon the Kahn's face, he might have spoken it aloud. Finally he said, "We shall do this."

"Good," said Amanander, speaking aloud for the first time since the introduction. "Bring your men and rendezvous with my cousin at the garrison at Meridien. I know you know the way."

The Kahn turned uneasily in his saddle, seeking out the eyes of Mamma-Doc. The woman sat entranced, her own eyes on Amanander. He willed her to smile, and obediently her lips turned up. As the Kahn nodded, Amanander felt a little shiver through his own mind. The hen was fighting him! He tightened his clamp upon her, showing her an image of her children torn and bleeding. The answering surge of emotion was overwhelming. Energy poured into his mind, unchanneled like a river at floodtide. He controlled his surprise with an effort and threw it back out, reaching into the minds of a few of the other companions on either side of her. They instantly focused their eyes on him.

From somewhere on the cliffs a hawk shrieked and dropped. "We shall meet again a week hence," said Amanander as he reinforced the image of the wide green plains in the minds of the Riders. It was easier now, he noticed, now that he'd had that little boost from the woman. For curiosity's sake, he gave her another image, this one of her man crucified. Again another blast of energy surged back, filling him with an overwhelming sense of strength. Almost as easily as he might crush a leaf, he let his mind flow over and into the others, until only the Kahn was untouched.

He nodded briefly at the Kahn, flapped his horse's reins, and guided the animal away, listening as Harland made some hurried excuse for a good-bye. He was halfway down the path when he heard the hooves of Harland's mount behind him. He didn't bother to turn around.

"Aman!" called Harland. "Why were you so rude? Turning your back on them like that? Don't you realize they could have thrown something at you? That's considered a grave slight among them. One never turns one's back upon a friend."

Amanander let a little smile appear around the corners of his mouth. "Yes, Harry. I know."

"And here they had agreed to help us—thank heavens for the Mamma-Doc. She must have liked what she saw, hmm?"

Amanander nodded. "Indeed."

"But, Aman." Harland rode up beside him and grabbed his arm. "We can't insult our allies like that. We need every friend. How do you expect to cement an alliance between the Kahn and his people and the Southern lords—"

"Harry, I think you misunderstand. I don't intend to be their friend. I intend to be their master."

"Aman!" Harland gazed at him, shocked, the reins limp in his fingers.

Amanander suppressed a laugh. Harland was so pathetic. "I was joking, Harry. Of course."

"Ah." Harland breathed a sigh and tightened his hands on the reins. "For-forgive me, Aman. I didn't mean to suggest—"

"Of course you didn't." Amanander felt his smile stretch his mouth like a taut bowstring. "We will begin with Dlas, I think."

Harland raised an eyebrow quizzically. "Dlas?"

Amanander nodded. "I don't want an enemy on my flank. I know that garrison like my own hand, its strengths and its weaknesses. It will be an easy thing to take it out."

"But—but, Aman—your nephew holds Dlas. Surely it would be better to at least offer him the chance to join with us? To explain things as we see them? Just as you did with Reginald?"

The horses' hooves beat a steady tattoo as they cantered down the highway. Amanander stroked his chin as though giving Harland's suggestion serious consideration. "You think we should send an envoy, then, Harry?"

"Oh, yes. Two or three men, no more."

"Two or three." Yes, thought Amanander. Two or three to go through the gates. And a pack of Harleys waiting in the hills. "Yes, Harry, I think you're right. I shall be sure to send a messenger with a proposal to Barran. Better to try to make as many allies as we can."

The sun briefly glinted out behind the lowering clouds. He smiled at his cousin, amused by the utter trust which stared from Harry's guileless eyes. With a little smile, Amanander delved, gently at first, then with greater insistence. He was rewarded when Harland's mouth slackened. This part was easy. Too easy, he thought. With slow deliberation, he gave Harland an image of Missiluse Castle in ruins, as it had been the day his father had died. Only a small trickle of emotion flowed back.

Amanander tried a harsher image, a woman raped and bleeding, lying on the ground, her legs spread wide. This time the emotion surged, raw, every bit as violent as that of Mamma-Doc's. Triumph, as hot and exhilarating as a sexual climax, rolled through his body. I have it, thought Amanander. He had the key. He thought of Reginald: clumsy, arrogant, defiant Reginald. Oh, he would have to summon Reginald here as quickly as possible, and Atland's sons—

"Summon Reginald," said Harland.

Amanander looked at his cousin with a start. "What did you say?"

"Summon Reginald immediately," repeated Harland.

A slow smile spread across Amanander's face. He'd had no idea it would be so effortless.

Chapter Fifteen

From the cover of the dense underbrush that lined the ancient road as it dipped down into the valley, eyes watched as the fourteen travelers guided their horses over the uneven blacktop. The highway, which had once been wider than thirty horses across, now barely accommodated four of the riders abreast. Low-hanging branches partially obscured their vision, and one of the observers leaned over to growl in another's ear. "Who are these humans?"

Jama shook his head, eyes narrowed in concentration, and motioned for his lieutenant to be quiet. This was most unexpected. Down in the hidden valley on the other side of the mountain pass was the College. It had taken weeks for his scouts to find the refuge of the Elders, so inaccessible were the inner hollows of the Pulatchian Highlands. And yet, here, on this sunny morning, more than a dozen humans came riding over the crest of the hill, their horses fat, their weapons shining, their clothing well worn but by no means threadbare. He leaned forward, his dark eyes scanning the company as they rounded a curve and breasted a slight rise. It was a company of soldiers—not the King's soldiers, for he knew those uniforms too well. These men wore dark brown leather breeches, and their shirts of unbleached linen were covered by cloaks woven in intricate patterns of predominantly browns and greens and blues. He craned his head, trying to get a better look. At the head of the group rode a tall thin man dressed in shades of grayish green. Jama sucked in his breath as he recognized Vere.

"Adanijah," he muttered. "Do you see who that is?"

Adanijah leaned forward, his headdress fluttering back as a breeze shifted the leaves. "At the head?"

"It's the one called Vere. Ridenau Prince and member of the College of the Elders."

Adanijah smiled, his uneven white teeth flashing in his terra-cotta face. His secondary arms jolted spasmodically against his chest. "Good then. He comes just in time."

Jama grunted an assent. "But who's he bringing with him? The Elders don't let humans into the College."

Adanijah smiled and glanced over his shoulder, where the rest of their forces lay concealed in the dense underbrush. "Maybe he comes to do our job."

Jama shot Adanijah a quelling look. Although he understood Amanander's order that the College be destroyed, he had grave doubts that this was the right course of action. There was something distasteful and disquieting about falling like vengeance on a refugee group of Elders, who, blind, deprived of hands and tongues by their own codes, could hardly defend themselves. He looked at the travelers, now nearly parallel to their hiding places. In the center of the company, in the most protected position, a slim rider garbed in a dark blue traveling cloak rode a dainty mare. He tugged at Adanijah's sleeve. "That's a woman," he hissed.

Adanijah glanced over. "So? Their women don't interest me."

With a hiss of disgust, Jama looked at Adanijah. "But obviously she interests the College, you fool, or Vere wouldn't be bringing her to them."

"You think he's taking her there?" Adanijah narrowed his eyes for another look.

Jama shook his head. "Have we seen any other sign of humans in these parts? And here comes more than a dozen of them, riding bold as you please in the direction of the College."

Adanijah gave the soldiers an appraising look. "You think they will interfere?"

Jama shrugged. "They are a dozen to our fifteen hundreds." He looked at his second in command, and bit back a chuckle. "I hardly think so."

The hair rose on the back of Deirdre's neck. She spurred her mount up to Vere's and leaned nearer to him in the saddle. "I don't like this."

Vere turned and gave her an inscrutable look. "This is what the Children have been reduced to, M'Callaster."

"No," she said, dismissing with a wave the huts which clung like scabs to the sides of the mountains. "That isn't what I meant. I don't like the feeling I have. I feel as though we are being watched."

"We are," Vere replied gravely. They rode side by side in silence, and then he pointed to pass in the road, high above them. "You will leave us there, for you can go no further. I am sworn to bring no outsiders into the College."

Deirdre raised an eyebrow. "I don't like that."

Vere shrugged. "That is the way it is, M'Callaster. We have our ways, as you have yours."

Deirdre gave Vere a hard look. "I swore to Roderic to bring his lady safe to the College—"

"Deirdre," Vere said gently. "You only promised Roderic you would take us to the pass there and you have. Trust me."

With a puckered frown, Deirdre turned away. "What about Alexander?"

Vere nodded. "I am going to take him with me. I want the Elders to speak to him—I think he may be able to tell them things about the Magic they don't know yet. Or at least give them some idea how Amanander and Ferad are likely to try to use it."

"So you expect us to wait for you?"

Vere shook his head. "No. Don't wait. I don't know how long I will be. And after consulting with the Elders, it may be that Alexander and I will go and look for Dad."

"Have all the Ridenau brothers gone mad?" Deirdre shook her head.

Vere gave her an amused look. "What do you mean?"

Deirdre made a derisive noise. "Well, look at you all. Reginald and Amanander traitors, you and Alexander about to go off on some wild quest. Phillip refuses to crawl out behind his mountains, leaving Everard to fight in the North, and here the only one with any sense to stand by Roderic is Brand—" She shook her head.

Vere looked up at the green mountains, rising sharply

on all sides. For a long moment, he said nothing, and then he nodded. "Indeed, M'Callaster. I see what you mean. We are a wayward lot. Makes one wonder how a country can be united, when even brothers cannot."

She met his eyes and nodded, saddened by his expression. "How much further?"

Vere glanced up. "Distances in these mountains are deceiving. We will reach the entrance to the pass by dusk. Camp there tonight, and then tomorrow be on your way."

Deirdre gave him a long, measuring look and looked away with a sigh of resignation. "Aye, Vere. As you say. I don't like it. But I will respect it."

His only answer was a smile which did not quite reach his eyes.

The long shadows fell early from the high peaks of the mountains. Adanijah cursed as he glared across the valley. "Why wait?"

Jama leaned against the trunk of the tree, chewing on a long stem of grass. The others eyed him cautiously. He knew the desperation which beat through his brothers' blood. "I say we allow the Ridenau to bring the woman into the Elders."

"And the soldiers?" An old, grizzled veteran of many battles spoke across the clearing.

"If they are there, kill them. But otherwise, remember what Amanander told us. We do nothing to alert the humans."

Adanijah spat. "Foolishness. What care we whether they know?"

Jama set the piece of grass aside and gazed up at his older companion with mild eyes. "Because. All along we have fretted that we would have no recognition from the humans. And now it is offered. And now, for right now, we will do as he asks."

"For right now." Adanijah met Jama's eyes with a long look.

"For right now. So long as his interests and ours are one."

"And when they are not?" Beside Jama, a comrade twisted off another piece of grass and slowly looked it over as though it were the choicest of morsels.

Something twisted in Jama's gut. His people had survived on grass like that, eaten boiled until the tough fibers broke down. There was little or no nourishment in it, but at least one died of starvation with one's belly full. "When they are not, Zell, then we shall turn upon the Ridenau as easily as he would turn upon us." In the fading light, Jama met Adanijah's eyes and was satisfied to see him nod approval.

The pass rose high and forbidding, the striated rock walls of pinks and browns and tans practically at right angles to the ground. Deirdre slid off her horse, patting the animal's rump. She hooked her thumbs in her swordbelt and shifted her plaid over her shoulder. "You know I don't like this, Vere. I would feel better if I saw the lady safe in the hands of the Elders myself."

Vere slid off the saddle, handing her the reins. "I know. But believe me, it is better this way."

Deirdre gave him a long look. She turned away and strode to Annandale. "My lady."

Annandale tightened her hands on the reins. "Tell Roderic I shall return as soon as possible."

Deirdre nodded. "I will send a messenger."

"A messenger?" Vere had come up behind her. "Why a messenger?"

Deirdre looked up at Annandale, her eyes steady. "I have other business."

"What other business?" Vere demanded. He tugged at her arm, and Deirdre spun on her heel to face him.

Angry words leapt to her lips and she bit them back. She tossed her head back and glanced at Annandale. "I am not going back to Ithan."

Vere gasped. "I—I thought you had agreed to stay— at least until the autumn—"

"I agreed to stay till Gost. But there have been changes—new information has come to light." She glanced back at Annandale once more. "I think Roderic needs me for what I am about to do more than he requires my presence in Ithan."

"And what is that?" Vere's face flushed scarlet beneath his tattoos, and he clenched his hands into fists. "Cross the Saranevas before the first frost?"

She regarded him with cool disdain. "I go to Owen Mortmain. To ask him to send Roderic reinforcements."

"Vada?" Vere whispered. "You go to Vada?"

"Aye. And if I don't leave now, I may not get back across the Saranevas by the first frost. You know how long a trip it is."

"But-but, M'Callaster—Deirdre, what made you think to do such a thing?"

"Take a look around you, Vere. The country's in chaos. Can Roderic risk allowing the West to stay uninvolved? How can he fight a war on so many fronts? Every man of the Congress is intent on protecting his piece of Meriga, which may be as it should be, and maybe I should be doing the same—but by the One, Vere, I cannot sit back and watch Roderic flounder for lack of troops and supplies."

Vere stared at her. "You really think Owen will come?"

She shrugged. "He's an old man. I doubt he will come. But under the circumstances—" She broke off and gazed over Vere's shoulder. "Aye. I think Owen will send troops to his grandson's aid."

Vere drew a deep breath. "In all these years, Owen has never sent men. The supplies have come, but only because Abelard's administrators have taken them. What is different now?"

"Well, for one thing," Deirdre said, "Roderic is of his blood. What man would deny his grandson aid?"

Vere shrugged. "It's a long risk, M'Callaster. You ride across the length of Meriga—ask an old man for aid— what if he says no?"

"Then I'll come back. And may the One forgive me for being a fool."

"Will you—will you be all right? It's dangerous—"

She gave a short laugh. "Aye—it's dangerous. If I don't return by Gost—count me lost."

"Gost? You'd hoped to be back in the Settle Islands by Gost."

"I guess my plans have changed." She met his eyes as a grim smile stretched his thin lips.

"Shall I—may I tell Roderic where you have gone?"

She shrugged. "As you please. If I succeed he'll find out, and if I fail it won't matter."

"Deirdre . . ." Vere began.

She looked at him expectantly and he continued. "Thank you. Thank you for your protection on this journey and forgive me for being angry with you just now. I—I didn't understand what you had in your mind to do. . . ."

She held up her hand and smiled up at Annandale, who was watching her with an unreadable expression. "'Tis of no consequence. And it isn't the first time I've been accused of being too close-mouthed about my intentions." She smiled at him. "Goddess blessings, Vere."

"And to you M'Callaster."

She looked at Annandale and gave her a crooked smile. "And to you, lady. I honor my oath to the Prince."

Annandale nodded, tears in her eyes. "Roderic is lucky to count you his friend, lady. You are the bravest woman I have ever met."

Deirdre shook her head. "No. Not I. You are." She backed away and offered her hand to Vere. "Farewell, my friend. Take care of the lady. She is well loved."

Vere nodded, and, motioning to Alexander, led Annandale's mare through the pass. Deirdre stood aside, surrounded by her men as she watched the three disappear into the dusk. She adjusted her plaid around her shoulders with a sigh.

"M'Callaster?" One of her men intruded on her thoughts. "We make camp here?"

Deirdre scanned the hills, the thickly wooded valley.

An owl hooted deep in the forest, and the hair rose on the back of her neck. "Aye, Donner. By the goddess I'll be glad to see the last of this place." And I don't know why, she added silently.

Vere was silent as he led Annandale's mare down the steeply curving path. In the deepening dusk, the shadows lay beneath the trees in dark pools and nothing moved in the branches. Doves cooed invisibly, and pale white flowers shone like stars in the shadows beneath the trees. A hush seemed to hang over the place. The only sounds were the clop of the horses' shoes on the broken surface of the ancient road.

Annandale looked over at Alexander. He took a deep breath and gave her a tight smile. Suddenly Vere stopped. Annandale looked up. In the road, silent as wraiths, three white-wrapped figures stood, arms tucked into the wide sleeves of their robes. Their hoods were pulled low over their faces, revealing nothing. Annandale gasped.

Fear not, said a musical voice in her mind. *Be welcome here at the College of the Elders, Daughter of the Greatest Magic.* Annandale glanced wonderingly at Alexander, knowing from the expression on his face that he had heard a voice, as well. A dove cooed again, and a soft breeze brought the scent of honeysuckle. *May the Power which orders the universe keep you in Its care.*

The words seemed to echo, reverberate into the deepest recesses of her mind and beyond, into the very core of her being, and an intrinsic rightness, almost a recognition, surged through her. Annandale smiled, feeling more at ease, more welcomed than she had ever felt in her entire life. This, she thought, this is what it feels like to come home.

Vere made a motion and the horses began to move down the path. The three hooded figures turned as one and led the way, their white robes gleaming in the twilight. The road seemed to fork off abruptly, but the three walked straight between two trees and disappeared.

Alexander gasped. "No," murmured Vere, "it's only an illusion. You will see."

He turned to Annandale, holding out his arms, and indicated she should dismount. As she slid from the saddle, two squat figures appeared from the trees. They took the reins from Vere, and Alexander slowly swung out of his saddle. Annandale winced as she heard his joints creak. He walked stiffly to join them. Vere gave them a tight-lipped smile. "Come."

He walked between the trunks of two of the great trees and reached out and pushed. A doorway materialized where none had been before, and Annandale gasped. She raised questioning eyes to Vere. He smiled. "I told you— the Elders are well hidden."

She followed Vere through the doorway and found herself on a landing at the top of a staircase. The air was stale and musty, the floor beneath her feet covered in a material of ancient manufacture. Torches burned in makeshift sockets, and Annandale shivered in the dampness.

Vere gestured toward the staircase. "Lady, I should warn you. The Elders are in hiding for their lives. There is not much comfort here, especially not the sort you are used to in Ahga, but what there is, you are welcome to."

Annandale raised her eyes to Vere. "I didn't come for comfort, Vere. Lead on."

Alexander coughed. Vere looked at him, an expression of sympathy and concern on his face. "Come on, Alex. We can rest here." Vere led the way down the steps and finally they reached the bottom.

"Vere, what is this place?" Alexander asked.

"The foundations of a high tower," Vere replied. "In the Armageddon, all this landscape changed. These are new mountains, raised by the earthshakes. There are many such places in these hills, if you know what to look for." He led the way down a long corridor. The floor was cracked in many places, and water dripped through the low ceiling to form shallow pools on the uneven surface. Finally, Vere paused before a door. He gave them both a crooked smile and opened it.

Annandale stepped over the threshold. The room extended further than she could see in the dim light, but she could see white-robed figures clustered around small fires. Near the doorway, a small cooking fire burned in the center of the floor. The woman who bent over the steaming iron pot which hung from a trivet looked up. "Vere," she said, a smile of welcome creasing her face in a web of wrinkles, "just in time for dinner. As always." The woman looked at Annandale as though she knew her. "I am glad to see you at last, my dear. I knew your mother. My name is J'lin."

Annandale blinked. More and more of the white-robed figures were coming forward, shuffling toward them, their backs bent, their faces hooded. In her mind, she seemed to hear whispers, and a myriad of emotion swept over and through her: welcome, trepidation, relief. She raised her eyes to Vere. He touched her arm.

"This is the Lady Annandale, J'lin." He touched Annandale's arm gently and led her forward to where a small, nearly child-sized figure sat hunched before a battered grate. He sat upon a carefully folded pile of threadbare blankets. "My Father," he murmured, bending down. "The Lady Annandale."

Annandale gasped as the figure on the ground looked up and she saw that, except for the one eye in the center of his forehead, his other eyes were gone, the sockets thick twists of scars.

Did you not warn her, my son? The voice which shivered through her mind was soft, kind, achingly gentle, and Annandale stared at the ruined face before her. *Fear not, daughter. This is but one of the precautions we take to ensure that our Magic will be safe.*

Annandale raised questioning eyes to Vere. He cleared his throat. "I'm sorry, lady. I forgot to warn you. When the Pr'fessors take their final vows, they give up their hands, their eyes and their tongues. It keeps the secrets safe. This is Sirak. He is the oldest of the Pr'fessors."

Annandale gazed down and the Muten's thin mouth curved in a smile. *Be welcome here, daughter. You are long awaited.*

But-but how, she thought.

Ah, you already know how to reach the mind of another. So effortless your gift. We shall do well together, you and I. Rest now, and eat. Tomorrow comes in its time.

He turned away, and Annandale knew she was dismissed. She looked at Vere once more. He gave her a crooked smile. "Let's eat."

Chapter Sixteen

∼

Annandale opened her eyes. A long shaft of light streamed through a window set close to the ceiling of the underground room. She lay on the narrow cot watching the dust motes twine like a ribbon through the gold light. Her thoughts were a jumble.

For the first time, she understood something of the grinding poverty the Mutens endured, the terrible chasm which separated them from the human population. Their deformities were not so appalling or disgusting once one became accustomed to them. Was it simply that humans were taught to find the Mutens repulsive and therefore did? She rolled on her side, her head pillowed on her arm.

The thin quilt which covered her was adequate for the cool June nights, but in the winter— She fingered the neat patches and hoped they had more blankets than these.

Her breasts ached, her nipples swollen and taut. She sighed. Rhodri, she thought. She closed her eyes and thoughts of her baby brought a rush of milk, the hot liquid gushing from her engorged breasts, soaking the front of her nightgown. She pressed her lips together as a tear slipped beneath her lashes. She thought of the last sight she had had of him, one tiny fist tucked securely in his mouth, the other beneath his chin. His lashes were small crescents over his plump rosy cheeks, his thatch of dark hair as downy as a baby bird. She remembered how Roderic had looked at her as she had turned away from the cradle, his mouth compressed and grim.

Let me go home, she prayed instinctively, knowing that someone, something listened. Give me strength to do whatever is required and then let me go home. For I do not want to die. I want to hold my baby again—lie in Roderic's arms again. Do not deny me. She shut her eyes as power from an unnamable source seemed to pour through her. The long shaft of light seemed to glow, until it seemed to be a living, shimmering thing, shifting into a million prisms of every shade of color. A voice seemed to fill her mind, a voice which spoke without words and yet seemed to be the embodiment of all that was good and right and true.

Your time of trial is upon you, daughter. Hold fast to the Pattern, for the Power of it will bring you home. Annandale sobbed. The light was unlike anything she had ever seen before, and yet she knew she had a place in it, knew she belonged to it, and it to her. She wanted to crawl into it and rest.

Not yet, soothed the awareness in the light. *Not yet. But soon you shall rest in the Pattern, for the Power which orders the universe holds you dear.*

Annandale took a deep breath and opened her eyes to see J'lin standing over her. "Child," whispered the Muten woman. "What is it?"

She swallowed hard and shook her head. How to explain what she had felt? The overwhelming sense of Power, of knowing, of something greater far than she, and yet, something to which she belonged, something she was of, and yet was not—her thoughts swirled.

"Ah, child." J'lin knelt by the cot, gathering her in her arms. "Dark days indeed these are that take a mother from her child, a woman from her husband."

Annandale sighed, sensing the kindness, the gentle acceptance. She pulled away and smiled. "You—you knew my mother?"

J'lin nodded, reaching up with a gnarled hand to smooth the tangled curls away from Annandale's face. "For a little while."

"She died."

J'lin nodded once more. "Too many have died."

Annandale drew a deep breath. "Was—was this her fault? All of this?"

"Nydia's fault?" J'lin frowned. "What do you mean?"

"If she hadn't used the Magic—if she had not agreed to bear me—to cause Roderic—"

J'lin shook her head. "Child. Listen to me." Dark eyes peered from the wrinkled face, kind and wise and knowing. "Each of us is responsible for what we do. Each of us bears the consequences of what we do here, in this life. But we do not live alone. Tell me, though, child. What do you mean, caused Roderic?"

With a halting voice, Annandale told the story. J'lin listened, her eyes troubled. When Annandale finished, J'lin breathed a soft sigh. "I see."

Annandale looked up. "Do you?"

J'lin nodded. "It wasn't just that Nydia enabled the Queen to conceive a son. We knew that, you see, guessed that. It was only a matter of time before Abelard convinced her that was necessary. But I did not know . . . the rest."

Annandale shifted her position.

J'lin pursed her lips. "I see now, more clearly, some of what has happened and why."

"Can you explain it to me?"

"You know that the Magic is a disruption in the natural order of the Pattern? That it enables one to control things which normally cannot be controlled?"

Annandale nodded.

"The Pattern always works to right itself, to restore the order of the universe. It cannot be changed, only disrupted, only tangled like a skein of yarn, but never altered. But the degree to which it is disrupted, the degree to which it is tangled . . . ah, this is where much of the pain of the world comes from. So many of us spend our lives at cross purposes to the Great Pattern, working for what we think we want, rather than allowing it to work through us. . . ." Her voice trailed off.

"Abelard didn't just want an heir. He wanted to twist the future itself. With what he did, what your mother did, they set into motion a knot which coils through time, space, every dimension. It is not for mortal men to control the future," J'lin finished sadly.

"So—so it was my mother's fault?"

J'lin shook her head. "Child, blame not your mother. There was nothing evil about her. She had choices, true, and maybe she did not choose wisely, but she did what she believed she had to. And she paid the price, did she not?"

Annandale nodded slowly.

"As have we all. As we will continue to, until the Power which orders the universe restores the Pattern." She drew a deep breath and a high wailing scream shattered the silence.

Annandale rose up on one elbow. "What's that?"

J'lin's terra-cotta face drained of color. "I—I don't know—stay here, child."

Without another word she rose to her feet, slipping away, and Annandale rose and tugged her clothes on, hastily lacing and tucking them into some semblance of order. A louder cry echoed down the long corridor and Annandale froze as a thunderous pounding charged down the corridor. The door was flung wide.

She gasped as six armed Muten soldiers rushed in, razor spears flashing in the light. The first one turned and looked over his shoulder, gobbling something in a language she didn't understand, the rest crowding in the door, grinning at her. The razor spears dripped with blood, and on their gray-green tunics blood was smeared. A shout echoed down the corridor, a brief order. The leader turned back to her, his broken teeth flashing in his wide grin. He raised the spear and reached for her, and Annandale felt her knees buckle, smelled the rank stink of their sweat and the coppery reek of the blood as they dragged her out of the room.

On the opposite side of the valley, Deirdre raised her head, turning back to look at the high mountain peaks which marked the entrance of the pass. She swore softly beneath her breath.

"M'Callaster?" Donner looked over at her. The sun had ridden just above the treetops, and the weather was fair. The day promised to be fine—with luck they could cover many miles.

"Just a feeling, Donner. Damn these mountains."

"I don't like them, either, M'Callaster." Donner caught her eye and grinned. He was a big man, broad in the shoulder, long in the leg. His beard was rough across his chin, his hair curled around his ears. "Do you want to go back?"

For a moment she hesitated, wishing she could shake the overwhelming sense that something was wrong. "No," she said finally. "We'll never reach Vada if we dally after mind-monsters." She looked over her men, assessing them thoughtfully. "You, Kell. At the crossroads, the rest of us will go west. You and Irec will go back to Ithan. Tell Roderic we delivered his lady safe— well, as safe as we could. Tell him his brother refused to let us go down into the College."

"Shall I tell him where you've gone, M'Callaster?" asked Kell.

"Aye." She flapped at the reins. "But don't be surprised if he doesn't believe you. Come, lads. We ride."

They led her down the corridor, thrusting her roughly into the main room. Soldiers milled, and here and there she caught a glimpse of a still, white-clad figure stained with blood. She bit down on her lip, hard, and moaned a little with relief when she saw Vere. Bruises darkened his cheek, and blood ran down one temple. Another stain spread down his sleeve. Alexander sat on the floor, arms bound behind his back, his head resting on his knees. Vere looked up when he saw her, the tattoos on his face startling against his pale skin.

The invaders grabbed her arms and tied her hands behind her back, then gave her a shove which sent her stumbling into Vere.

"Vere," she whispered. "What has happened? Where's J'lin, the Pr'fessors? What is—"

"Silence!" The Muten guard raised his hand as though to strike and she cringed.

Vere gazed up at him, contempt in his eyes. "You would strike a woman?"

The Muten spat. "Your kind do." He raised the butt of his spear at Vere.

"Hold!"

Annandale recognized the order more by the tone in which it was given than in the heavily accented words. The guard stared at a young Muten, who wore plain white robes, much as the Pr'fessors did. His thumbs were hooked in his swordbelt, and a long dagger slapped against his thigh. His secondary arms were crossed over his chest. He spoke harshly in the Muten tongue.

The guard lowered his spear and backed away, a sneer still curling his lip.

The newcomer strode over to the three captives. He stared down at them, and Annandale saw that he was very young. His gaze lingered on her face, as though transfixed, and she felt a slow blush creep up her cheeks. She looked down as another Muten, this one taller and heavier, with an immense barrel-chest and secondary arms that seemed larger than most of the creatures', walked up behind him. He made a low comment and a gesture of contempt.

In reply, the younger Muten shook his head. He looked at Vere. "Do you know me?"

Vere nodded slowly. "You are Jama-taw. Son of Ebram, the one the Children call the Hope. Why have you done this shameful thing?"

A sudden flush suffused Jama's face. "No shame to rid the Children of the shackles which have bound us for generations."

Vere looked at him with something like pity. "These weren't the shackles, and you know it. Why have you done this? And how shall you answer before the Nine Tribes?"

"The Nine Tribes shall answer to me." Jama met Vere's eyes squarely, his chest thrust out. From the folds of his robe, Annandale saw the tiny secondary arms clench into deliberate fists.

"You may well make the Nine Tribes answer to you," Vere murmured, still with the look of pity. "And you may annihilate all of the College, until every Elder is dead. But you shall not make your children answer to you . . . someday, you will answer to them."

The burly Muten said something which could only be a curse, and Vere raised his head and looked beyond Jama's shoulder at him. "You, as well, Adanijah—oh, yes, I know you, too."

Adanijah looked down at Vere, shock plain on his face. "What will you do with the humans, Lord Jama?"

"We will take them to the Ridenau Prince and allow him to decide what to do with them," said Jama as he spun on his heel.

"He'll take us to Roderic," Alexander whispered, hope breaking on his face. A cold chill ran down Annandale's spine at the look Jama turned upon them all.

"No," he answered. "Not the Butcher. To Amanander Ridenau. The true Ridenau Prince."

Chapter Seventeen

Amanander watched with satisfaction the relentless activity in the courtyard below his window. The outpost garrison, only a few weeks ago nothing more than a small fortified hill, now hummed with activity as the soldiers of the Southern Alliance and the Harleyriders prepared for war. In only the space of a few weeks, barracks had been erected, the inner ward enlarged, the outer walls torn down and rebuilt.

He stood with folded arms, watching the infantry drill with short swords, the Harleyriders beyond the perimeter of the walls raising clouds of dust as they rode their shaggy ponies at straw targets, their chilling whoops penetrating the glass. It was well, he thought, satisfied. The Southern lords had no history of enmity against the Harleyriders; their lands were not part of any territory the Harleys were likely to claim.

Behind him Reginald droned on, his voice a dull monotone as he recited the reports of the scouts who monitored Roderic's presence at Ithan. A fairly sizable force had left Ithan and was moving southwest; messengers came and went with predictable regularity. Nothing unexpected.

Amanander smiled as he listened, Reginald's words echoing in his mind before being spoken aloud. Like a thin thread, the connection to Reginald wound inexorably tighter. Or maybe, thought Amanander, pleased with his own imagery, like a vein, slowly bleeding. Harland and Reginald shared more with him than blood. He had realized that the longer the men were held in his thrall, the stronger he grew, the easier he found it to control minds at greater and greater distances. Ferad had missed the link with emotion altogether. Poor Ferad.

As an exercise, he focused upon the drill sergeant shouting orders to the men below.

The sergeant suddenly closed his mouth in midsentence. A few of the men paused in the drill, glancing over at the change in the sergeant. Even from this distance, Amanander could see that his face had gone slack. The man's mind slid open before his will, like soft cheese yielding to a knife. In the jumble of memories, some sweet, some bitter, he found a face, a name, and pulled up a half-forgotten memory. A first love.

Delicately as a spider, he twisted the sergeant's memory of the face, wrenching the features into a misshapen lump of tortured clay. The battle-hardened face crumpled as the backlash of horror roared into his mind. The sergeant fell to his knees in the dusty yard, covering his eyes with his hands, mouth working, tears streaming down his cheeks. The men muttered amongst themselves.

Abruptly, Amanander pulled out. The sergeant collapsed in a heap. He turned away from the window as the first shouts filtered through the humid air for help. He felt nourished, satisfied, as though he had just helped himself to a succulent peach. These men had such simple minds. It was so easy to pluck from them anything he wanted.

A short, hard knock on the door disturbed his reverie. With a scowl, he crossed his arms over his chest. "Enter."

The door swung open and Gerik, the second son of the Senador of Atland, strode into the room. His face was twisted in a scowl.

Amanander raised his eyebrow. "Yes?" Gerik was supposed to be overseeing the inventorying of supplies.

Gerik strode into the room, his thumbs hooked in his swordbelt. "Word has come from Cort in Atland," he began, ignoring Reginald's drone. "My brother says that Kye and more than ten thousand men are marching toward Atland garrison. The war begins."

"Yes." Amanander held up a hand and Reginald silenced.

Gerik glanced at Reginald with narrowed eyes, then looked at Amanander, his chin thrust forward. "Well?"

"Well?"

Gerik lowered his head. He was a huge man, well over six feet, his reddish brown hair clumsily hacked away above his ears. He looked like a bull about to charge. "You summon us here, while Roderic begins to position his troops. You risk placing us in a vulnerable position. He could trap us in this place, close the gap. And what will we have to show for it?"

Amanander raised an eyebrow and looked at Harland. Harland stirred to life. "Gerik . . ." he began.

Gerik's eyes narrowed even further. "You know this

land as well as I do, Harry. If Kye is able to take the high ground running from the old gorge, our forces will be split in half."

"And then we will crush him, like a vise," replied Harland, his speech slurred. "See here, Gerik." With a shaking finger, Harland began to trace a line down the center of the map.

With a restlessness borne of frustration, Gerik seized a chair away from the table. The wood creaked in protest as he slammed it down again. "Crush him? In order to do that, we have to have the men in position. And here the main body of our force sits. I say we ride now and strengthen our position on the border between Missiluse and Atland. If he takes the garrison at God's Deen, he will use it to establish a base for himself—"

"If," Amanander whispered. He glanced once more at Harland and Harland blinked, his face as blank as a frog's on a lily pad.

"What?" Gerik looked at Amanander with an expression of intense dislike.

Amanander smiled at Gerik. "I said 'if.'"

"I heard you." Gerik folded his arms over his chest. "I know your game. You intend to use my men to bleed for your cause. You're no more than a dispossessed Prince, without land or men, or title either, for that matter, and you seem to think you can assume command here without so much as a by-your-leave. You've nothing but promises to offer any of us. And I'm not so sure I want to buy what you have to offer, especially when the price is the blood of myself and my—" Abruptly his words ended in a choked sound.

Amanander looked Gerik up and down. Reginald and Harland stared at him impassively. Gerik's eyes darted from side to side, his hands worked in impotent fists at his sides. Amanander sat down at the table. He crossed his long legs at the knee and leaned back in the wooden chair. The whites of Gerik's eyes were shot through with pale red veins. The man was like a bull, he thought, in more ways than one.

He probed cautiously around the edges of Gerik's awareness. His mind was like thick syrup, the kind of mind which, once made up, clung to an idea with stubborn determination. Deftly, with an ease that was becoming second nature, Amanander closed his eyes, envisioning a hot brand burning deep into the core of Gerik's very self. He could almost smell the sickly sweet odor, feeling the surge of power as the man's defenses melted under the assault.

When at last he opened his eyes, Gerik's face was laced with sweat, his breathing deep and slow. Time to return to the troops, thought Amanander.

"Must return," whispered Gerik. "Your pardon, Lord Prince."

With a little smile, Amanander waved him away. Gerik fumbled with the door. Amanander watched indifferently. Such was the price one paid for disobedience.

As Gerik slipped out of the room, Amanander drew a deep breath as another awareness flickered through his mind, sharp with anger and spiced with the least bit of fear. Ferad, he thought.

He deliberately turned to look out the window as the

door swung open and Ferad stepped over the threshold, his robes rustling around his squat frame.

Unbidden an image of the Kahn exploded into Amanander's mind. So, he thought, that's what he wants. Still apparently ignoring Ferad, Amanander closed his eyes, allowing his mind to roam. He could feel the soldiers in the courtyard and in the barracks, the servants in the kitchens and in the stables. There were so few he couldn't touch. His mind glanced over Gartred, where she huddled in their bedchamber, and whispered over the prisoner in the dungeons beneath the keep. Only a few of the Harleyriders were beyond his reach, and even those numbers shrank as his sphere of influence grew. Only the Kahn truly eluded him.

"My Prince." Ferad's voice was oily. "What do you hope to gain by this alliance with the Harleyriders?" The door slammed shut behind him and suppressed anger pulsed through every word.

Amanander swung back to look at his former tutor. Ever since the Harleys had begun arriving, Ferad had been on edge. He cocked his head. He had expected Ferad to be less than pleased by the news of the alliance he had made with the Harleyriders, but he had not expected him to come barging into his inner chamber without so much as a knock on the door. He wondered, not for the first time, if perhaps Ferad had outlived his usefulness.

"Well?" Ferad sat without waiting for permission.

Would it matter what he said? Amanander wondered. He no longer relied upon Ferad, no longer cared for Ferad. It was odd, he reflected, that with this new use for the Magic, he had felt himself becoming more and more detached from those around him, even as he became more and more adept at gauging the emotions of others.

The boy Jama, for whom he had entertained a brief moment of respect, Harland, for whom he had never had anything but contempt, even Ferad, who had for a long time been the closest Amanander had ever had to a friend, was slowly slipping away in some sense. All forms of connection seemed to have less and less meaning, the more he put this new ability of his into play.

Now he noted the grime around the cuffs of Ferad's robes, the tattered neckline, the patched folds. The Muten's hair was nearly completely the color of steel, the three eyes lost in folds of wrinkles. "This alliance with the Harleyriders has nothing to do with you, Ferad."

"I beg to differ with you, my Prince. The Harleyriders have always held my people in utmost contempt . . . more so even than yours. This alliance with them jeopardizes everything Jama and his forces hope to accomplish. How can you trust these men who have betrayed every treaty, every agreement ever made with them? Did your history tutor teach you nothing?"

"I will take my chances. Now, if you don't mind, Ferad, I have work to do." Amanander nodded a dismissal.

Ferad stared at him with something like surprise. "What?"

"I don't wish to discuss this with you, Ferad."

"Jama will hear of this."

Amanander shrugged. "I'm sure he will as soon as he gets here. But it isn't any of my concern if my alliance with the Harleys jeopardizes what the Muten faction seeks to accomplish. I doubt the Harleys are interested in being bounded by mountains in far-off Nourk. They want free access to the Plains. How does that jeopardize everything Jama hopes to accomplish?" Amanander leaned back in his chair, pinning Ferad with his gaze as surely as with an arrow to the wall.

Ferad only shifted his eyes.

"Or is it possible, Ferad, that you and your Brotherhood have other goals? Goals which Jama isn't aware of—or maybe he is aware of them and only I am not. Let me think." Amanander steepled his fingertips. "What goals could those be? You don't seek to reign in Ahga, do you, Ferad? You surely wouldn't be so foolish as to think that you could use me to get yourself a safe position, and then at some point strike at the very hand that fed you? You wouldn't have that in your mind to do, would you?

"Because if you did, I can certainly see why the Harley alliance would interfere with plans like those. I might be able to call upon the Harleys once again, and use them to wipe your miserable backsides from the face of the earth, or at least send you screaming back to your warrens."

Ferad's skin flushed an ugly shade of dark red. "You forget yourself, Prince."

"Do I, Ferad?" Amanander sat perfectly still. Fear flickered in Ferad's eyes, and Amanander saw his opening. Into the mind of his master, Amanander surged, like a snake through slippery reeds, insinuating himself into the dark crevices of Ferad's mind. With no more thought than he would give to crushing an insect, Amanander ripped through the defenses of Ferad's mind, laying waste the mind of his former tutor, exposing every secret he'd ever had.

Images swirled through his mind: faces, places, names, words in languages that had no meaning to him. Memories rose, chaotic glimpses into the dregs of Ferad's self.

With every ounce of power he could summon, Amanander ripped through the fibers which held Ferad's conscious mind together. In a place so closely hidden, even Amanander nearly missed it, he found the plan. He had not been far from the truth. In less time than it took to shape the thought, Amanander destroyed the last vestiges of the man who had been his tutor, and who had so very nearly betrayed him.

At last, Amanander leaned his head back against his chair, sweat pouring down his face. Ferad had collapsed into a heap on the floor, gazing up at the ceiling with blank eyes. A thin thread of spittle leaked from the corner of his mouth and drooled down his chin. Amanander rose, and with the tip of one toe, he prodded Ferad. The Muten did not move, only gurgled as more saliva bubbled from his mouth.

Amanander smiled. He felt as though he had eaten an extremely satisfying meal, without the heaviness that accompanies such an act of physical fulfillment.

He sank down in a chair, his long legs stretched before him. He sensed the presence of the servant at the door before the man knocked. "Come in," he called.

"My lord," the man entered, looking perplexed. "The Khan begs a word."

Amanander looked the man up and down, reading into his mind as easily as through a clear glass. The Khan had not begged for a word; he had demanded it at full bellow. Well, thought Amanander, let him have it. He smiled at the servant. "Of course," he said. "Of course. Send him to me. And—" Amanander paused. "But first summon another servant or two. My poor tutor has met with an unfortunate illness. He is no longer quite himself. Remove him, please."

The man looked at the wreck of Ferad huddled on the floor over by the window, and his face drained of color. "Yes, my lord," he whispered. "It shall be done."

"Good." Amanander smiled. "I know I can trust you to see it done properly."

The man swallowed hard and withdrew, his hand shaking as he closed the door. Amanander turned back to the window, where a fresh squad of soldiers practiced relentless drills. He smiled. Oh, yes. He could trust everyone around him. They no longer had any choice.

Chapter Eighteen

❧

Annandale glanced at the boy who rode so easily beside the wagon. She squinted overhead at the harsh sun. Mid-Year. In Ahga a holiday, celebrated with feasting and dancing, at Minnis a day of picnics beneath the oaks on the dappled lawns of the great gardens. Would she ever see Ahga again?

The thought of the four towers, the precision of the design altered now forever by Ferad's Magic, brought thoughts of her son. Rhodri, she thought with sudden longing, so intense it took her breath away. Rhodri. She bent her head and wept.

On the opposite side of the wagon, Vere stared into the distance, wisps of gray hair straggling down the sides of his tattooed cheeks. Although his hands were bound behind his back even as hers were, his shoulders were squared, his eyes steady on the moving horizon as the cart lurched over the uneven road. Next to him, Alexander's iron gray head rested on his knees. Although his face was turned away from her, Annandale knew that his eyes were closed, his mouth compressed into that thin line that emphasized his resemblance to Amanander.

She could hear the wheezing pull of breath as his lungs labored to breathe in the hot, humid air.

She raised her face and stared at Jama. The days following their capture had stretched into two weeks, and as inexorably as the cart bore them closer to Amanander, she knew that Jama's lieutenants argued nightly for their murder. What perverse streak was it in the Muten youth, she wondered, that kept them alive? He of all people had reason to hate Roderic with a passion. Did he understand that to take them to Amanander was in some way a worse fate than death?

As if he heard an echo of her thoughts, he turned to her, his three dark eyes meeting hers with a hesitancy she had come to expect. Something about her unnerved him, she thought. Instead of breaking the look and glancing away, she kept her eyes focused steadily on him. A slow flush crept up his throat, and Annandale understood. He thinks I am beautiful, she thought. Does he truly believe that to bring us to Amanander is a kindness?

The cart lumbered over the potholed surface of the road with a jerk, up a small rise, and down again. On either side of the road, great trees hung with weird gray-green shrouds bent like widows in mourning weeds. A miasma was in the air, the stench of poison pits, open sewers bare beneath the burning sky. No wind, no breeze eased the heat, and Annandale felt a trickle of sweat between her shoulders. Her thin cotton gown was dirty and reeked of days and nights of constant wearing. She bowed her head, searching for that peace, that sense of something greater than herself. Even here, even in this benighted land of swamps and evil-smelling fens, even here she should be able to feel it. She drew a deep breath, though her lungs burned as they filled with the noxious fumes, and shut her eyes. The blight ran deep into the land. She forced herself to breathe evenly, and gradually she felt the same peace fill her. Slowly she raised her head and opened her eyes. The twisted trees, the blistering air, the landscape itself, all were the results of the efforts of the Pattern to heal itself of the Armageddon. There was nothing evil, no dark or sinister purpose to the oppression she sensed all around her. In time, the land would be restored, and all of this would be some half-remembered nightmare. She looked up and saw, on a low hanging branch, a pale pink flower, its waxy petals incandescent in the murky light.

She smiled. Not even the sudden frantic calls for the ranks disturbed her, though out of the corner of her eye, she saw Jama speak sharply to the wagon driver. He reined in as a soldier ran up beside him, the bridle of a horse clutched in his hands. The rider slumped over the neck of the horse, his hands hanging slack by his side.

Jama looked stricken. He raised his hand and shouted an order to halt. The cart jolted to a stop. Annandale looked at him curiously. His face was creased in a mixture of fear, concern, and some nameless grief. He slid off his horse and went at once to the rider.

He tugged at the prone body, and the heavy form slipped out of the saddle and tumbled into his arms. She heard the quick intake of his breath.

The face of his second-in-command, Adanijah, was marred by purplish lesions that oozed a greenish yellow pus. Blood ran from the corners of his eyes like red tears, and a thin line of blood-tinged mucous spooled from one nostril.

The soldier who brought Adanijah up to the front fell back, crossing himself in a gesture Annandale had seen the Pr'fessors make, and as she looked back, she saw fear ripple down the long line of troops behind the cart like a wave.

"The purple sickness," Vere whispered.

Instantly she understood. Nothing was so virulent as the purple sickness among the Mutens. Humans were immune, but it could kill whole villages of Mutens within hours. It arose suddenly, silently, killing fiercely and fast. Once the contagion was sparked, there was nothing to do but to let it run its course. The entire Muten force was certain to die all around them. Jama raised a stricken face to the sky even as he slowly let Adanijah fall to the ground. Annandale peered over the edge. The Muten still lived. His chest rose and fell sporadically, and she could hear a phlegmy rattle in his throat.

Jama dropped his head and sobbed like a child, his shoulders heaving.

She looked at Vere. There was no pity on his face, only a certain grim satisfaction. The Mutens would die very quickly, she knew, and then they could escape. As her eyes met Vere's, something spoke, deep in her mind.

Right the balance.

She gasped. Surely the Voice was mistaken. This couldn't be—this was the chance for escape.

Right the balance.

She bowed her head, her body quivering. While part of her rebelled, another part responded instinctively, gladly. She swallowed hard. "Jama-taw," she said, her voice as clear and firm as a bell in the stricken silence. "Let me touch him."

Jama raised his head, meeting her eyes uncomprehendingly. "What?"

Vere looked at her in shock. "Lady, do you know what you do?"

Annandale nodded. "I must. Don't ask me why—I only know I must."

"Untie her," put in Vere. "And let her touch him, quickly before he dies."

"Why?"

"You don't have the time to ask these questions," Vere spit out in Muten, the harsh syllables falling from his tongue like acid, and with a start, Annandale realized she understood what he said.

With a gesture from Jama, one of the guards untied her bonds and helped Annandale slip from the cart. She gathered her skirts and gently touched Jama on the shoulder. Immediately a wave of grief swept over and through her. He loves him like a brother, she thought. But she sank to her knees beside him, willfully ignoring his grief. She reached over him and gathered the heavy Muten in her arms.

Instantly, as their skin made contact, agony roared through her, pain unlike any she had ever felt before, ripping at every nerve and sinew. Her blood seemed to boil and she felt the horrible lesions burst forth on every surface of her skin, blood leaking from her eyes and nose. She tasted it on her tongue. She closed her eyes and moaned. Her muscles seemed to turn to jelly, her bones felt like fiery brands. This was unlike anything she had ever healed in her life.

She drew a deep quivering breath as the pain began to fade, draining out of her body. She opened her eyes. Adanijah lay in her arms, his head pillowed on her breast. His breathing was firm and steady, and the awful lesions were gone. Only a few traces of blood on his face showed that he had ever been ill.

"Lady," breathed Jama. "By the Power—"

"A bit late to swear by that Power," snapped Vere, in Merigan.

Annandale gently disengaged herself from the heavy body and shakily rose to her feet, gripping the wheel of the cart as she rose.

Jama was looking at her with something like awe. "What are you, lady? How—how—"

Annandale shook her head wearily. "It doesn't matter, Jama. It doesn't matter."

She raised her head and looked down the road, her shoulders bowed beneath a nameless weight. Jama looked up, following her gaze. Six black-garbed soldiers were bearing down upon the company. A familiar fear constricted her throat. Despite the hot sun, they were fully uniformed in leather armor, their tunics emblazoned with an inverted triangle topped by a silver crescent. A new moon, she wondered, and then she realized that the image on their chests reminded her more than anything of an animal skull left to bleach in the merciless sun.

"By the One." The ragged whisper seem to tear out of Alexander's throat.

"Steady, Alex," muttered Vere.

"You—you don't understand." Alexander turned to look at them both, his dark eyes shadowed by the huge shadows beneath his eyes. "That emblem—that badge—in all the dreams I've had of Dad, that was the badge his guards wore."

His eyes met Annandale's, and despite the heat an icy finger of fear traced a cold path down her spine. Her eyes locked on his. Could it be possible, after all the missing years, that Abelard was alive? The shadows around the bases of the trees seemed to congeal into pools of bottomless blackness, and the air grew more oppressive. She whispered a prayer to that nameless source for strength.

The soldiers reined their horses several yards from where the Muten party had stopped. Jama cleared his throat and addressed the center rider. "We come at the bidding of Prince Amanander."

The horseman said nothing. Jama frowned and began again. "I am Jama-taw. I bring—"

The rider cocked his head as though listening intently, then raised his arm and pulled on the reins so that his stallion wheeled. "You are known to the Prince. Come with me."

Adanijah struggled to sit, then rose unsteadily to his feet. He muttered something beneath his breath in the Muten tongue that Annandale did not hear, but which made Vere whip his head around to stare at him.

Jama nodded slowly.

"Vere?" whispered Annandale. "What did they say?"

Vere's tattooed cheeks were pale, his gray eyes dark. "He said—" Vere paused as though struggling with the translation. "Un-dead—or not live. Either one—and both."

"Undead?" Alexander muttered, his shoulders bent as an old man's. "Not live? What does that mean?"

Annandale took a deep breath. They knew, she thought. All of them, whether they wished to deny it or not. They knew exactly what it meant.

As the cart jolted through the gates, Annandale gazed around at the frenzied activity. Men swarmed over the walls, constructing watchtowers, mortaring the walls, engaged in hundreds of tasks, scurrying like ants with some intent purpose. The courtyard teemed with activity, and yet she had never had such a sense of death in her life. It was as though she sat in the middle of a graveyard. A dark shape loomed in the doorway of the central keep and Annandale looked up as Vere hissed and Alexander moaned softly.

Her belly contracted with fear. Annandale ran her parched tongue over dry lips. This was the man who had staked everything on his ability to bend her to his will and who had tortured innocent people in the attempt to break her resistance to him. He had killed without thought, without remorse, all in his effort to force her to allow him to use her. What did he want with her now? she wondered as she stared up at him. What did he want with any of them now?

Amanander gazed down at them, his face registering no emotion whatsoever, not even surprise. It was as if, Annandale thought, they were expected. His eyes flickered over to Jama-taw. "Well?"

"The College of the Elders is no more," Jama said, his voice low.

Annandale turned to look at him. Was that an undercurrent of shame she heard?

Amanander snapped his fingers and spoke to one of the soldiers who hovered by his elbow. "Take the prisoners to the cells beneath the keep." His eyes flitted over each of them in turn, not pausing, as though they had no more interest to him than cattle brought for inspection. His very detachment made Annandale shiver and wonder what Amanander intended for them. Briefly his gaze rested on Alexander. "I would bid you welcome, brother, but I don't think any of you are glad to see me. So I will spare you all the trouble of unmeant courtesy." He turned on his heel and paused, thoughtfully, as though considering something. "Oh, yes," he said, with a smile which did nothing to warm the chill which went down Annandale's spine, "you'll find the very person you've been looking for, Alexander. Though I doubt he will be able to express just how glad he will be to see you all once more."

Chapter Nineteen

"Captain Barran?"

The deep voice of his lieutenant interrupted Barran's thoughts as he struggled to put his jumbled fears into words on the parchment before him. He laid the pen down and looked up. "Yes, Rone?"

The lieutenant wet his lips. "The scouts, sir. They are reporting increasing numbers of Harleyriders gathering just to the west."

Barran frowned. "Which direction are they traveling?"

Rone shook his head. "They aren't. They've made a camp, sir, and it appears they intend to stay."

At that Barran pushed away from his desk, biting back a curse. He strode to the window and stared out into the inner courtyard of the desert garrison. In the heat of the noon sun, the guards drowsed at their posts, and the men off duty lounged in the small pockets of shade. He could hear the low murmur of their voices, the soft rattle of the dice as they cast lots. Barran turned back to Rone. "Exactly how far west?"

"A day's ride."

Barran swore softly beneath his breath. "Numbers?"

"Between five or six hundred. But really, Captain—" Rone cleared his throat before continuing "—you don't think it likely they plan to attack the garrison?"

There was the faintest trace of condescension in Rone's voice. He was nearly twenty years older than Barran and had not at all been happy to be sent to Dlas when Barran had assumed command. He much preferred the easy life in Ahga, and made no secret of the fact that he thought his talents wasted. Barran plopped back into his chair. He was used to Rone's attitude. "You tell me. Six hundred Harleyriders gathered to the west—just within striking distance. A kingdom messenger comes from Roderic, telling me my uncle and his cousin have likely formed an alliance with the Harleyriders, and that I am to watch any unusual movements closely and to prepare for an attack."

Rone raised one eyebrow. "Harleys don't attack garrisons. Not in the last twenty years."

"That doesn't mean they've forgotten how, or don't plan to try again. I don't intend to take any chances. Make sure the outer perimeter is secure. Double the watch. And send me a messenger. This should be reported back to Ithan at once."

When Rone had gone, Barran rose once more and walked to the window. He didn't like this news. Foreboding swept through him, he narrowed his eyes and watched as the guard changed. The desert garrison was a long, low structure. Only the watchtowers rose above the high walls. He had been in charge of the desert garrison for more than a year, an unusual command for one so young, but not unheard of given who his father was, and where he potentially could expect to rise.

Someday, thought Barran, someday, I will sit in Ahga at Roderic's right hand, the captain of the King's Guard. A grim smile did little to soften his face as he thought about Roderic, about the annoying, pesky child he'd always treated more as a brother than as a royal heir. Just old enough to be thrown together constantly, just young enough to be annoying was how he had always thought of Roderic. He had had to share his mother— Abruptly he swallowed hard and blinked back unexpected tears. His mother. His mother who had never harmed a living soul, now dead in the earthshake which had enabled Amanander to escape. The more rational part of him knew it was futile to blame Amanander for the earthshake, that no mortal man could have caused such a thing to happen, and yet, despite all the warnings of his rational mind, Barran did just that.

He drew a deep breath and cleared his throat. His father would not allow his grief to interfere with his adherence to duty. Brand was devoted, trustworthy, utterly loyal, the best of all the soldiers in the army and the Guard. He had earned the honor of his position not by blood, but by years of hard fighting across the miles of Meriga. If he wished to someday take his father's place, he must not let his own grief interfere.

He gripped the rough wooden windowframe, mentally ticking off the preparations he had made. The guards, the supplies, the weapons polished and ready, the rations carefully allotted, the water cisterns full to overflowing. He wondered where the promised reinforcements from

Roderic were. The messenger had come nearly a month ago; he was expecting them to arrive any day, but so far there had been no signs of them.

He thought about all the stories his father had told him about his years in Arkan fighting the Harleys, when he was just an infant and Roderic was not even yet born, trying to draw on every scrap of information he could remember. Something crossed his mind, something so small and yet significant, he wondered why he hadn't thought to ask it before.

In a few quick strides he was across the room, bounding into the outer room so suddenly that the guard at the door was surprised in mid-yawn. The soldier immediately snapped to attention.

"Find the scouts who just came in," he barked.

"As you say, sir." The soldier saluted and took off.

He was back in less than five minutes with a bare-chested man who clutched a tunic in one hand. Soap froth still clung to his half-shaven chin. Barran ignored the details of his appearance.

"Sir." Both men saluted and the guard took his post.

Barran met the dark eyes of the scout. "Tell me," he began slowly, "in the Harley camp, were there any signs of women or children?"

Without hesitation the scout shook his head. "No, sir. None."

"Why didn't you report this to Rone?"

"I did, sir."

Barran turned away with a soldier's curse. Damn the man. How could he fail to see the importance of that detail. "Put your shirt on, soldier. I think I need to speak with you myself. And you—" He looked at the guard in the doorway, standing motionless once more. "Find Lieutenant Rone and tell him I want to see him immediately."

With another quick salute, the man was gone, trotting away in little clouds of dusty sand across the sunny yard. Barran met the eyes of the scout, who was just finishing lacing his shirt.

"It's been more than twenty years since the Harleys attacked a garrison, Captain."

"Indeed," said Barran as he stalked into his office. "But do you care to wager your life on history?"

Barran fled. The sand was thick and ankle deep, the gently quivering surface giving way beneath his boots. Sweat rolled down his back, made the gritty grains cling to his skin beneath his thick leather armor and the soaked linen shirt. He bore a sword three times heavier than it should be, and all around him he heard the cries of his men, screaming in the flame-filled night for mercy. But there was no mercy, and as he turned at the sound of his own name, a dark shape bore down upon him, a Harleyrider in black leathers, shiny with blood, and chains which gleamed red in the awful light. He glimpsed crosses being erected upon the walls, his own men writhing in agony. Barran threw up his arms, his sword quivering in his trembling hands, and the Rider bore down, driving the shaggy short-legged horse across the sand.

Light flashed off the edge of the weapon, a weird unearthly light, and as the Rider threw back his head, the heavy fall of hair fell back over its shoulder, and Barran looked up into the face of Amanander.

"Uncle!" he cried, more out of surprise than fright.

Amanander laughed, low and long, and the sound made the gooseflesh rise on Barran's arms. A shiver ran down his spine and his bowels loosened. Every ounce of will he had was required to stand against that awful sound, and Barran stared into the face of his kinsman, who was and somehow was not the man he remembered. "Uncle?" he whispered.

Amanander raised his hand and the scene seemed to swirl, the landscape wheeled as though on a giant revolving plate, and Barran saw the gates of the desert garrison, one gate torn off the huge hinges, the other—

A sob rose in his throat.

A figure was nailed to the great crosspiece, his face a rictus of agony, his body twisted in a final death throe. Barran stared at the dark head, the blood which streamed down the tortured cheeks, the bluish tinge which colored the hawk-nose and the grimacing lips.

"Dad," he whispered. He raised his eyes to Amanander. "Why—how—please—"

"Open the gates," said Amanander, his black-gloved hands caressing the leather reins like a lover. "Open the gates."

The landscape wheeled, a crazy kaleidoscope of stone and light, blood and sand, bone and sinews stretched to the point of breaking. "Never," whispered Barran as he stared into a face which was suddenly hideous. "Never."

"Then so be it," said Amanander with a smile.

The world spun once more and Barran fell to the

ground, his cheek pressed against the warm, gritty sand. He struggled to cling to earth which writhed beneath his hands like a beast in its death agony.

"Captain, Captain—"

The voices seemed to come from a long way off. Barran opened his eyes. Immediately he heard the clang of metal on metal and smelled the acrid stink of burning pitch, the unmistakable sounds and smells of battle.

A young recruit stood by his bed, sweat plastering his hair to his forehead, fear as plain as dawn in the desert on his face. Before the words were out of his mouth, Barran knew what he would say. "Wake up, sir, please, wake up. The garrison's under attack."

Chapter Twenty

❧

*R*oderic paused in the doorway of the nursery. Unobserved, he watched Tavia change Rhodri's soiled linen, while Melisande, now more than two, kept up a running commentary. Her hair and eyes were dark, reminding him of her mother, Peregrine. She had been one of the first, he thought, one of the first casualties in this war, one of the first of the women whom he had loved to die in the cause of the heir of Meriga. Now the child extended both arms over her head and pirouetted into the center of the room, humming a little tune. When she caught sight of him in the doorway, she stopped and beamed. "Dada!"

With a little shriek of delight, she launched herself into his arms, her white petticoats flashing around her plump legs. He lifted her up and hugged her tightly, gazing over her shoulder to the baby, who had been alerted by his sister's shriek. "Hello, Meli," he whispered against the thick fall of her dark curls. "How's my sweetest girl today?"

Melisande giggled and took his face in both of her hands. "I'm a good girl, Dada. Rhodri, he's been bad!"

"Bad?" Roderic smiled, in spite of himself. Tavia

wrapped the infant in a light cotton blanket and raised him to her shoulder, where his head bobbed in the direction of his sister's voice, like a heavy tulip on a too-fragile stem.

Melisande giggled and whispered something in his ear, something breathy and indistinguishable, and Roderic shook his head. "My, my. Extra guard duty for him, don't you think?"

Melisande shrieked with giggles. "Oh, Dada, he can't even walk." She struggled in his embrace. "Watch me dance."

Obligingly he set her down, and she stood on her tiptoes, humming a tuneless little song. As Tavia crossed the room, Melisande jumped and kicked, her arms held high over her head, and Roderic realized she imitated the Islanders and their energetic dances. Abruptly he was reminded that Deirdre should have returned by now. He frowned.

Tavia spoke softly. "Say hello to your Dada, young Prince."

In spite of everything, Roderic had to smile back as the baby, as though obedient to his aunt's order, broke out into a wreath of toothless grins. His deep blue eyes crinkled at the corners and he made a soft coo. Roderic stroked the back of the baby's downy head, where the hair still stuck up in all directions. "He's doing well."

"Yes." Tavia nodded. "They both are." She looked at Roderic sharply and her motherly face was wreathed with concern.

"Dada." Melisande tugged at the hem of his tunic. "When's Nanny coming home?"

Roderic drew a sharp breath and tried to suppress a sigh. Everyone missed Annandale, especially Meli, for Annandale was the closest to a mother she had ever known. "Soon, sweetheart. Nanny will be home as soon as she can."

"Meli," Tavia said, "go and find Kaitlan. She's right next door sorting laundry."

"Is it time for cakes?" asked Melisande, her cheeks pink.

"Nearly," replied Tavia. "When you find her it will be."

"Bye, Dada!"

The child disappeared through a door. Tavia gave Roderic a long, considering look. "Come." She led the way onto a balcony, where two chairs were placed side by side in the shade. A soft breeze stirred the baby's hair. Roderic sat in one of the chairs and Tavia placed the infant in his arms, smiling down at him. "He's growing beautifully, Roderic."

The child looked at him with a grave expression in those blue, blue eyes. His little mouth was rosy, his cheeks softly plump. His hands were clasped loosely on his chest. He looked for all the world like an old man at peace with the world. Roderic touched his fingertip to the very tip of the tiny nose and smiled sadly. He drew a deep breath.

"You miss her."

He nodded, his eyes not leaving the baby's face. "I hope she made it there all right. I expected Deirdre back by now. I'm sure Alexander convinced Vere to go off on some wild goose chase after Dad." He raised his head

232   *Anne Kelleher Bush*

and sighed. He had been tempted to go off after Alexander when it was discovered his brother was missing, but Brand had quickly convinced him of the folly that would be. Alexander might be an invalid, but he was a grown man and an experienced soldier. If he insisted on traipsing alone through enemy territory and Vere was foolish enough to go with him . . . well, there wasn't really anything Roderic could do about it.

"You don't look happy, Roderic." Tavia spoke as gently as she might to the child in his arms.

"I have a bad feeling." He did not take his eyes off the infant, but a frown deepened the new furrow between his brows. "I can't explain it, but I have a terrible feeling."

"Tell me." She leaned back in her chair.

"There's a border garrison south of here, called God's Deen. It's right at the border of Missiluse and Atland. You know Kye has gone to secure a position there. Frankly I expected Deirdre to return by now . . ." His voice trailed off, and he raised his eyes to the horizon, where the mountains rose purple against the clear blue sky.

"What about Dlas?"

He shot her a sharp look. "Have you been talking to Brand?"

"He's worried about his son, Roderic."

Roderic sighed. "I know and I understand. The reinforcements left here a month ago. They should be there by now. I expect dispatches soon."

"And Everard?"

"The fighting in the North seems to have abated." Roderic shrugged. "So here we wait, like pieces on a chess board. Kye is to march east to Atland garrison. Depending on the resistance he encounters, I expect to send Brand with more troops. And once we secure Atland, we will turn on Missiluse."

"Do you have the troops to send?"

Roderic nodded slowly, holding out one finger for the infant to grasp. "Barely." He gazed at the baby. "Do you think I was right to let her go, Tavvy?"

Tavia sighed. "I—I don't know, Roderic. I know Annandale is—special. But it seems that all the world's at war right now." Tavia shook her head. "She was very brave to leave these walls. I wouldn't want to do it."

"I almost felt I had no choice but to let her go."

"Perhaps you didn't," Tavia said gently.

Roderic sighed again. "So many decisions, Tavvy. So many variables."

"So many depending upon you to do what is best."

He looked up then and met his sister's gentle eyes. What would she say, he wondered, if he told her the truth? Would she tell him to stop the fighting? Tell him to open negotiations with Amanander for the throne? And even if Amanander was not the rightful King, there was still Brand, still Alexander or Everard or Phillip or Vere. His mind rejected Phillip outright—in all the years of fighting, Phillip had offered nothing but excuses. He was safe behind the walls of Nourk and he intended to stay there. Vere would have no part of the throne, of that he was certain. But Brand, or Alexander or Everard— any of them—they were fit to rule. What did an ancient prophecy matter now? Nydia was dead and gone, and so was Abelard, too, for all they knew.

The baby screwed up his face and mewed, waving his fists. Roderic instinctively raised the child to his shoulder and patted his back. The infant quieted momentarily, and Tavia looked at him with motherly concern. "We all miss her, Roderic."

Roderic nodded. "I wish—"

"Yes?"

He handed the baby to Tavia and rose to pace the length of the balcony. The wind ruffled the shock of hair which fell across his brow. "I wish I could shake this feeling, Tavvy. I keep feeling that something very bad has happened. And I just can't say what it is."

In the room there was a knocking on the door and a nursery maid opened it as Roderic peered into the interior of the room. A soldier stood in the doorway. "I was told that the Lord Prince was here," he said to the maidservant.

With an anxious glance at Tavia, Roderic stepped back inside the room. "I'm right here." He beckoned to the man. "What is it?"

The soldier saluted. "Scout came in a few minutes ago, sir. He found two bodies, about three days ride from here."

Roderic nodded for the man to continue, squaring his shoulders instinctively. "Well?"

"Two of the M'Callaster's men, sir. They were wearing plaids."

Roderic closed his eyes as Tavia rushed to his side with a little cry. "Any sign—any sign of my wife?"

The man shook his head. "No, sir. No sign of either the lady or the M'Callaster."

"No indication what happened to them?"

"Mutens, apparently. The wounds on the bodies look like razor spears. They were heading through Muten territory after all. The scouts are waiting in the hall, if you would like to speak to them for yourself, Lord Prince."

"I'll be right there."

As the soldier saluted once more and withdrew, Roderic looked at Tavia and knew she could see the unvoiced fear in his eyes.

"We'll pray, Roderic," she said as she patted the infant's back. "We'll pray that all is well."

"I think the time is come for more than prayers, Tavvy. It's time to act."

Chapter Twenty-one

Across the barren plains of central Arkan, Deirdre and her men rode, pausing only long enough to rest their horses and replenish their dwindling supplies. They stopped at the garrisons, where the wary commanders welcomed them guardedly, gave them food and drink and places to sleep, then sent them on their way with admonitions to be wary.

The western horizon stretched away in the distance, mile after mile of barren, dusty land. Deirdre remembered that Roderic had told her once that the Arkan Plains had been a land of plenty. The crops had grown from horizon to horizon, he'd said, and the bread of Arkan fed the whole of Meriga.

They rode through scattered villages, where men in tattered clothes scratched a living from the dust, and women with faces lined with grief and care eyed them suspiciously from the doorways of hovels. They never stopped in those places, never begged so much as a crust of bread or a cup of water, even for their animals. Silver was next to worthless here. Only food had value, and Deirdre could not bear the thought of taking even a scrap away from people who had so little.

The garrison commanders were stern, tight-lipped men who asked many questions and provided little information. They did give her directions readily enough to the next garrison. Deirdre suspected that her progress was being reported upon. Well, let it be, she thought, though she doubted Roderic would be relieved to hear that she headed west. Doubtless he would suspect she had deserted his cause.

But she had learned to dismiss such thoughts from her mind. The days were long and demanding enough without worrying about something which might not come to pass. So she thanked the garrison commanders and always made sure they knew her name, even if they didn't believe her title.

They were courteous enough, though, and more than once she had seen the soldiers on the walls, watching as she and her companions rode away, onto the highways which ran across the landscape, testimony to Abelard's unceasing care, stretching across the measureless miles.

Time and again they were warned about the Harleyriders, who emerged from their camps in the deep deserts south of Loma and who were expected on their customary migrations. "In this part of the country, we let them be," explained the lieutenant of one lonely outpost as he watched them prepare to leave. "But this year we've seen damn few—too few if you want my opinion."

Deirdre paused. His opinion might count for something, she thought. She had learned long ago that the soldiers in the field often had a better idea of conditions than their superiors in their keeps. She shifted her plaid and settled her swordbelt across her hip. "The spring was late in coming. Is it possible it's kept them in their lairs?"

The lieutenant, a tall man weathered beyond his years, stared down at her, something like respect warring with condescension in his expression. "Perhaps you are right, lady. We'll hope it isn't something more."

"What have your scouts told you?"

For answer he gazed beyond the opened gates. "Well that's the trouble. They haven't been able to tell us anything. There's been hardly any signs of the Harleys at all."

"And that worries you?"

"We know they're out there. And if they aren't here— and if the other garrisons report no signs of them . . . then where are they?"

Deirdre shrugged. Harleyriders were a legend to her people, wild tales told around the fires at night. The Sascatch Tribes, who ranged across the northern borders of Meriga and who sacrificed human prisoners to their gods and ate their flesh, they were more of a real threat than Harleyriders.

"You be careful, lady," the soldier said grimly. "Just because we can't see them doesn't mean they aren't there. Somewhere. And you're a stranger to this part of the country, no matter who or what you are in your own lands. I can tell you don't quite believe how dangerous they are."

Deirdre considered his warning. There was a certain amount of truth in what he said. He was a skinny giant of a man, so tall that even she had to look up. Deep lines ran down the corners of his mouth. This was a man whose face reflected the harshness of the land where he had spent his life. "Don't believe in them?"

"Lady, you rode in here as bold as any man I've ever seen; you carry yourself like a soldier and speak like a lord. Your men answer to you as readily as mine do to me. But don't underestimate the dangers of this land, lady, for there's more out there than you care to imagine. Do you know what the Harleys do to their enemies? The ones they respect, I mean?"

"No. Tell me."

"They crucify them. They take them to the nearest building—even if it is just a ruin, or a tree if they can find one—and tie the prisoner to it, arms outstretched, feet together, maybe as high as ten feet or so in the air. Sometimes they use nails. But either way it's a long, slow, cruel way to die. I've seen what the bodies look like. And it isn't a pretty sight."

Deirdre swallowed hard, listening to the mutters of her men as they paused in their preparations. "I don't imagine it is." She met his eyes, refusing to show fear or the slightest hesitation. "I appreciate your warning, lieutenant, and I will be careful. Now, how many days till the next garrison?"

"Ford-Gunn lies ten days ride from here, due west. There's a village between here and there, Gassapeak. You'll find water, but don't look there for provisions. You'll have more luck relying on your bow."

She nodded her thanks, threw her bedroll on top of the pack behind the saddle, and gripped the reins in both hands. As she swung up into the saddle, she looked at him once more. "Tell me, lieutenant—" He raised a look of grave concern. "Is there any news of the Prince? Or the situation in the South?"

He shook his head. "Last messenger came in over two weeks ago, lady. We're at full alert—but so far nothing more."

She nodded a brief farewell, tugged at the reins, and rode through the high gates, ignoring the stares of the curious men who watched as the company rode away.

Spring might have come slowly to this land, she thought, but summer was here with a vengeance. Their horses' hooves struck the paved surface of the highway with a loud echo. The landscape was barren and sere, a few scrawny trees clung to the surface of the dusty soil, here and there a few hardy flowers bloomed in the crevices of what could only be ruins of the Armageddon. She followed the road, which led along the steep banks of the river, a river which flowed sluggishly, its water muddy and unappealing, reflecting a few of the clouds scudding across the lowering sky.

Four days out of the garrison, at a hot dry noon, she reined her horse and squinted ahead in the distance. Sweat trickled down her neck between her shoulder blades, and her linen shirt clung to her body like a damp skin. Her plaid, woven against the chill and damp of the North, lay in a roll behind her saddle. Even the horses seemed to gasp for breath.

Ahead of her lay the ruins of a city, the high towers gaping empty. She drew a deep breath.

Darmot looked around. "You want to go through there?"

"Is there a way around it?" She looked at the steep riverbank, the high hills which cradled the little city.

He stared all around. "Will take us an extra day to ride around it. There's no way across the river."

Deirdre nodded slowly. "Aye, and once across, could we get back so easily?"

Darmot shook his head. "I don't like the look of that, M'Callaster. 'Tis an ambush waiting to happen in there."

She glanced at him. "But there's no time. Every day we lose—"

"Aye, M'Callaster, I know your mind." He glanced over his shoulders at the other men. "Draw in, lads. Weapons ready."

The little company drew together in close formation, and Deirdre kicked at her horse. The hooves rang with eerie echoes through the stillness. They cantered down the road, the dust flying up in their eyes and mouths, hands at their swords.

Through the main thoroughfare of what had once been a city, beneath the ruins, empty shells where everything one might even think could be useful has been carted away long ago, they rode. The hair rose at the back of Deirdre's neck. The gaping glassless windows reminded her of eyes, of mouths full of jagged teeth. At the many crossroads they paused, glancing down the empty roads, the cross streets where twisted lines of rotted steel swayed in the breeze. Flat sheets of metal, long ago scoured bare by the relentless weather, hung at haphazard angles off poles. The eerie emptiness coupled with the debris caused Deirdre to shiver. She touched her spurs to her horse's side and raised her hand. "Let's get out of here."

As one, the company galloped out of the ruined city. Deirdre breathed a low sigh of relief as they passed the last of the rubbled buildings and the open roadway loomed ahead of them. She turned to Darmot with a rueful smile. "I suppose we're getting to be worse than a couple of old wives?"

He opened his mouth to answer, and from the buildings, a low keening wail swept across them. The hair rose once more on her neck, and she wheeled her horse, drawing her sword in one fast smooth motion.

As one man, the six drew their weapons, drawing close in tight formation. Deirdre half rose in the stirrups. "Donner, Darmot, do you see?—" She broke off as a hawk rose from a building, a struggling rabbit gripped in its talons. Deirdre relaxed with a curse. "I see demons in shadows," she muttered. "Come, let's ride on."

"Alert formation?" asked Donner.

"Why not?" Deirdre shrugged. "At least **until** we're well clear of this accursed place."

In a tight wedge, the men drew together, horses responding to the unspoken commands of the riders as if one flesh. The road led out of the city, down and over the dusty hills. Deirdre glanced suspiciously left and right. Her mount threw back its head repeatedly, nostrils flaring. She patted its neck and saw the whites of its eyes. "Easy, boy," she soothed, even as she craned her head, trying to guess the source of the animal's discomfort.

Over the rise of the next hill, she had her answer. Donner, riding in the front, paused and gagged. "Mother goddess," he choked. "M'Callaster, look."

"Mother goddess, indeed," muttered Deirdre, scarcely able to believe the grisly sight.

On either side of the road, crucifixes of varying sizes sprouted like a gruesome parodies of trees. She reined in her horse to a slow walk. The stallion whickered nervously. "Easy, easy," she murmured as she guided the animal between the row of tortured corpses.

"M'Callaster," whispered Donner.

"Aye?"

"Look—see the bodies?"

"Aye?" Deirdre snapped. Looking at the bodies was the last thing she wanted to do.

"Did the lieutenant at the last garrison not say the Harleys crucified their enemies?"

"Aye," she said again. "What of it?"

"These are no enemies—unless they have launched a war against themselves. These are their own women— and their own children. Look, M'Callaster—do you see?"

With a sharp glance at Donner, Deirdre peered more closely at the bodies which hung upon the crosses. He was right. The Harleys—or whoever had done this—had nailed Harley women to the crosses. And children. Bile rose in her throat, and with a muttered curse, Deirdre put the spurs to her stallion and galloped down the road, away from the awful sight. Her men, needing no urging beyond that, galloped after her. A little ways past the last of the crosses, she reined her horse to a halt. The horse slowed obediently. The stench of blood was still thick in the air, and the beast pawed the ground nervously. She looked back over her shoulder, quelling her nausea with some difficulty.

"What does it mean, M'Callaster?" Darmot pulled hard at the reins of his own beast, struggling to bring it under control.

She shook her head. "The goddess only knows, Darmot. They would have said something if there was war between the Harleys—I thought the crosses were for warriors. The Harley women may be tough, but I have never heard they take up arms and fight with their men." She drew a deep breath and gazed into the west. "Well, if nothing else, this tells us that there is more afoot here than even the men in the garrison know. From now on, we ride with even more caution. Time grows short, and I have a feeling 'tis even shorter than any of us have guessed."

Chapter Twenty-two

❦⁓

"*L*ady." The word shivered through her mind, caressed her ear as softly as a breeze. Annandale looked up from the low pile of blankets on which Abelard lay. In the weeks of their captivity since their arrival, there had been no change in his condition. The King's eyes were closed, as usual, his breathing was shallow. The skin sagged from his cheekbones, and beneath the ragged garments he wore, his body was little more than bones and sinew covered with a leathery husk. She could feel his mind, however, and the never-ending torment in which he existed as his body and the last vestiges of his will fought Amanander's enchantment, and she did what she could to ease the misery. But her attempts were futile; nothing short of her own death could wrest Abelard from Amanander's control, and she knew that even were she to make such a sacrifice, the King would only die.

"Lady." The word whispered through her consciousness once more, and this time she turned around. In the doorway of the prison, a white-robed figure gripped the damp steel bars with hands that shook.

She rose to her feet and drew the blanket which served as a shawl around her shoulders. Despite the heat outside, the chill of the basement dungeons penetrated her to the bone. "What do you want, Jama-taw?"

"I-I've come to beg you to forgive me, lady, if you can. I-I understand now what a terrible thing I did to bring you here." Misery was in every youthful line of his face as he stared into the cell at the four human prisoners.

"Do you, Jama?" Annandale could not help the bitterness which crept into her voice. "Have you really any idea what it is you've done?"

"Ah, lady—I cannot begin to tell you." He groaned, then, a sound of purest anguish, and this time, Annandale closed her eyes against his grief.

Behind her, Alexander coughed, and Vere came to stand beside her. "It's too late, Jama-taw," he said evenly. "Apologies don't really matter. My brother lies close to death; my father cannot die. The College of the Elders is no more. And this lady suffers most of all, since she can feel everyone's torment in addition to her own. You only add to her grief. Go and spare us all."

Jama looked down, mortally stricken. "I was wrong, Lord Vere. I believed Ferad would help our people. The Elders never would."

"You never understood what the Elders tried to do for your people. Most of your people never understood. And now they are destroyed." Another spasm of coughing erupted from Alexander and Vere spun on his heel. "Hold on, Alex. I'm here."

"Jama, what's happening up there?" Annandale asked, to divert her attention from the sound of Alexander's misery as it shuddered through her. Vere was right. Here there was nothing but constant pain, and no respite even in sleep, for her dreams were tortured by the memories of the inhuman look in Amanander's eyes, his expression devoid of emotion or caring. She remembered the frigid chill which went down her spine as his gaze had fallen on her, the prickling sensation at the back of her neck as he had looked her up and down. She had known then that Amanander cared not whether every man in the fortress died.

Jama glanced anxiously over one shoulder. "Lady, I want to try and get you out of here. You must understand, I did not know—how could I know? When I brought you here—"

She could no longer resist the siren call of his pain. With a little sigh, she covered his hands with hers. A thin light flared, and her eyes flooded with tears. As the light faded, the tears spilled down her face and she brushed them away with the back of one hand. "Hush, Jama," she soothed. "Tell me—what did you not know?"

"The Prince!" Beads of sweat popped out across his forehead. "I-I—he's a monster, lady. I know you may not believe me—but lady, I do not lie!"

She drew a deep breath. "I know you don't lie, Jama. I know exactly what he is—the Elders of the College were trying to stop him. That's why I was there. He's found a way to use Old Magic in a new and completely different way. With my help, they could have fought him."

The boy stared at her, eyes wide. Tears seeped down his cheeks. "Oh, lady," he whispered. "Forgive me."

She shook her head sadly. "It isn't me who must forgive you."

"Jama-taw," said Vere, from his place by Alexander,

"what you wanted for your people was nothing less and nothing more than what your father wanted, and his father and his father before him. But each thing comes in its time. You alone decided to use the destruction of your own people as a means to achieve an end."

With a vestige of dignity, Jama raised his head. "There's nothing I can do, Lord Vere, except to try and get you all out. Reparation must be made in small stages." He looked Annandale in the eyes. "Lady, has he touched you? Harmed you in any way?"

Annandale shook her head. "No. It seems he has forgotten we are even here."

"Oh . . ." Jama looked over his shoulder again with a visible shudder. "He hasn't forgotten. He forgets nothing, I think. He can—"

"Tell me, Jama, what can he do?"

"He—" Once more Jama turned and looked over his shoulder. "He can reach into your mind. He takes you—do you understand what I mean? He takes whatever part of you is you and uses it—somehow—and puts himself there instead. The men here—everyone here—all serve him. They have no will of their own. Lady, can you imagine such a thing?"

Annandale nodded. "Oh, yes, I can well imagine it. Look at how he keeps the King alive. Abelard can neither eat nor drink, but his body lives on. And Amanander did something like that, before—only not as well. Not on such a large scale—how many men are here in the garrison?"

Jama glanced up at the low ceiling, where ancient lines and pipes dripped corroded rust. "The army here is at least twenty-five thousand. Then you must also count the Harleyriders, all of them, from everywhere, for all I know."

"What?" Annandale whispered, shocked.

"Yes." Jama pressed his head against the bars. "Lady, I—I can't tell you—"

"Stop it," she hissed. He looked at her, surprised. "There's no point in endless apologies at this point. What is done is done. There has to be a way to get some word to Roderic—to warn him of what he faces."

"I haven't told you everything, lady."

"What more, then?"

"The men—when they die—he still uses them. Dead men walk till their legs rot and they can walk no more. I have seen it myself."

"Jama," Annandale said, her mind reeling beneath the weight of the information, "how is it you are here?"

Jama looked once more over his shoulder. "He can't reach me."

"Why not?"

"I—I saw the men as soon as they met us on the road. I—I have certain gifts—it's not unusual among my people for some of us to have what we call mindskill—do you know of what I speak?"

Annandale nodded. "I think so. So you are able to fight him?"

"Only because I expected it—and it is hard, and growing harder. His strength is increasing. Every day it grows." He dropped his gaze. "He comes to me in dreams. Every night. He shows me terrible things—things to make me fear, to hate—it is on these which he feeds. And once he feeds upon your fear, your hatred, he has his way into your soul."

"What do you do to fight him?"

"Refuse. My will is my own. I tell myself not to hate semblances of what might never be—or to waste time hating things about which I can do nothing. It is harder not to be afraid."

In the sudden silence, Annandale touched his hand once more, gently. "I know."

"Do you, lady? There are only a few of us he cannot reach so far—three or four of my party. The rest of my men are his. They still answer to me, but they are his—I know it, and so does he."

"You must leave, Jama."

"That is what I came to tell you. I will leave, and I will take you with me. I swear it."

"Oh, Jama." Annandale shook her head. "Surely I would only hinder you. Better to go yourself when you can. And get to Roderic—here—" She looked down at her hand, the nails ragged and caked with dirt. On her right hand, the little pearl ring Roderic had given her so long ago gleamed like a moon in the dim cell. She remembered the day he had given it to her—years ago now it seemed. If you should be in any danger, he had said, send me this ring, and I will come. He had spoken with such quiet conviction. Such innocents they were, then. She wriggled the ring off her finger and pressed it into Jama's palm. "Take this ring to Roderic. He will know you speak the truth if you have it. Tell him what you have told me, and any other information you can possibly give him. And tell him I love him, with my life."

Jama fingered the ring as though it were the most precious jewel he had ever beheld. "Lady—I want you to come with me. I owe you a great debt. You saved the life of my best friend, and my life and the lives of all my men. I cannot leave you here."

Annandale sighed. "I don't want to stay here, either, Jama. But surely you see it would be better for you to get out while you can. And as for me—" She looked over her shoulder, where Abelard lay on a bed of rags, his breathing so soft as to be nearly soundless "—I cannot leave the King. Amanander seems to have forgotten about him, too, and yet—"

"He forgets nothing. And no one." The young Muten's three eyes burned in his face. "All right. We'll try to find a way to take him, too. I owe you all."

Annandale sighed. "If it can be done, Jama. Only if it can be done. I would rather see you escape and get to Roderic."

Jama looked over his shoulder once more. "We need to go quickly if we are to be of any use to Roderic. He has laid a trap—"

"A trap?"

"Yes." Jama nodded. "He hopes to lure Roderic and a main part of his army into Dlas."

Annandale shuddered. "Then go, Jama. Go and make what plans you can. But please, remember what I said. Better that one of us gets to Roderic than all of us die trying."

"Lady," Jama met her eyes squarely, "better that all of us die trying than for one of us to live here."

She squeezed his fingers and was rewarded by the

blush which suffused his thin cheeks. He gave her a quick smile that might have been a grin and pulled his hood over his face. He scurried away down the corridor and disappeared into the darkness.

"I don't like that," said Vere softly. He came to stand beside Annandale, peering down the corridor after Jama.

She looked up at him, surprised. "Why not?"

"I wonder if he isn't setting a trap for us," replied Vere. "You were right. It's foolishness to think he can get two sick, no, dying men out of here with a woman and another man. And Dad's condition is so bad, I doubt he can be moved. In fact, so closely is he linked to Amanander, I doubt he can be moved at all without Aman knowing about it." He broke off and gazed down at her speculatively. "One thing's become clear to me, though."

"What's that?"

"The reason Amanander has left you alone is that he no longer needs your help in working the Magic. He seems to have found a way to prevent the backlash. But he may need Alexander."

"Alex? Why?"

Vere sighed. "It's obvious that Amanander is able to draw upon a person's will. But somehow, he has to be getting the energy in order to do that. He must be feeding on people in some way—some way I can't quite understand. But it seems to me that it must take a tremendous amount of energy in order to do what he does. And Alex is essentially the same person as Amanander. It would seem to me that if Aman needs energy, the first source, or maybe the most potent source, would be the person most like himself." He glanced over his shoulder. Alexander lay near Abelard, shivering.

"It's as if we don't exist," Annandale said slowly.

"You're right." Vere sighed once more, his thin shoulders rising and falling in the gloom. "He has you now. I wonder what he intends to do with you."

Annandale shivered. A sudden stab of longing for Rhodri, for Roderic, pierced her so poignantly that tears welled in her eyes. "I don't even want to think about it."

"My dear, sweet lady." He threw his arm around her awkwardly and hugged her. For a moment, she allowed herself to relax against him, and then, as the residue of his pain filtered into her awareness, she drew back.

"He could keep us here long enough to make us despair," she murmured. "Make us give up hope. If we despair, he's won."

"And then we will all belong to him." Vere stroked his beard. "All of us. He doesn't *need* you, not anymore, or he would have tried to use you as soon as we arrived."

"But if he can make us give up, surrender of our own accord, then he's won." She pressed her lips together and straightened her shoulders. "So we mustn't give up hope and we mustn't despair, because if we do that—"

"We belong to him."

A wave of loathing swept over her, nausea so acute she felt as though she might vomit. *Hold fast, daughter.* The voice whispered through her mind, like a scent of roses in the midst of offal. She closed her eyes, concentrating on the voice. Hold fast? she wondered. For how long?

There was a long silence, and then Vere spoke so softly in the shadows, she had to strain to hear him. "If any-one gets out," Vere said finally, "I think it's important to try and get Alexander out. You and I may be expendable, lady. But I would wager anything that Amanander has plans for his twin."

Chapter Twenty-three

Despite Roderic's impatience, several more days passed in slow progression, bringing news of neither Deirdre nor Annandale. Only a desultory progression of messages from the North trickled in, with Everard's assurances that for now, at least, the Muten Tribes were being held in check.

Finally, frantic with worry and angry with himself for listening to Annandale's plea, he ordered a contingent of scouts to head into the inaccessible interior of the Pulatchians. The uncertainty was driving him mad.

He was reviewing the maps with the leader of the scouting party when there was a knock at the door.

"Lord Prince." The captain of the watch stood in the doorway, uncertainly. He had left his command, which was a punishable offense, and he knew it. Roderic looked up and frowned. "What's the problem, Captain?"

"In the distance, my lord, there is a column of soldiers approaching. Coming up from the south."

"What? We're being attacked?"

"No, my lord. They're ours. They look like they're in retreat."

"Retreat? Come with me." He hurried to the top of the

keep, calling for Brand and Miles. As he stepped out onto the windswept roof, he could see, in the distance, a ragged column of men coming ever closer. "Captain," Roderic ordered over his shoulder, "get men out there, horses, litters—see to their needs."

"At once, Lord Prince."

Heedless of the sun's glare and the gusting breeze, Roderic watched as the battered regiments staggered through the main thoroughfare of the tent city surrounding Ithan and disappeared through the gates. He frowned as he recognized the colors of the regiments. These were the men he had sent to Dlas with orders to reinforce the garrison there. Brand was going to be frantic.

Grim-faced, he marched down to the hall, to find a scene bordering on chaos. The exhausted men were slumped on every available bench or chair. The wounded lay in long rows near the dais, and Lady Norah, with the other women of the household, bustled about, finding blankets, offering cups of hot wine and cider steaming with spices, or pieces of bread and hastily sliced meats and cheese. Among the wounded, the physicians bent here and there, calling for bandages, ointments, and salves, and more than once, a sheet to place over the face of a dead soldier.

Roderic glanced around the room. Brand and Miles were nowhere to be seen. He squatted next to a man who huddled by one of the hearths, hands cradling a goblet. On the tattered tunic were the remnants of a captain's insignia. "What happened, Captain?"

"Lord Prince." The man offered a weary salute. "I didn't think we'd make it back. We were lucky to get so far, and then we ran into the bad weather. Storms, Lord Prince, swirling clouds of dust which reached from the sky to the ground. They came up out of nowhere, it seemed. We must have lost almost half again as many on the Arkan Plains."

"Did the Harleyriders attack?" Brand spoke quietly, grimly, and Roderic looked up to see his brother standing over his shoulder. He knew by the look on Brand's face that he, too, had recognized the troops.

"Harleyriders? Monsters. They looked like Harleyriders, Lord Prince. But—"

"What do you mean?" Brand demanded, and Roderic knew that worry for his son made him sound harsher than he would ever intend otherwise. "Was it Harleyriders, or wasn't it?"

The other man stared up at him. "I wish I could say, Captain Brand. But in truth—yes, they were Harleyriders. They looked like Harleyriders and smelled like Harleyriders. But they fought like no other men I have ever encountered in my life." He shuddered and, despite the heat of the day, pulled the blanket tighter around him.

Brand narrowed his eyes. "Captain—"

Roderic rose and put his hand on Brand's arm. It was obvious to him that the men had been through a great deal. There would be plenty of time to hear them out, to ask questions and gather information.

"Lord Prince," said a man who wore a sergeant's stripes on his bloodstained sleeve, "Captain Brand. It wasn't Harleys. Was monsters dressed as Harleys. I've never seen the like. They looked like men from a distance, but when we got up close, it was like they were already dead."

"What?" The hair rose on the back of Roderic's neck.

"Where did you meet these—these monsters?" asked Brand, his voice taut with suspicion.

"When we reached the border of Dlas, Captain," answered the sergeant. "We never made it to the garrison. They just appeared out of the desert and kept coming."

"What do you mean by that?" A tic had appeared beneath Brand's left eye.

"We crossed into Dlas, and right on the Loma border, in the hills, they were waiting for us. We couldn't shake them—they just kept coming."

"Day and night, Lord Prince," said the captain. He stared into the cold hearth with dull eyes. "We had no sleep—they followed us all the way back to Arkan, and then the dust storms hit."

"What's your name, Captain?" Brand bit out the words.

"Jonovon, captain of the Fourth Regiment, Fifth Division."

"Your orders were clear," Brand said.

Jonovon raised his face and met Brand's angry eyes calmly, wearing the expression of a man who knows he has done his duty. "Captain, I am well aware what my orders were. But you have to believe me when I tell you I have never seen anything like this. These soldiers, whatever they were, had such accuracy—whatever they took aim at, they hit."

"Lord Prince." Another man, roused from a fitful sleep by the voices, struggled to a sitting position near the sergeant, "My name is Athal. The captain's right. These Harleys weren't like any others I have ever seen in my life. I saw them take direct hits and just ignore them. There was no way we could have gotten any further in Dlas without losing every man."

"Lord Prince—" Another tugged at Roderic's hand. His voice was no more than a weak whisper, and Roderic bent down on one knee to hear him. "The winds, Lord Prince, when the enemy stopped, the winds followed us, as though some hand controlled nature itself."

Roderic looked at Brand. He got to his feet once more. "All right, men. Thank you for the information. We'll need to talk more with you, but for right now, rest. Lady Norah will see you have all you need." He cleared his throat and gestured to Brand. "Come."

The two threaded their way through the ranks. In the doorway of the council room, Roderic paused and saw Miles cross the hall, dismay plain on his face. He motioned to Miles. As the Senador made his way to the council room, Roderic shivered, despite the warmth of the stuffy room. "What do you think of this?"

"Call up every available reserve. Someone's got to get down there and relieve the garrison at Dlas as soon as possible. If those things—whatever they are—intercepted these men, then there's a likely chance the garrison is besieged."

Roderic caught Miles's eye. The Senador's face was set and grim, but there was a wordless pity in his expression as he looked at Brand. Miles understood that Brand spoke as a father. "First," Roderic said, choosing his words carefully, "I need reports from all those men, especially the officers. We have to know what we are dealing with."

"I agree," Brand said, still frowning, "but dispatches should go out immediately to the reserves held at Ahga."

Miles drew a sharp breath and Roderic shot him a cautionary look. "Why don't you do that now, Brand? I'll have Henrode and his scribes begin to take down the reports. It won't take long to find out what we need to know."

Brand spun on his heel and was gone before Roderic had the chance to say anything more. Miles let out a long breath. "He's more upset than I've ever seen him."

Roderic nodded. "He's lost his wife in this war. He can't stand the thought of losing his son, too."

Miles nodded slowly, and the two men stared a few minutes as the hall was gradually restored to some semblance of order under Norah's capable ministrations. Roderic watched her moving amongst the wounded men and something twisted in his gut. The thought of losing Annandale was more than he could bear.

Long into the night, Roderic read the reports scribbled in Henrode's hastiest hand. As dawn approached, he put the last piece of parchment down on the stack piled high on his desk and covered his tired eyes with one hand. What the reports amounted to was terrifying in its simplicity. Ordered to reinforce the garrison at Dlas, the army had met no resistance at all, until they had crossed the Loma border. There, as they headed toward Dlas, they encountered an enemy such as they had never met before. Although the soldiers looked like Harleyriders, they didn't fight like Harleyriders. Some were clad in rags, and some wore the black leather of the Riders. All fought with polished steel. They fought with grim ferocity, stopped by neither dark, nor weather, nor lack of food or sleep. Their numbers were impossible to estimate.

In their thousands, they pursued the hapless troops across Loma, through swirling storms of dust and debris, then, as if by some internal signal, the enemy stopped in a silent line at the Loma desert, in an eerie row, staring north at the escaping troops.

As Roderic shuffled through the pages, reading the grim news over and over, one parchment caught his attention. He paused, fingering the report as a chill shuddered through him. In the center of the page, one poor wretch had drawn the symbol on the shields carried by these unknown foes: an inverted triangle topped by a crescent. The hair on the back of his neck rose. It was the same sign he had seen in Nydia's flames all those months and months ago, on the day he had first met Annandale.

He wet his lips and closed his eyes, and Annandale's face rose before him. Those eyes, blue as the summer sea beneath a cloudless sky, gazed back at him, and he remembered the nights spent in her arms, her gentle smile, her merry laugh. What if she were lost to him forever? he wondered. How could he endure her loss?

He shoved the thought aside. Nothing was to be gained by brooding upon things which had not yet come to pass. Annandale was safe among the Mutens. She had to be. The remains of the fire hissed in the hearth and a low wind moaned. He glanced outside the window, where a gray dawn was spreading behind the purple mountains.

He rubbed his eyes, gathered the parchments together in one neat heap, and went to dress. There was no chance of sleep for him.

Henrode was waiting as he strode into the council room, his ink-stained fingers already scratching his pen over parchment. "Henrode," Roderic said, surprised, "what are you doing here?"

The scribe shot Roderic a look of exasperation. "Lord Prince, I have been your scribe for more than three years now. I know when you will want to send out dispatches. Here. You might sign these."

Amused, despite the situation, Roderic picked up the papers. Among them were the summons to the last of the reserves held at Ahga. Roderic picked up Henrode's pen and scrawled his signature at the bottom. A small stab of anxiety quivered through him. These were the last of the professional troops. It would be well to order a conscription of the able-bodied men amongst the farmers and the merchants. As he opened his mouth to tell Henrode to write an additional order, Brand entered the room.

"Good morning, Roderic." Brand's face was pale and the shadows were dark beneath his eyes. He looked like a man who had spent the night fighting demons.

Before Roderic could respond, bearers carrying Phineas's litter marched into the room, followed by a yawning Miles.

Roderic took his customary seat at the head of the table. A servant brought food and set plates and goblets on the table. He bowed briefly, then shut the door behind him. Roderic reached for a piece of bread and gestured to the other men to help themselves. He tapped the stack of parchments on the table. "I will assume you all are aware of what is in these reports."

Miles nodded slowly. "I'm not sure I believe it. I've never heard of anything like this before in my life."

"There're too many men involved not to believe it," Roderic replied.

"Oh, I agree, Roderic. The question isn't whether it's real or not, it's—"

"How we fight it," interrupted Brand.

"Exactly." Roderic pushed back his chair and walked over to the windows. "Recommendations, gentlemen?"

"We must get down there as quickly as we possibly can," said Brand. "Are those dispatches ready to go out?" He glanced at Henrode.

"I signed them this morning," answered Roderic.

"Gentlemen," Phineas said softly, "I agree that the garrison at Dlas must be relieved. But I think the reports we have all heard warrant greater caution. Given the depleted state of our men and our supplies, sending more troops down there may be suicidal."

"Phineas," Brand said, "Dlas is too important—"

"Brand." The older man spoke so quietly, Roderic had to strain to hear him. "Dlas is of minor strategic importance at the moment. I know the safety of the men at the garrison means a great deal to you—it means a great deal to us all. But this is an enemy unlike any our men have ever faced. We have to consider how best to fight him."

"Him?" Miles asked.

"Amanander's behind this," said Roderic. "The reports are too similar to the soldiers Amanander used last summer. The only difference is he seems to have recruited Harleyriders."

"We suspected that from the beginning," said Brand. "What does it matter who fights for him? And I beg to differ with you, Phineas. Dlas is of strategic importance and always has been. Dlas protects the underbelly of Arkan. From Dlas, it's an easy march into Missiluse. We lose Dlas and we lose a key position."

"We don't know yet if we've lost Dlas," replied Phineas. "You are making an assumption that the garrison has either been attacked and is lost, or is under attack and must be relieved. Neither is certain."

"So you're suggesting we sit and wait? For what?" Brand thrust his chair back from the table. "Must Amanander's army come knocking on the walls of Ithan?"

Roderic exchanged a glance with Miles. "We haven't exactly been idle here, Brand. Fighting a war on this many fronts requires a certain amount of coordination—"

"Indeed. And while we coordinate, Amanander gains ground."

"What ground has Amanander gained?" Roderic shot back. "Our troops were beaten once. Kye maintains his position in Atland, the Arkan lords hold fast, Everard has contained the Mutens in the North. Yes, I agree that the time is coming soon for us to plan a major offensive. But, Brand, we have to know what we're fighting in order to win."

"So what are you suggesting, Roderic?"

"I am suggesting that a scouting party be sent into Dlas. We need to know everything we can learn about these Harleyriders. It won't take the scouts long to return. And by the time they do, the reserves I've called from Ahga will be here. Then we can act."

"And in the meantime, brave men at Dlas may be under siege or worse, while we sit and wait for information?" Brand got to his feet. "No. That's not acceptable."

"Then what would you find acceptable?' asked Phineas.

Brand stared at Phineas and force of long discipline made him square his shoulders. "Let me take some men down there. Send the scouts with me—you know I have more years fighting the Harleys than almost anyone here. That way I will be in position to command the reserves from Ahga—to secure the roads from here to there—"

"And to ensure that Barran is alive and safe?" Phineas spoke gently.

Brand's mouth tightened into a grim line. "Are you suggesting—?"

"No," interrupted Phineas. "I understand your concern for your son, Brand." He cleared his throat and looked at Roderic. "What do you say to the captain's suggestion, Lord Prince?"

Roderic thought quickly, and looked from one man to the other. He loved both of them, had trusted their counsel for as long as he had been Regent. He understood Brand's fear for his son. Forcing Brand to stay at Ithan would only further frustrate him. "I think," he said slowly, "I shall miss your presence, Brand. But I also think your absence may serve us well."

He saw the satisfaction leap into Brand's eyes and knew that Phineas watched them both with a troubled frown.

A cold sun rose on the day Roderic bid good-bye to Brand. The calendar proclaimed it the first of Gost; Roderic, shivering as he rose before the stars had set, thought it felt more like the first of Tober. There was an autumnal chill in the morning air as Roderic walked down the steps of Ithan where his brother awaited him, already mounted on his horse.

As the heralds blew the orders to move out, Roderic reached for his brother's hand. "The One be with you."

"And keep you," Brand answered.

"Remember, don't provoke an attack. We need information more than anything."

"Roderic, you sound like an old woman."

"I'll send those reserves out as soon I can."

"I know. Farewell, little brother."

Unexpectedly, Roderic's throat thickened and his vision blurred. He had relied upon Brand's experience and his advice for so long, it seemed unbelievable that his brother was leaving without him. "Farewell."

With a grim little smile, Brand tugged at the reins and turned his horse. He rode out the gates after the long column of men and wagons.

Roderic stood watching as the regiments were lost in the misty dawn. He heard a distant cheer go up as Brand galloped past the lines to take his place at the head of the army. Would Brand have been so eager, Roderic wondered, if he knew that the Prince he fought for was not the true heir? If he knew that the man whose blood he sought to shed was more his brother's than the man whose blood he'd pledged to die for? Yes, he decided at last, it wouldn't matter to Brand. For Brand went to fight for his son, and Barran meant more to him than all the gold in Ahga. He thought of Rhodri, of the child who lay sleeping in his cradle, of Melisande who played and danced and laughed with such abandon. Perhaps Brand was right, he thought. Perhaps children were the only thing worth fighting for.

Chapter Twenty-four

*L*ess than a week after Brand's departure, the first of the reports from the scouts began to filter into Ithan, and Roderic lingered long into the nights with Phineas and Miles, drawing upon every scrap of information they could glean from the soldiers who had returned from Loma. On a chilly Gost night, it seemed Roderic had just closed his eyes when frantic knocking at the door of the outer room made him bolt awake.

By reflex, he grabbed for his sword, encountered a bed robe instead, and threw it over his shoulders. He hurried into the outer room to see a sleepy Ben opening the door. "I'm coming, I'm coming." Roderic tied the belt around his waist as the old man threw open the door. "What's wrong?"

In the rushlit hall, a sentry stood at attention. "You must come at once, Lord Prince."

"What's going on? Has anyone died?"

"No, Lord Prince. Chiavett Kahn, Lord Prince. He arrived moments ago."

"Who?"

"He claims to be the leader of the Harleyriders."

"What? A Harleyrider? Here? In Ithan?"

"As I said, Lord Prince."

Roderic stared at the man. His stolid face was set. "Where is he now?"

"In the hall, Lord Prince."

"All right. I'll be there as soon as I dress. Take him—have someone take him to the council room. I'll be there as soon as I can."

"As you say, Lord Prince."

Roderic shut the door and walked back into the bedroom, beckoning to Ben. The old man scurried after him. "What does it mean, Lord Prince?"

Roderic pushed his hair off his forehead. "I don't know, Ben. One of the Harleyriders here? The One only knows what it could possibly mean."

Roderic reached for his clothes and stripped off his robe. "Go back to bed, Ben. You need your sleep more than I do."

The old servant handed Roderic his boots. "I've been your bodyservant since you were twelve, Lord Prince. Won't be the first time I've waited to see you to bed."

"No, Ben." Roderic hid a smile as he tugged on his boot. "Though this is the first time you've waited because a Harleyrider has come to me."

Roderic was immediately sorry that he had told them to bring the Harleyrider to the council room. He had forgotten about the smell. The Kahn was a big man, tall as Roderic, but broader, his chest and arms huge slabs of muscle. He wore skins and leather breeches, and across his chest were thick silver chains. His hair was dark and hung in lank strands over his chest and back, and his beard was braided in what looked to be hundreds of tiny plaits. Four of Roderic's men at arms surrounded him. He loomed in their midst and the soldiers snapped to attention as Roderic entered.

"Lord Prince," said their captain. "I hope I was not wrong, sir, to waken you. This—this man came in around midnight, demanding to see you immediately, and I thought you would want to know."

"Of course, Captain. You did right." Roderic looked the outlaw over. "Why have you come to Ithan?"

He pulled himself to his full height, and Roderic recognized the indefinable quality of nobility despite the grime. This man was every bit as much a Prince as he. "I need your help."

"Help?"

"My people are in danger."

"Danger? What kind of danger?" Roderic knew that his amazement was plain on his face.

"I want to talk to you alone, Prince Roderic."

Roderic looked at the soldiers, who exchanged warning looks with their captain. "Why?"

"I didn't come here to be a hostage. I'm here for some help."

"Surely you understand that the relationship between our peoples has not been an easy one?"

"Do you think I'd come at all if I thought I had another choice?"

"Wait outside." Roderic waved the guards away and sat down in one of the chairs, as far away from the Kahn as he could get. "Now. What exactly are you talking about?"

"Look, Man," he said. Roderic raised an eyebrow at the Harley title of respect. "There isn't much. Back about two winters ago, my old lady, my Mamma-Doc, had a spirit dream of death with two faces walking across the land. The pattern, she said, the pattern was broken, and had to be restored. And there was something about a tree, a tree that put forth many branches and had flowered in this generation. All sorts of stuff. None of it made much sense to me. I listen to my Mamma-Doc; don't get me wrong. But it isn't the right thing for a man to listen to his woman too closely, you know? And besides, death is everywhere." He shrugged, and for some reason, Roderic felt sorry for him.

"Go on, please." Roderic nodded.

"Then she had another spirit dream. This time was about her and me. We were walking through the Plains and the road split. We had to make a choice, she said, and she had told me to take one path, but it was the wrong path in the end, she said when she woke up. And she made me swear to remember that. That she had told me to take one path and that it had turned out to be wrong." He shrugged again. "So I swore. Didn't seem like it mattered much." He paused and stared into the space over Roderic's shoulder. "But then Harry Onrada came to me."

"Harry Onrada? Harland? The lord of Missiluse?"

"Him." The Kahn's mouth twisted in outright disgust. "Said we had a chance to claim our space. So we went to meet him and my Mamma-Doc came along. We met the Ridenau—the one who claims your throne. And my Mamma-Doc—she told me to join with him."

There was a long silence. Roderic considered the man carefully. "What happened?" he asked at last.

"So we joined up. We gave our word, sealed it in spit. With my men, I went to his fortress. I ordered them to obey him—"

"Who?" interrupted Roderic. "Harland?"

"Nah. Amanander. The Ridenau. At first it was all drills and practice—I thought nothing of it. And then, I began to notice changes in my men."

"What kinds of changes?" Roderic leaned forward, forgetting the stench.

"They—they no longer respected me. No longer listened to me. It was as if they were always listening to someone—something—else. Someone or something I couldn't hear. And then one day, I saw the son of one of my oldest friends die on the practice fields. It was an accident—I saw it with my own eyes. They carried his body away. And the next day, I saw him in the hall, by the Ridenau's right arm."

"What?" Roderic sat back in disbelief.

"Yah. Sounds worse than any dream, doesn't it?" The Kahn gave a short, bitter laugh. "My men aren't mine anymore. The ones who live are his slaves, and the ones who are dead walk still."

"You've seen him raise the dead?" whispered Roderic.

"Nah. I don't know how he does it. I can only tell you I've seen dead men walk. I should've remembered the spirit dream. For now my Mamma-Doc is dead, and my men are no longer mine."

"How did she die?"

"My men killed her."

"What? Why?"

"The men are killing all the women. And the kiddens."

Roderic stared in disbelief at the man who sat at the opposite end of the table. "Your own people?"

"Yes." The Kahn raised his eyes to Roderic, and in their depths, Roderic saw utter hopelessness.

"But why? Are these factions within your families?"

"Nah." The Kahn shook his head vehemently. "We do not crucify women or kiddens. It is the sacred death. We only crucify people we respect. Like you, Prince. We would crucify you."

Roderic swallowed hard. "I'm honored. How do you know it's your own men?"

"I've seen it happen." He pressed his lips together. "I went with my men—though I knew even then they weren't mine anymore—on a recon, to check out what was up ahead. And we came to what was left of Mamma-Doc's family. And I saw the men doing it—nailing the women to the crosses and standing them up. I ordered them to stop it—ordered my men to take them down. And they refused. I saw my Mamma-Doc on her cross, and I had to fight ten of my own men to get to her. It's a slow death, you know, and she was still alive. I cut her down, and took her away, and before she died, she told me to come to you."

"What do you want from me?"

"I told you. Help."

"What kind of help?"

"The Ridenau must be stopped. If he falls, my people will be my own again."

Roderic shifted uncomfortably in his chair. "How do I know this isn't a trap? Or that you've been sent here by Amanander with this story—"

The Kahn moved in his chair, a vaguely threatening gesture which Roderic understood was born of frustration. "You have to listen to me. The men don't die. They don't need food and they don't need drink. They walk with dead men's eyes. Wide open. I have lived among them. They walk till their legs rot and they can walk no more." His expression was one of disgust. He rose to his feet and paced to the window, where the first gray light of dawn lightened the sky.

"I haven't much to offer you, Prince, but what I can do to help you, I will. Someone must stop this, and stop it now."

"Can you tell us how to kill them?"

"Cut off their heads. It's the only way."

Roderic was silent, wondering what Brand would have said to this, and what Phineas would say. He shifted in his chair. "I will speak to my advisors in the morning."

"You should know that over forty hundreds of my men have answered the Ridenau's call. I have risked much to come to you. You will not answer me?"

Roderic frowned. "I said I would take the matter under advisement. I will consider your request, as I consider all the appeals for aid to my court."

"Then you consider this, Prince. For centuries my people have roamed the Loma deserts and the Arkan Plains, and we go where we want, and do what we please. When we have to act, we act, and when we have to wait we wait. And we know the difference between the two. But you—you sit like spiders spinning webs. Don't waste too much time. The enemy will come for you whether you listen to me or not." His shadow loomed on the walls.

Roderic stood up. He went to the door and called for the guards. When they had come in, he said: "Take our guest to the barracks and find him lodging there."

"Under guard, Lord Prince?"

Roderic hesitated. "See to his needs: give him whatever he wants, except a weapon."

The Kahn laughed as he was led away. "Believe me, Prince, if I wanted one, you and all your men could not stop me."

There was a reason, Brand thought, as he squinted in the hot glare of the noon sun, that younger men went on campaign and older men stayed home. His back itched and his boots were full of sand. The light reflected off the pale yellow grit, and in the far distance, the walls of the garrison of Dlas seemed to shimmer.

"There it is, Captain!" One of those younger men, a man at least thirty years his junior, raised an arm and pointed. The scouts had headed out at dawn, and now, seeing the walls of Dlas rising out of the desert, he understood why they had not returned. The march through Tennessy and into Loma had been fairly uneventful. They had surprised a few odd packs of Harleyriders here and there, but nothing of the scope the regiments fleeing back to Ithan had described.

There had been one village, where the women and

children had been crucified. Brand had paused a long time there, thinking. He had never seen a woman crucified. Nor a child, for that matter. The old Harley legends made it a sacred death, one reserved only for warriors and enemies worthy of their mettle. In all his years of campaigning in Arkan and in Loma, he had never seen the Harleys crucify even an enemy woman. He would have lingered there longer, but his men were impatient to be off and away from such a sight. But the image of those tortured faces was burned into his brain, and he thought it would be a long time before he was able to forget.

Now, he turned and smiled at the junior officer, one of the newer ones promoted during the course of the last two years. So many men had been lost in this war, he thought, too many. He tightened his mouth in a grim line and refused to think about Jaboa.

A small dust cloud in the distance disgorged two riders. He nodded. "Looks like Barran has sent a welcome out to meet us."

The smile died on his lips as he saw the state of the men on horseback. Their hair was lopped off in clumsy fashion, their faces were unshaven, and more than a few days growth of beard roughened their chins. Their uniforms were stained and reeked of sweat. Brand noticed his men exchanging glances. In the field, it was understood that proper grooming was not easy to achieve. But at the garrisons, even the outpost garrisons, it was expected that discipline would be maintained. He frowned. He would have to speak to Barran.

The soldiers galloped up to greet him, and Brand turned away at the ripe odor emanating from their bodies. Even the horses looked as though they hadn't been brushed in days. What in the name of the One, he wondered, was wrong with his son?

But their salutes were crisp enough, and their voices properly subdued. "Your son, Captain Barran, sends you his greetings and begs us to take you to him with all haste, sir."

Brand coughed. "Lead on, then, soldier." He gestured for the men to ride ahead.

Within the garrison walls, the guards stood at ramrod attention and the dusty courtyard was neat and bare. Brand noted with satisfaction that at least something was maintained with military precision. He slid off his saddle and threw the reins in the direction of a waiting groom. At least, the man appeared to be a groom. They were all so unkempt, so stained and shabby, it was hard to tell. He waved away the guards who would have guided him. "I know the way."

He walked eagerly into the garrison. He knew the garrison at Dlas from all his years spent fighting here. And it looked as though nothing had changed, except perhaps the discipline among the men. Well. He would have a word with Barran about that, and then everything would be fine.

A slight buzzing sound seemed to come from behind the closed door of Barran's office, and as Brand touched the knob, he was struck by a faint, sweetish smell. The smell grew stronger as he opened the door. It struck him full in the face as he gagged at the sight before his eyes.

Barran, or what was left of him, had been nailed to the open windowframe. Flies crawled over his rotting, bloated body. Brand grasped the doorknob as his knees buckled. He looked back over his shoulder, ready to demand an answer from the slack-faced sergeant who sat behind the desk, when he heard his men begin to scream. And then there was no more time to wonder what had happened.

Chapter Twenty-five

There was no moon on the night Jama came for them. The dark was as thick as the shrouds which draped the trees, as black as the moonless sky. On the walls, the torches cast flickering shadows. He hissed her name in the middle of that moonless night, and Annandale was instantly awake. She sat up, clutching the ragged blanket to her chest, her hair tumbling lank and heavy about her shoulders.

In the darkness came the jangled sound of keys fumbling in the locks on the barred door, and across the room she heard Vere leap to his feet.

"Lady, Lord Vere." Jama spoke so softly she had to strain to hear him over Alexander's labored breathing.

"I'm here," she called softly. In the murky gloom, she saw Vere stand, a gray ghost, and swiftly cross the room. The door swung open with a creak of ancient hinges, and in the silence, it sounded like a scream. Annandale jumped.

Jama stepped past Vere, and in his arms he carried a large bundle. "I have uniforms here—please, put them on over your clothes."

Vere caught Jama's arm. "What is your plan?"

"The guards are changing in two turns of the glass, Lord Vere. When the gates are open to let the guards in and out, we will slip in amongst them. There's a wagon waiting in the grove of trees past the bend in the road. Hopefully the night is so dark no one will notice six extra men."

In the darkness, Annandale heard Vere's quick intake of breath. "It's a long shot, Jama-taw."

"It's the only one we have." He handed Vere several pieces of clothing. "Here. Put these things on."

Annandale took the cloak and leather tunic he offered her, shrugging it on over her clothes. It reeked of old sweat, but it was not the smell which turned her stomach. A miasma clung to it, as though the last person to wear the garments had died while wearing them. Which, she thought, pressing her lips together, was exactly what had happened.

She helped Vere pull the tunic over Alexander's head and helped him stand. He leaned weakly against the wall, waving them away. In the darkness, the two of them fumbled to wrap a cloak around Abelard.

Vere motioned her aside and picked Abelard up, lifting him as easily as he might a child. Annandale winced to see how frail the King had become. She hastened to Alexander's side, and beckoned to Jama. He wrapped an arm around Alexander's waist and turned his head to look around at Vere. "Come," he whispered. "We must go swift and silent."

Only Alexander's steps dragged across the ancient floor. From the depths of his robe, Jama pulled out a slender cylinder. There was a soft click and a small beam pierced the thick night. He smiled around Alexander's bulk at Annandale. "Cold fire," he whispered.

"Yes," answered Vere. "Explain the miracle to her when we are safe outside the walls." He gave a soft snort of derision.

Jama subsided into hurt silence. Annandale clutched Alexander closer. She could hear the heavy beating of his heart, the wheeze as his lungs struggled to breathe. She gripped his back harder, fighting the seductive urge to heal. She had no time now. Later, she promised herself. Later, when they were beyond the walls and safely on the way to Ithan—then, then she would give into the demanding call of the healing.

The corridor was long and straight, and they were forced to go so slowly, it seemed the corridor would never end. Finally, Jama gestured with the lamp. "This way."

Annandale looked up. A thick cobweb hung in the air. With a deep shudder, she tightened her arm around Alexander and helped him up the steps. The door swung open with a painful creak, and she jumped. Slowly, she and Jama managed to haul Alexander to the top of the steps. Vere followed with relative ease. Annandale turned to look back and saw, with disbelief, the King open his eyes and stare at the star-studded sky.

"Vere." His voice was less than a whisper, not much more than a sigh.

"Dad?" Vere looked down at the man in his arms in disbelief.

"Be—" The King's voice ended in a choke.

Jama made a kind of strangled noise, and Alexander

drew in a deep breath. As Annandale turned back, she gasped as her eyes met Amanander's.

"Good evening. A pleasant night, indeed." His eyes glittered in the starlight and his voice was colder than the basement dungeon.

Jama gazed at Amanander, his face blanched white with shock.

"If you thought the prisoners needed an airing, Jama, you had but to suggest it," Amanander continued. He stared at Jama the way a spider might at a smaller insect.

"What in the name of One do you think you're doing with us, Amanander?" Vere asked through tight lips. Annandale looked at him over her shoulder. He shifted the King's long frame as easily as he might a child's and met Amanander's cold stare with one of his own.

Amanander slid his gaze over each of them in turn and Annandale quivered, feeling as though something foul had brushed against her bare skin. "My plans don't concern you, Vere." There was no hint of taunting malice in that voice, and it was the lack of it that made Annandale shudder once more. "But, Jama, it's as well you brought the King from below. It's time to send him home."

Vere tightened his grip on the fragile King. "Home? What are you talking about?"

"I'm sending him back to Roderic," Amanander answered. "He's served his purpose here. And I want Roderic to understand just exactly what I am capable of, dear brother. Because the next one I send back will be you. Or maybe even you, my dear." His dark eyes flickered with an inhuman light as they glanced over Annandale. "Pity we're brother and sister."

"Brother and sister?" blurted Vere. "What are you talking about?"

"Didn't you know, Vere?" Amanander spoke as casually as if he might have been discussing the weather. "Roderic isn't our father's get. *She* is. By the witch. There isn't a drop of Ridenau blood in him. He's a pretender. And yes, Dad knows. In fact, it was by his command the misbegotten Prince was conceived. So you see, Vere, I am the rightful heir of Meriga." Without waiting to see what sort of reaction this revelation drew from Vere, Amanander snapped his fingers. Instantly a dozen dark shapes emerged from the night. "Take the King and place him in the cart just outside the gates. You'll find it in a stand of trees, hidden from view. As for my brothers and my sister, take them to the keep and place them in the room near mine. I need to keep a closer eye upon them."

Jama trembled. Amanander's gaze fell upon him.

"The Muten?" asked one of the soldiers in a dull voice.

"I'll take care of him myself." Amanander snapped his fingers once more. "Don't resist them, Vere. Let them take the King."

Vere's shoulders went rigid. He allowed one of the leather-clad soldiers to take the King from his arms, and in the flickering light of the torches, Annandale saw tears on his face. She turned to the King with a little cry and placed both hands on his skeletal arm. Instantly, a bright blue light flared in the dark night, illuminating the whole scene with a luminous, unearthly light. Strength poured through her hands, and her whole body convulsed as Abelard's body went rigid beneath her hands.

"Stop her!" commanded Amanander, and two of the guards dragged her some paces away. She struggled helplessly, sweat rolling down her face, her frame still trembling.

Some residue of the light still limned Abelard's face, and he turned to gaze at Amanander. "You—" he whispered, his voice only marginally stronger than before. "You will never reign in Ahga."

For the first time, Amanander showed some emotion. Scorn twisted his mouth. "That's an old prophecy, Lord King. It lost its meaning long ago. Soon Ahga will be mine, and all Meriga with it. And it's curious, Dad." The sarcastic edge in his tone cut like a knife. "I used to want you to live to see that day. But now—" He shrugged. "I don't care anymore. So go back to Roderic and give him whatever warning you think you can. But tell him I am coming for him. Soon."

Abelard made a sound that might have been a curse.

"Save your breath, Lord King, what's left of it. It's too late to damn me." Amanander looked from Abelard to Jama, who stood beside Alexander. His arm snaked out, and he wrapped his fist in the Muten's robe. Jama stumbled and fell, and Amanander hauled him close. With a swift upthrust, Amanander stabbed his dagger deep into Jama's chest. The boy died with a gurgle and a look of shocked surprise on his face.

Amanander let the body fall to the ground. "Now. Do we understand each other?"

Annandale pressed her fist against her mouth. It was not the first time she had seen Amanander kill in cold blood, but there seemed to be something so effortless about the killing, no hesitation whatsoever, that chilled her to the very marrow of her bones. She swallowed hard.

"Good." He spun on his heel and faded into the night, his black garments blending so easily with the shadows it was as if he had never been there. Silently the guards guided Annandale, Vere and Alexander to the steps of the keep, while the others carried the King to the gates. Jama's cooling body lay untended in the dust.

Chapter Twenty-six

❧

The dust upon the wooden floor was thick enough to leave footprints, noticed Annandale, as she was escorted into the room by one of the black-clad soldiers who served Amanander. She clasped her hands and looked around, grateful to be left alone for even the briefest span of time. Although the guard had not touched her, or made the least lewd or threatening gesture, still his presence was anathema. She had felt soiled, sticky, and generally unclean as he had escorted her down the hall to this room which looked like a private office of sorts. At least, the large desk against one wall and the rickety wooden chair which stood before it seemed to indicate that it was.

She clasped her hands and walked to the window. Dust was thick upon the pane and grime smudged the peeling paint. The smell of mildew reached her nostrils. Everywhere in this accursed fortress was decay.

She gazed outside. Despite the heat, the men-at-arms drilled, and the servants scurried back and forth across the crowded courtyard. To what purpose? she wondered. She shivered despite the stuffy air. The black-garbed figures reminded her of termites, and the entire garrison reminded her of nothing so much as a hive.

She drew a deep breath and sat gingerly in the rickety chair. Only Amanander would have had her brought here. Only Amanander would wish something of her. But what? A kind of weary resignation filled her mind. The walls of the garrison seemed so high, the outer world so remote. Jama had offered their only chance of escape, and now he was dead. What chance did any of them have?

She heard soft footsteps outside the room, and she raised her head in time to see Amanander enter, dressed in the same unrelieved black as his soldiers. He paused in the doorway, and she raised her chin, meeting his gaze with all the defiance she could muster.

"So lovely," he murmured, and his voice shivered through her and down her spine like a cold raindrop.

She swallowed hard. "What do you want of me, Amanander?"

He smiled, a travesty of a smile which stretched his lips and raised his cheekbones and did not quite reach his eyes. "I've come to offer you a chance to change your mind, my dear."

"Change my mind? What do I have to change my mind about?"

He shook his head and gave a soft laugh. "Ever the defiant one, aren't you? So small, so soft, so brave."

She dropped her eyes. "You don't scare me, Amanander."

"Oh—" he advanced further into the room and she stifled the impulse to gag "—but I do."

She twisted her fingers in the filthy fabric of her dress. He was right. His very presence terrified her, his nearness sickened her. She raised her head but could not bring herself to meet his eyes. "What do you want of me?"

"I've come to offer you a chance, my dear. To change your mind. To renounce Roderic, and to take your place at my side—"

"As your Queen?" she spat.

"No," he answered, evenly. "As my sister. Cherished. Loved. Adored." He allowed his voice to slide over the last word, and she shuddered.

"You sicken me, Amanander. I would never renounce Roderic—never. You know that."

"Then are you prepared to watch him die?"

"You'll kill him if you have the chance whether I change my mind or not. Don't imply you'll let him live."

He shrugged. "I imply no such thing, my dear. Of course Roderic has to die. But you don't have to watch."

Bile rose in her throat and she nearly gagged. "You'd make me—"

"Yes. Of course. His death wouldn't have the same sense of purposelessness, and utter defeat, if you weren't there to watch. But if you agree to renounce him—as well as your own claim to the throne—then I shall excuse you."

"You disgust me, Amanander. You make me want to vomit."

"I know." He smiled then, and this time the smile did reach the dark depths of his eyes. He walked closer and reached out one gloved hand. She forced herself to stay absolutely still as he stroked her cheek. "But you are still the loveliest creature I have ever seen in my life. And that includes your own mother."

She closed her eyes, pressing the lids shut tight against her cheeks. She thought about Roderic, about the gentle expression in his eyes when he looked at her, the loving expression he wore when he kissed her—abruptly the image shifted and Roderic's expression changed to the look of disgust he had worn on the night she had told him the truth of his parentage. She blinked and another image rose before her: little Rhodri, his small body white and still on bloodstained sheets. She gasped and jerked away from Amanander's touch. "Leave me alone!"

He chuckled softly. "As you wish, my dear." He leaned back against the edge of the desk, stretched out his long legs, and crossed his arms over his chest. "You simply don't understand what Roderic faces."

"What do you mean?" she asked in spite of herself.

"Don't you understand, my dear? I can use the Magic at will. I have discovered the key of controlling the consequences—I no longer am bound by the constraints of the threat of what might be unleashed. I can work my Magic when and where I please."

"You lie."

He raised a brow. "You are brave. Foolishly so, I think. You want a demonstration?"

She swallowed hard and bit her lip. "I don't believe you. You're only trying to make me give up hope, give up believing that there is any escape, any way out. I know Roderic is coming—"

"Yes," he said, so softly she had to strain to hear him. "Of course he's coming. But can he save you this time? That's the question, isn't it?" Before she could speak, he raised his hand and snapped his fingers. She looked from him to the door questioningly. "Just wait, my dear. You'll see."

She eyed him suspiciously. From the corridor came the clump of heavy footsteps. The door swung open and two men-at-arms dragged a white-wrapped body into the center of the room. Amanander snapped his fingers once more, and the guards left.

He smiled at Annandale almost pityingly. "Now. Watch." He closed his eyes. A second might have passed, or maybe a minute or two, and something snaked through the room, slithering and coiling around Annandale. She startled in alarm. The hair on her arms rose, and gooseflesh prickled her skin. Deep within her being, the healing impulse flared, a surge that took her breath away. What Magic was this?

She stared at Amanander, gripping the splintered arms of the chair, and felt as though from a distance the sharp wood dig into her palms. The shape on the floor at their feet quivered.

She looked down to see a pale hand reach out, the nails blue, the flesh mottled. The hand tore at the covering, and Jama-taw sat up, his eyes dull and unfocused. The reek of the grave was on him, and she pressed the back of one bleeding hand to her mouth. "The One save us," she whispered.

Amanander snorted. "The One save you, indeed, my dear. Now do you see? How can you expect Roderic to save you when he won't be able to save himself?"

The sound of his soft chuckle lingered in her ears long into the night.

Chapter Twenty-seven

❦

"*T*his way." The servant's clipped tones made clear in no uncertain terms exactly what he thought of the Islanders. Deirdre slung her travel-stained plaid over one shoulder and pushed her sword further behind her hip. Her dagger slapped against her thigh with each step. Her boots clicked against the polished tiles of Owen Mortmain's castle. She stared around her curiously and wondered what Prince the keep of Lost Vegas was had been built for. Unlike most of the structures which pre-dated the Armageddon, it was clear to her that whoever had ordered the construction of this place had had in mind a palace.

Two sets of broad staircases swept gracefully from the central hall beneath huge windows which still, despite the passing of centuries and the ravages of time, opened to the cloudless blue of the Vada sky. The hall itself was cavernous, enormous, the central floor some feet below the ground, so that one had to step down almost half a flight of steps in order to reach the great feasting hall. Traces of former magnificence were evident in the crystal lights which hung from the ceilings, thousands of beeswax candles set into the arms.

Deirdre looked back over her shoulder at her men, huddled in a tired and weary-looking little band around a long table, hungrily gnawing on the first cooked meal they had had in weeks. After they had seen the first set of crucifixes, they had become even warier and decided fire was something that was likely to call attention to themselves, and something they could all live without.

From across the long space, she caught Donner's eye. He grinned as he raised a knife laden with meat to his lips. Something in her quivered in response. It had been so long since she'd taken a man. She thought of Donner once more, the hard muscles of his arms, his merry grin, his eyes which seemed to dance, even under danger. She could do much worse. Why not? she thought. Roderic was so far away. Instantly she bit her lip as the servant indicated a long corridor at the top of the steps which led down to another staircase, this one smaller but nearly as ornate. Why did she automatically think of Roderic every time she thought of bedding anyone?

She suppressed a sigh as the servant led her to a door on the floor above. The evidence of the Armageddon was clearer here, the walls showed signs of patching, of repairs. She looked up at the roof. Even a child knew the stories of the fearsome ravages the Armageddon had brought to the lands west of the Saranevas. The wrath of the One, the priests of the Church all said. The Island Keepers, who in general espoused a much more gentle and forgiving goddess, were hard put to understand the ways of their deity.

There was no discernible response to the servant's knock, but the door swung open on well-oiled hinges, and the servant stepped to one side, allowing Deirdre to enter the room ahead of him.

"Lord Senador." The servant bowed. "Deirdre M'Callaster of the Settle Islands."

She stepped past the servant and into the room, where the light momentarily blinded her. As her eyes adjusted to the brilliant sunlight which streamed unimpeded through a sheer wall of glass, she gradually focused on a short, dark figure seated beside the window.

"Deirdre M'Callaster?" whispered the voice from the figure by the window. "Old Cormall's daughter?"

"Aye, Lord." She crossed the space across the room in several long strides and swept a low bow. Something stuck in her craw about bowing to this man—any man— but one didn't come begging for troops and not show respect.

"Cormall's daughter?" The voice rose in disbelief. "You don't even look like a woman."

She raised her eyes and met the faded hazel stare of Owen Mortmain. So this, she thought, is what it looks like to be broken.

His face was lined, his hair white, although a good lot of it still clung to his scalp. He wore it clipped close about his ears, in a soldier's fashion. There was nothing of the dandy about Mortmain. His body was soft, gone to fat long ago, the body of a man forced by infirmity or age to surrender an active life. But it was his eyes, more than anything else, in which Deirdre read defeat. There was no light in them, no sparkle, no grace. He simply looked her up and down with the dumb mute gaze of a beast.

"Not just Cormall's daughter," she said, wondering how to broach the subject. Now that she stood in his presence, she wondered if Mortmain had the spirit to order anyone to do anything. "His heir."

"You?" Mortmain's voice rose sharply. "You are the M'Callaster in his place?"

"Aye." She nodded gruffly. "Chief of all the Chiefs of the Settle Islands."

He ran his eyes over her frame, measuring and assessing, and Deirdre was half surprised. She hadn't thought the man had it in him to care.

To her further surprise, he looked past her to the servant, who still hovered in the doorway. "Wine, Jem, if you please. And something to eat. Our guest has traveled a long way."

She fancied she could hear the servant's muttered comments despite the audible assent. The door closed softly and Mortmain folded his hands loosely on his chest.

"Come, sit." He turned to look back out the window. "See this, lady? It pleases me greatly to watch the tending of my orchards."

With a wave of his hand he indicated the scene beneath the window, and Deirdre, leaning over from the chair he offered her, saw the servants in the fruit trees, with baskets and shears and other implements. They moved slowly, deliberately, as though each knew exactly what it was that needed doing, and each was wholly devoted to the task of seeing it done. "'Tis a pretty sight, Lord Senador."

He shot her a quick look from under silvery brows.

"Very pretty. But I don't fancy you rode all the way from the Settle Islands to Vada to look at fruit trees. Why have you come?"

"I didn't come from the Islands. I've ridden from Ithan Ford—"

"Tennessy? What are you doing there?"

"The country's at war, Lord Senador. Roderic's gone to Tennessy to consolidate a position there—"

Mortmain waved a hand. "There is something very comforting about growing old, my dear. One finds one need no longer concern oneself with petty quarrels."

"'Tis much more than a petty quarrel. The lesser lords of the Southern estates have risen against the throne; the Mutens rebel in the mountains. The Harleyriders move across Arkan. Oh, no, Lord Senador, 'tis so much more than just a petty quarrel."

Mortmain shrugged. "For an old man like me, that is indeed all it is. The length of Meriga is between me and the Pulatchian Mountains. If the Harleys come, let them come. I will be dead soon, anyway."

Deirdre narrowed her eyes. "You surprise me, Lord Senador. You aren't the man I thought you'd be."

"Oh?" His gaze was fixed on the scene outside the window. "And what sort of man was that?"

"The Settle Islands is far from Vada, but even when I was a girl, the Keepers told the tales of your exploits, how you rose against the power of the Ridenau Kings and sought to make a place for yourself independent of the central power." He shot her a surprised look. "That surprises you, does it? Do you think we Islanders care any more for the Ridenau Kings than you do?"

Mortmain narrowed his eyes. "But you fight for them—old Cormall fought for them—"

"Aye." Deirdre waved her hand in the same dismissive gesture Mortmain had used. "Of course. 'Tis a way to balance the power in the North. But we heard of you—I heard of you, even as a child. And the stories that are told are grand."

Mortmain snorted softly. "Grand." He shook his head. "Grand in defeat, I suppose." He glanced out the window and then back at Deirdre. "So now you have seen the fallen idol. You still haven't told me why you have come."

"I come on Roderic's behalf." She wet her lips and cursed herself for sudden cowardice. There was a presence about this little man, defeated though he might be, or was it simply the tales of the Keepers reverberating through her childhood memories, ghostly voices rising from the firesides, telling the tales of warriors, ancient and new?

Mortmain shook his head. "His sheriffs take all they please."

Deirdre wet her lips and began again. "'Tis not supplies I come to beg you for. 'Tis men."

"Men?" Mortmain's disbelief was plain. "I would not ask my men to fight for the Ridenau cause—"

"Lord Senador, the country verges on chaos. Roderic has done all he can—is doing all he can—but the lines are stretched to the limit and beyond. I saw the Harleys ride across the plains on my way here—greater doings are afoot than any of us knew or realized. They have taken to crucifying their own women—please, Lord Senador, you must understand me."

"I do understand you, child," Mortmain said gently, staring at her impassioned face with something like pity. "But I swore long ago never to ride to the defense of the Ridenau, and I will not risk my men's lives to do what I will not. Abelard has his pound of flesh. But he'll not have one drop of Vada blood."

"Abelard is gone." Deirdre resisted the urge to leap to her feet. "'Tis not Abelard you aid. 'Tis your grandson— the son of your daughter. Will you turn your back on him?"

The arrow hit home. Mortmain dropped his eyes. "I know whose grandson he is—" Abruptly she saw his mouth work and he brushed a hand over his eyes. "Why do you come to me now?"

"Because Roderic needs your help. Because no one else would dare. And because Roderic is not Abelard's son at all."

"What?" Mortmain whispered.

"You heard me, Lord Senador. I don't know who's son he is—but he discovered the truth just before I left. He is the Queen's son—of that there is no doubt. But someone else fathered him—someone else with Abelard's blessing."

"Explain this." Mortmain's gaze fastened on her face and Deirdre felt the full force of his faded will. For the first time she could nearly believe this man was capable of a rebellion against the throne.

With halting words, she told the story as Roderic had told her, and when she was finished, she looked carefully at the old man. He was no longer staring at her. He was watching the gardeners among the fruit trees. A bee buzzed and butted against the windowpane. Mortmain wet his lips. "Phineas," he murmured.

"I beg your pardon, sir?"

"Is Phineas still alive?"

"The King's chief councilor? Lord Phineas? Aye— very old and sick, but still alive. He is Roderic's main advisor."

Mortmain nodded. "I knew him, you see—long ago." He squared his shoulders and looked Deirdre full in the face. "You tell a fairly unbelievable tale."

"Aye." There was no point denying it.

"And on the strength of this tale, you expect me to send regiments of troops with you? Back to Ithan?"

Deirdre nodded. "Aye. I do."

"You honor more than your oath, Lord Senador." It was Mortmain's turn to strike a sore spot.

Deirdre gritted her teeth. "Aye." She nodded. "I do."

"Tell me how you came to be the M'Callaster—how you came to rule in your father's stead. I never heard that the Settle Islanders ever accepted the rule of a woman."

"They don't, as a general rule." Deirdre grinned in spite of herself. "But when the woman beats every man who challenges her, they have no choice. Even their heads aren't quite that thick."

Mortmain laughed softly. "Go on."

Deirdre clasped her hands over her knee and launched into the tale, her voice falling into the cadence of the Keepers, who told the stories of her people. Mortmain nodded, his eyes never leaving her face as she spoke, and when the tale was finished, he nodded.

"I see."

"What do you see, Lord Senador?" Deirdre tried not to bristle.

"More than you might believe." He got to his feet, and Deirdre was struck by how short Mortmain was. Sitting, he had the appearance of a man much taller. "Let me send you off to rest, M'Callaster. I will think on this and give you my answer within a day."

Deirdre recognized the dismissal and rose to her feet, adjusting her plaid. "Time grows short, Lord Mortmain."

Owen nodded. "I understand. Your faith serves Roderic well. I hope he knows just how well."

Deirdre grinned. "He will, Lord Mortmain. Believe me, he will."

Chapter Twenty-eight

❧

The reserves from Ahga arrived in record time, their march aided in some part by the unseasonably cool weather. "A man can go further when he's not burdened by the sun, Lord Prince," cheerfully explained one of the sergeant's of the regiments as Roderic strode up and down the lines, inspecting the new arrivals.

Roderic forced himself to return the man's grin. It wouldn't do to let these new arrivals see the toll the stress and strain of the last weeks had taken upon him. Every day that went by without word of Deirdre, every hour which passed without any sign of Vere or word of Annandale, only made the burden heavier. He exchanged a few more pleasantries with the rest of the men, but his eyes automatically scanned the road leading up to the opened gates every few minutes. It had rapidly become a habit with him every time he found himself out in the inner ward.

He was conferring with the captains of the regiments when he noticed it. A cart was coming up from the main road, drawn by two horses which stumbled and seemed to stagger, driven by a figure wrapped in a shapeless gray cloak. He realized, as he squinted his eyes against the

sun, that it was the same color as the Muten camouflage
Vere usually wore. He broke off in midsentence and
stared.

The captains followed his gaze.

"Looks like a farmer, Lord Prince?" asked one, glancing back at Roderic's face curiously.

Roderic narrowed his eyes and took a few steps closer to the gate. "No," he murmured, half to himself,
"that's no farmer's wagon, that's a military supply
wagon—see the broad base? The cover's off, but—" He
peered over the men. Was that a bloodstain on the front
of the driver's cloak? "Excuse me, will you, gentlemen?"

Foreboding descended as he walked toward the gates.
The driver had a hood pulled down over his face, but
there was no doubt that the cloak he wore was of Muten
weave. A sunbeam struck the clasp at his shoulder and
glinted off it, and Roderic's heart leapt in his chest. It was
Vere. It had to be Vere. He broke into a trot, calling to a
guard at the gates, and ran down to meet the wagon. A
few yards away, he stopped.

The reins hung loosely in the driver's hands, so loosely it was clear to Roderic that the figure in the wagon did
not control the horses. The horses themselves wheezed
up the rise, their massive ribs showing through dry,
unhealthy coats. A chill went up and down his spine. The
guard halted by his side, and his hand automatically fingered his spear. "Careful, Lord Prince—that might be a
trap."

Roderic nodded, watching the horses stagger up the
slight incline. A few paces from where they stood, one of
the animals fell to its knees. The entire wagon shuddered

and the driver fell sideways, tumbling off the seat to lie in the road. The guard put a restraining hand on Roderic's arm. "Allow me, Lord Prince."

Cautiously, the man approached the still figure. A few people had gathered to watch the unusual progress of the strange cart, and now they crept closer, whispering warily to themselves. Roderic edged closer to the dying animal. The guard nudged the still driver with the butt of his spear gently. There was no reaction at all from the form. Gently, the guard edged the hood back off the face, and gasped.

Roderic craned his head. The Muten was dead, his face blotted and pale. He walked to stand beside the guard. Despite the wave of disgust and pity he felt, his primary emotion was one of relief. The unfortunate driver had clearly been a Muten. "By the One," he muttered. From the state of decomposition, it appeared that it had been dead for at least a week. Flies buzzed and crawled from the neck of the corpse's garment. The guard eased the body over on its back, and Roderic saw that death had most likely been caused by whatever had made the wound in the Muten's chest.

"Burn this thing," he said. "And do what must be done for the animals." He swiped his hair off his face.

"Lord Prince," asked the guard, as he leaned upon his spear, his eyes scanning the horizon, "how do you suppose a Muten got one of our wagons? Or why was he on his way here?"

Roderic shrugged. "Not likely he was on his way here. The One knows we've lost enough wagons in these mountains, and probably the horses drew it here after this wretch was killed—" A low moan from the cart interrupted him.

He turned slowly and peered into the cart. The world seemed to spin and tilt, and he grasped at the rough wooden sides with shaking hands. On a bed of straw, a long figure lay beneath a moth-eaten purple cloak. The hair and beard were long and filthy and lay in matted locks over his chest and shoulders. But there was no denying the jutting nose, the high cheekbones, now as stark as a skull's in the sunken face. Roderic whispered, "Dad."

Unbelievably, the red-rimmed eyes opened, blinked, and focused. "Roderic?" The King's voice was a harsh, hoarse rasp. "My son?"

Roderic jerked his face toward the keep. "Summon the physicians," he cried. "Guards—bring a litter—now! The King's returned!"

Galvanized by Roderic's words, the soldiers sprang into action. He gazed down at his father's face. "You'll be all right, Dad. We'll get you cleaned up, fed, don't worry—" He raised his head to see guards running down the path, removing the bridles from the two dying animals, ready to pull the cart themselves into the inner ward. Roderic stood back, watching as they dragged the wagon up the hill.

On the steps of the keep, Tavia stood waiting. "Roderic!" she cried, when she saw him coming behind the cart. "Is it true?"

He nodded. "Get the physicians. He must be seen to at once."

As the wagon was brought to a halt beside the steps,

Tavia gathered her skirts and gazed down at her father. "Dad," she whispered.

His blue eyes fluttered open and closed.

"He's very weak," said Roderic.

"Let's get him inside," Tavia said.

Roderic reached into the wagon and gathered Abelard in his arms. He cringed when he felt how light the King was, not much more than skin and bones, not much heavier than Melisande. He carried the King into the hall, where a crowd of servants and retainers were fluttering at the entrances. Gently Roderic laid him on a low, fur-covered bench beside one of the hearths. A gray-bearded physician stepped forward. He touched Roderic's shoulder.

"Can you do something for him?" Roderic asked. Out of the corner of his eye, he saw Norah bustle into the hall, followed by Phineas on his litter.

"I can try, Lord Prince."

Roderic stepped back. The physician touched the King's cheek with the back of one hand, felt at his throat for a pulse. He raised troubled eyes to Roderic. "He should be taken to a room where I can examine him properly, Lord Prince."

Lady Norah pressed through the crowd, two burly menservants at her heels. "Come, I have a room prepared." She snapped her fingers and the servants moved to lift the King. Roderic stopped them with a glance.

"I'll take him," he said. Once more he gathered the King in his arms and carried him out of the hall. He passed Phineas on his litter. "Wait in the council room for me, Phineas," he said as he went past. He thought he saw a shadow of a reaction cross Abelard's face at the mention of Phineas' name.

In the cool, white bedroom, he placed Abelard on the clean linen sheets and slowly straightened. "Everything—" He felt his throat thicken with emotion. No matter what this man was, he was the man Roderic had always thought of as a father, the man who had always treated Roderic as a son. "Everything will be fine, Dad."

The King stirred and his swollen tongue touched his cracked and leathery lips. He groaned.

"It will be all right, Dad."

The physician touched his arm. "If I may have a few moments alone with the King, Lord Prince?"

Grimly, Roderic nodded. "I'll be in the council room with Phineas." He nodded at Tavia and Norah, who stood in the doorway, and pushed through the servants crowding the corridor.

On the threshold of the council room, he paused. Phineas lay beside the window, his face turned to the light as though he could see the view. Phineas turned his head.

"Phineas?"

"Roderic, how is the King?"

Roderic shook his head and sighed. "Very weak, to say the least. He's—he's so thin, Phineas. It feels as though he doesn't weigh more than Melisande."

"You understand it is all still up to you?"

"Yes. I know."

Phineas drew a deep breath. "I suppose we have to ask ourselves the larger question."

"What do you mean?"

"What this means—where he's been—why he's come back now. All those answers may have some bearing on the war."

"I suppose we'll have to hope he recovers enough to tell us."

Phineas shook his head. "Roderic—Abelard won't recover."

"Why do you say that?" Roderic stared at the old man.

"Since I've been blind, my other senses have grown more acute—including my sense of smell. I could smell death as Abelard went by me. He will be dead soon, I know it."

"No." Roderic sank into a chair. That wasn't possible. Abelard had returned. Surely he would recover at least something of his old strength, the Congress would rally around him, and surely Amanander would be beaten once and forever. And then Annandale would come back and they would live with Rhodri—

"What happens next, then?"

"After Abelard dies, you mean?" Phineas shifted uncomfortably on his litter. "There must be a Convening of the Congress. Abelard's will will be read—the same as when you were acclaimed Regent. And the Congress will vote whether to accept you as King. It will be very much like before, Roderic."

"That's not what I meant." Roderic plucked at the frayed fabric of his sleeve. "I meant what happens when it is brought before the Congress that I am not his son."

"What makes you think that's going to happen?"

"What if it does?"

"Roderic." The old man's voice was firm. "Much of

this—all of this—depends upon you. If you stop believing that you are the rightful heir of Meriga, and someday the rightful King, then we have already lost."

"But, by what right, Phineas? Not by blood—"

"Think you blood is the only way to earn something, Roderic? If you do, I am sorely disappointed in you."

"Roderic?" Tavia's voice from the doorway shattered his concentration.

"Yes?" Roderic looked up, almost glad for the interruption.

"Dad's asking for you. You better come now." Something in the low urgency of her tone made him bolt out of the chair.

"I'll be waiting," said Phineas softly.

He followed his sister down the corridor, back to the room in which the King lay, and he saw at once from the look on the physician's face, from the tears on Norah's cheeks, that Phineas had spoken the truth. He pushed past them all and went at once to Abelard's side.

The papery lids fluttered and the King drew a deep gasping breath. "Leave us," he breathed.

With a wave of his hand, Roderic dismissed them all, and when they were alone, he turned back to the King. "Dad—"

"Listen," the King gasped. "Annan—your wife—Aman has her. Mutens betrayed—" He seemed to choke on the air. "Aman had me all this time—I was sent back to show you what he can do—his power is great. Yours must be greater."

Roderic stared down at the dying man. "What can I do?"

"He survives on—" Abelard choked. "On fear. Fear

him not, my son—be strong—" A skeletal claw plucked at the white blanket which covered his withered frame.

"It hasn't been easy, Dad."

"No," rasped the King, as his laboring chest heaved with the effort to speak. "Faith shall finish what hope begins—never forget." Abelard's bloodshot eyes slid shut.

Roderic took a deep breath. There was so much he wanted to say to the King, so much he wanted to ask. Suddenly he felt defeated. Abelard had returned only to die. In the filtered afternoon light, he saw the ruined frame of the man Abelard had been, the great arms and chest now sunken and withered, the long legs which had walked so firmly through the halls of Ahga now little more than bone. Roderic touched his cheek. "Good-bye, Dad," he whispered.

The blue eyes opened once more, and in the watery depths, Roderic read a father's love and pride. "Have faith—" His voice trailed off into labored breathing.

Roderic closed his eyes against the tears. He pressed a kiss against the King's forehead and went to call for Tavia. Abelard would not recover. Except for Phineas, he truly was alone.

Chapter Twenty-nine

"*D*ead?" The word slipped from his lips as Roderic stared uncomprehending at the man who knelt before him. His uniform, or what was left of it, was tattered and torn. A wound had opened in his back and blood spread in a slow stain, darkening the already blood-stained fabric. The messenger raised tortured eyes to Roderic.

"Yes, Lord Prince. I saw it with these eyes." A tear slipped down his weathered cheek.

Roderic turned away and raised his eyes as Tavia rushed into the hall. "Roderic! What word?"

"He's dead," Roderic said, scarcely believing the words as he said them. "Brand. Brand is dead."

"Dead?" Tavia pressed her fist to her mouth. "How?"

The soldier rose awkwardly to his feet. "In Dlas, lady. They were waiting for us. I have never seen their like before and I have served twenty years in this army. They fell upon us like locusts, Lord Prince. We had no chance at all."

"And you—only you—escaped?"

"There were a few of us, Lord Prince. But the others died on the way back."

"Go—eat, rest. You've earned it, soldier." Roderic met Tavia's troubled eyes.

"What will you do, Roderic?" Tavia asked.

Roderic shook his head. "Talk to Phineas. What else can I do?"

With a heavy heart and a slow step, Roderic walked down the corridor to Phineas' chambers. The servant who opened the door raised his eyebrow as he saw Roderic's expression, but knew better than to dare question him. "Lord Phineas is resting, Lord Prince." With a quick gesture, he indicated the inner room.

Without a word, Roderic walked into Phineas' bedroom and paused. The old man lay on the bed, beneath a white sheet, his hands loosely clasped on his chest. His chest moved so faintly Roderic feared he might be dead. Then Phineas shifted. "Phineas," Roderic said gently. "Phineas. We must talk."

The old man turned his head at once in the direction of Roderic's voice. "What's happened?"

Momentarily Roderic marveled at the speed with which the old man awoke, and then he remembered that Phineas, too, was once a soldier. "It's Brand. He's dead. His whole force slaughtered with him. Only one survivor made it back."

The color drained from Phineas' face. "Brand dead?" he whispered.

"Yes."

"By the One."

"What are we to do, Phineas?"

"Come, Roderic." Phineas spread his hands and indicated the chair beside his bed. "Come and sit."

"This—this— Phineas," Roderic said as he moved to take the place the old man motioned to, "I can't replace those troops. Shall I call the men in Atland to fall back? If Amanander launches another such attack on Atland, there is no hope. They are in danger of being completely cut off—I need the men here—"

"Roderic." Phineas spoke softly but sharply. "This is a great blow. We can summon troops from Arkan. The Harleyriders have not invaded as Gredahl feared. There are troops in reserve at all the outpost garrisons. If messengers go out today, we can field an army within—"

"Within two months if we are lucky, Phineas. You know as well as I that to send word—"

"Yes, it will take time, but what is the alternative? I warned Brand not to go rushing off into Dlas until we had a better idea of what we faced—" Phineas broke off and choked, swallowing hard. "Garrick used to say there always was too much of the puppy about Brand."

Roderic turned away in the face of the old man's grief. Garrick. There was another name lost in the cause of Amanander. He thought of the words of the dying King. Have faith. Never give up hope. He got to his feet and paced to the window. "How many more must we lose, Phineas?"

"Eh?" the old man asked.

"Is this what the King envisioned, Phineas? Is this really what he had in mind? Oh, I know it's wrong to speak ill of him, but answer me honestly—how many more must we lose? Brand and Jaboa, Barran, Garrick, Peregrine—look how many we've lost. Why in the name of the One, Phineas, did he have to be so single-minded? Is a united Meriga really worth the cost?"

"You tell me, Roderic."

Roderic ran his fingers through his hair. "I can't answer that, Phineas. I used to think we fought for something greater than ourselves. I used to think that I could make a difference. And now—so many dead who shouldn't have died. I wonder if in the end I'll only question what it was all for."

"Listen to me, Roderic. I know things look bleak right now. I know you are imagining that nothing could possibly be much worse. But let's assess the situation. Amanander seems to move his men in concert. They can't make individual decisions. The leaders—if indeed they are leaders at all—can only do as Amanander directs. Well. What general can be everywhere on the field at once? Don't you rely on your officers to make split decisions for you?"

"Well, yes, but—"

"Roderic, think. What has Amanander truly accomplished? Other than to seriously demoralize you?"

"Brand's dead. Barran is dead. At least five thousand men are dead. Dlas is lost. My troops in Atland are in danger of being cut off."

"Roderic, we've been here at Ithan for nearly four months. In all that time, has Amanander attacked?"

Roderic paused. "Other than Dlas? No . . . no, he hasn't."

Phineas drew a deep breath. "Think about this. If we summon all the reserves held at the garrisons in Arkan, we can easily field as many men as Amanander. Now. If

Kye and our men attack—not as one body, but as bits and pieces, gnawing away at the edges—there is a chance, I believe, a slight chance, to turn Amanander's own strength to our advantage. We must use the element of surprise, the unexpected."

Roderic shook his head. "I understand, Phineas. But there are only so many men. Didn't you hear the reports? The dead rise and fight for Amanander."

"Roderic." Phineas's voice was gentle. "Would you entrust a battle to dead men?"

Roderic turned to stare at Phineas. The question was so ludicrous as to be unanswerable. As he drew a breath to try to answer, the door to the outer room was flung wide, and Phineas' bodyservant burst into the room. "Lord Phineas, your pardon—but, Lord Prince, you must come at once."

"What's wrong now?" Roderic was across the room in three strides.

"An army, Lord Prince. Coming this way. The people are panicking. Please—"

He didn't wait to hear the rest. In the hall he found Miles giving orders to the captains of the regiments. "Get those civilians inside the walls as quickly as possible and then raise the drawbridge—" Miles broke off in midsentence as Roderic grasped his arm. "Roderic, it looks as though he's made his final move."

Roderic nodded. "How many?"

Miles shook his head. "The road is black with them— the line stretches on for miles. You can't see the road for the foot soldiers and the horsemen."

"Damn." Roderic turned away with a curse. "I'm

going up to the top of the tower. I want to see this for myself."

Miles nodded. "As you say, Lord Prince—do you understand the orders, Captain?"

The captain saluted, and together Miles and Roderic climbed the steps of the tower two and three at a time. They burst out onto the windy height, and Roderic glanced around, seeking his bearings. "Over here." Miles gripped his arm and pointed west.

Roderic leaned over the battlement. In the distance, still some miles away, an army was indeed advancing. The line of men stretched as far as he could see, toward the horizon, and ahead rode at least two hundred horsemen. They carried standards, and he could just make out the colors snapping in the breeze.

He bit his lip. "Damn, Miles, what would you estimate?"

Miles shook his head. "Ten—fifteen thousand, maybe? Look at that cloud of dust—there're more horsemen behind the first ranks of foot."

Roderic swore, a coarse soldier's oath he had often heard Brand use. Well, so be it, he thought. If this was to be the last stand, so be it. "How are we provisioned?" he asked.

Miles shrugged. "Fairly well. Lots of mouths to feed, though—we'll have to see what kind of an assault they plan and ration as we must."

"Yes . . ." Roderic let his voice trail off. He squinted down at the approaching horsemen. The standards dipped and swirled in the afternoon light, and as he watched, one of them put his spurs to his stallion and galloped on ahead of the rest. "Miles," he began. "Those aren't Harland's colors—see there?"

Miles followed Roderic's gaze. "Hmmm. Not any I recognize, either—must be one of the lesser lords."

But Roderic stared over the battlements, not hearing the recitation of the possibilities. The rider who galloped on ahead wore plaid: brown and rusty red on a background so dirty it appeared gray. "By the One," he muttered in disbelief. "By the One."

Miles turned to him. "What is it, Roderic?"

"Look—down there. That's Deirdre. The M'Callaster. And she's brought an army with her." He turned to Miles with blazing eyes. "Open the gates. Let her in. Do it, now."

Without protest, Miles took off down the steps. Roderic paused just another moment more. The horsemen behind her rode easily, weapons sheathed; the foot soldiers marched in orderly formation, pikes and long bows slung over their shoulders. As they crested the rise in the road, Roderic could see the heavy supply wagons lurching along behind.

Deirdre's braids fell free and her plaid swirled out behind her as the horse gained the tent city around Ithan. "By the One," Roderic whispered once more. He took off down the steps and reached the courtyard in time to see the heavy gates swing open. The crowd looked at him expectantly. He ignored everyone but the woman who guided her black stallion through the gates, her cheeks pink, a ready grin on her face. Through the gates, he could see the standards of the army snap in the breeze, and a few horsemen trotted in behind Deirdre.

She rode up to the steps of the keep and swung out of her saddle. He stared at her, almost unable to believe that after all these months she had returned. "Deirdre," he said, so softly he doubted she could hear.

She walked up the steps and went down on one knee. "Lord Prince," she said, her eyes dancing in her solemn face. "The Senator of the Vada Valley sends his regrets that he cannot join you personally, and hopes these troops will aid his grandson's cause."

Roderic suppressed an urge to let his jaw drop in shock. He looked up as Deirdre's companions walked up behind her and knelt on one knee before him. "Lord Prince," said the first, "we come to pledge allegiance."

"Will you not bid us welcome, Lord Prince?" Deirdre rose to her feet, her mouth curving in the grin she could no longer suppress.

"Be welcome—" He turned to Miles. "Miles—"

"Come, come, welcome to Ithan Ford." Miles stepped forward on cue, beckoning to the captain of his guard as he did.

Roderic looked at Deirdre. "And you, M'Callaster—"

"Aye?"

"You have some explaining to do, I think."

She winked and tossed her braids over her shoulder. "Say but the word, Lord Prince. I stand at your disposal and wait upon your grace."

It was then the crowd began to cheer.

Chapter Thirty

On a gray and cheerless dawn, Roderic led the combined armies of the Estates of Meriga down the ancient highway leading out of Ithan. Deirdre and Miles, as well as Chiavett Khan, rode by his side, the standards of Arkan and Kora-lado, of Vada and Tennessy and the Settle Islands snapping proudly in the early morning breeze. The people who lined the roads were silent, grim, as though they knew that this, no matter the outcome, would be the final battle.

If he had thought the country desolate on his first march to Atland, which seemed so long ago, it was because he had had nothing to compare it with then. Now, the land south of Ithan lay like a spent beast, gasping its last. The villages they passed were deserted, the people fled north into the Tennessy Fall and beyond. No sign of human occupation except those abandoned dwellings greeted them on the long march.

Ten days out of Ithan, they made camp beside the Misspy Gorge where it opened out into the Missiluse lowlands. In the low-lying valleys, white bones lay in heaps, stripped clean of flesh by carrion animals. At least, thought Roderic, he hoped it was by carrion animals.

He found Deirdre staring south on a rocky ledge over-looking the gorge. "Can't you feel it, Roderic?" She spoke without looking at him. "There's a sickness, a rot upon the land. It turns my stomach." She spat, as though to clear a bad taste from her mouth. "Faugh."

"It seems the closer we come to Amanander the worse things look."

Deirdre turned and looked at him with faraway eyes. "He knows we're coming."

"Good," Roderic said grimly. "I hope he trembles." Before Roderic could say more, a sergeant ran up from the ranks.

"Lord Prince!" He paused to catch his breath. "From the West, there is a host approaching—at least a thousand horse, three thousand foot."

Roderic frowned. "Who—Harleyriders? Amanander's men?"

"No, Lord Prince, it cannot be. They carry a standard of a noble house—and the heralds say it is one of the Western lords."

Intrigued, Roderic hastened to the periphery of the camp, Deirdre at his heels. "Do you recognize those col-ors, Deirdre?"

"Aye," she murmured, her voice breathy with disbe-lief. "'Tis Ragonn's colors reversed. 'Tis his heir that comes."

As they watched, two figures detached from the main body of the oncoming cavalry and galloped towards them. One carried a long staff from which blew a bright green-and-yellow standard, and beneath it, a white flag of truce.

About a hundred yards away, the rider lowered his standard, and both horses slowed to a walk.

"We come in peace." The rider without the standard held up one hand, to show he was unarmed. He reined his stallion twenty paces away. "I seek Roderic Ridenau, Prince of Meriga. Can you take me to him?"

Roderic bowed briefly. "You've brought yourselves. I'm Roderic."

He spurred his horse closer. He was young, as young as Roderic, and his hair was black, his eyes dark brown in a sun-browned face. "Then I greet you, Roderic Ridenau. I am Evan Lewis, heir to the Senador of Ragonn." He slid out of his saddle. "Old Owen sent word to my father of your need, and I have come to pledge my allegiance. I bring you a thousand horse, thirty-five hundred foot."

Roderic glanced at Deirdre, too stunned for speech. Deirdre looked at least as surprised. "Lewis of Ragonn?"

He nodded, a grin creasing his face. "Will you accept my pledge?"

Roderic hesitated. The other Senadors had sworn the pledge to the King and were bound to his heir only through him. If Roderic accepted Evan's pledge, was it not tantamount to claiming the throne before he was confirmed? Should not the Congress decide who had the better right to rule after the war was ended? He remembered his last conversation with Phineas.

Young Lewis frowned, not understanding Roderic's reluctance. Roderic glanced once more at Deirdre, who shrugged and raised one eyebrow. Roderic felt like an impostor as he slowly extended his hand. "Will you witness, M'Callaster?"

"Aye." She nodded and adjusted her plaid.

Lewis bowed in her direction, then fell to one knee before Roderic. Roderic placed his left hand on Lewis' shoulder and took both of Lewis' hands in his right. "Do you know the words?"

He nodded eagerly. "I have practiced them across the length of Meriga." He took a deep breath. "I pledge allegiance to the Prince of the United Estates of Meriga, and to the kingdom for which he stands, one nation, indivisible, and upon my honor, I forever swear to do whatever he might require, to uphold my Prince and his kingdom, even unto my death."

Roderic raised Lewis to his feet and, as Abelard had done, touched Lewis' lips with his own. "In the presence of these witnesses, Lord Lewis of Ragonn, I accept your pledge, and seal the bond between us with this kiss." Roderic drew a deep breath. "Tell your men to camp here, next to ours. Come and meet Miles of the Tennessy Fall."

As they sat around the campfire in the evening, they heard shouts go up at the periphery of the camp, and even before Roderic could send a guard to find out what had happened, one of the sentries appeared, supporting an exhausted-looking man. "Lord Prince, forgive me—"

"What is it?"

"Messenger, sir. From Ithan."

"Yes? What news?" One look at the man's face told Roderic what he was going to say before he spoke the words.

* * *

Tears ran down the messenger's hardened face. "The King, Lord Prince. King Abelard is dead."

An immediate hush fell over the entire group as Roderic slowly rose to his feet. "When?"

"Two days, ago. Your lady sister said to tell you he didn't suffer at the end—just slipped away."

Roderic nodded automatically. "Thank you, soldier. Captain, see to this man's needs."

He did not wait for the salute. There was a hollow feeling in his chest, as though there were only empty space where his heart had beat a moment ago. He was surprised his knees did not shake. With measured steps, Roderic walked like one blinded beyond the perimeter of the camp. He threw back his cloak, said his name, and the sentry let him pass.

On a slight rise, he paused. The dark sky was silent, the stars stared back at him, and if they guarded some portent, they shared it not. Was Abelard among them, now? he wondered. The puny, flickering watch fires could not penetrate the darkness of that void. He stared south: blacker land under black sky. He raised his fist and the muscles of his arms and chest flexed, and he relished the weight of the King's sword across his shoulders. "Amanander!" He bellowed the challenge into the desolation. "I'm coming!" The bloodrage burned hot and bright, and he shook his fist to the impassive heavens.

"By what right?" The unbidden answer was a sibilant whisper in his mind. "By what right, Prince Roderic?" A mocking emphasis on the title made him stagger. The words faded away until it would have been easy to pretend he heard them not at all.

* * *

When they crossed into Missiluse, the horrors began. First there were the crosses. In scattered clumps, they rose across the landscape like parodies of trees, bearing their hideous fruit. Many of the corpses had been stripped of flesh, so that only skeletons remained pinioned to their branches, or in piles of desiccated bone around the bases. Carrion birds flocked the skies and the buzz of insects was a constant hum.

Vapor steamed through deep cracks in the ground, and here and there boiling springs of sulfurous water spouted without warning. But nothing challenged the passing of the great army as they moved with ponderous pacing.

Their passage was often blocked by the rubble of the ruins of old roads, torn from their beds of earth, heaved in great piles to the sides in gorges deep and rocky. The bodies of animals of every description lay rotting beneath the merciless sun. The air was wet and dank; a man could move no more than two or three feet before he was soaked to the skin.

The swamps seethed with unseen life; at night the men were wary and silent. More than once there were reports that a soldier had lain down to sleep and had disappeared by morning. At last, the scouts reported word of Amanander's position. "Less than two days march, Lord Prince," they said, twisting their hands nervously. "There's something—something bad about that place."

Roderic scanned their faces and did not press. Instead, he surveyed the ruins of the ancient city which lay around them.

"And that's not all. We can go no further, Lord

Prince." The scout wiped the sweat off his face with a grimy linen square. It left a smudge across his forehead. "The river south of here is fouled; this is the last fresh water supply."

Roderic nodded. "Then we have our answer." He pointed to a jagged spur that rose out of the swamp, the highest ground for miles. One side rose nearly a hundred feet, the sheer rock raw and striated. The other side sloped gently to the river's edge. "There. If the engineers say that ground's stable, we'll move up there."

The men were set to the task of constructing the fortifications. Near the top of the crest of the rise, the remains of a high tower rose three stories in the air. Once the engineers determined that the foundations were stable, Roderic gave orders to make that the center of command.

As the days passed, he watched the endless digging and hauling, and partly out of restlessness, took a turn riding out with the patrols. Less than six hours from the keep, he found a sloping hill which rolled down onto level ground. He turned to look at Deirdre. "What do you think?"

She scanned the area with a practiced eye, taking in the natural contours of the land. "Looks like a good place for a battle to me, Lord Prince. This slope gives us some advantage—those trees will make good cover for our men."

"I say we make our move, Deirdre."

She grinned, even as the sweat rolled down her face and trickled down the collar of her opened shirt. "Thought you'd never say so, Prince. Me and the boys, we're itching to get home."

Chapter Thirty-one

The scouts reported movement in the swamps as Roderic ordered the army into position on the battlefield he had selected. From the top of the ridge, he stared out over the plain, fancying that beneath the moon he could see the gray, ghostly forms of those men whose eyes had haunted his dreams for so long. The full moon stared like the flat eye of some uncaring god, casting a cold light over that land of nightmares. In the distance, over the trees, he saw a dark smudge on the horizon which was Amanander's keep.

"What are those things we fight?" Evan Lewis spoke quietly behind him. Lewis had spent a lot of time listening to the scouts, as well as the survivors from the Dlas expedition. He, too, had ridden out with the patrols, and he had seen firsthand what the enemy looked like.

"Only bodies, without mind or will or spirit." The Kahn's voice sounded harsh in the soft night air. "They do their lord's bidding; 'tis all they exist for."

A flash of orange lightning split the night sky and Roderic was reminded suddenly of the battle at Minnis. The flames of the campfires of the foot soldiers in their trenches twinkled, like fallen stars.

Roderic squared his shoulders. "Come, gentlemen. I want to review our strategy for tomorrow."

Miles nodded. "I shall summon the captains of the regiments to join us."

"And my men, Prince," said the Kahn.

Lewis followed Miles and the Kahn down the hill. Roderic watched them leave and turned to Deirdre. Her face was blank, her eyes unreadable in the dark. "You know, Roderic, despite our numbers, we face long odds tomorrow?"

"Yes," he answered softly. "I know."

"If one man out of a hundred still lives by this time tomorrow, you may count yourself a wise general. Our men, these armies, they are nothing—he uses mindless minions against them. The only life which counts tomorrow is yours. Yours is the only life he wants."

"What about Annandale?"

"I do not mean that others are unimportant. But if you fall, all will be lost."

He stared at the southern horizon. "You've been with me all through this, Deirdre. No man could ask for a more loyal ally, a more faithful friend. I'll never forget what you've done."

She shrugged, and for a moment, her face softened and she looked almost girlish. "Then don't betray my trust, Prince."

"How can you still call me that? You know the truth—why do you call me Prince even when we are alone?"

She sighed and shook her head. "A Prince isn't something you're born. A Prince is something you live. There are men among my people who are born in places not much better than byres and they are Princes. For to be a Prince means you know how to show other men how to live, and how to die."

Her voice was not much more than a husky whisper.

"And you think I am a Prince? After all you know about me?"

"I know you are, Lord Prince. The question is—do you? A man may go crazy from time to time. 'Tis how he acts afterwards that matters. You win tomorrow, you will be King. Can you do that, Roderic? Can you show other men how to live, and how to die?"

The question was nearly unanswerable. "Deirdre, do you think she's still alive?"

"Aye." Deirdre nodded. "She's stronger than anyone I have ever met—though it worries me how he got to her. I don't understand that part at all. I wish your father had been able to tell us more."

"Yes," Roderic agreed. "If I lose her, Deirdre, I don't know what I will do."

She looked at him sharply. "You'll go on, that's what you'll do. You'll raise your son in her memory, and you'll make this land a better place. If you choose to be King."

"Choose to be King?"

"Aye. Didn't that ever occur to you? You could lay all this down and walk away. You've been so worried that the people might not want you, you've forgotten that you, too, have a choice. The choice has always been yours, Roderic. You could have gone a long time ago."

"But—"

"But you didn't. That's what I meant when I said you

were a Prince." She gave him a crooked grin and pushed her sleeves further up her tanned forearms. "Come. The captains await."

"Deirdre—" His words stopped her as she turned on her heel. "I haven't forgotten our bargain."

"No, Prince. And neither have I." She winked at him over her shoulder and strode away, whistling.

Like the breaking of an enormous wave, the battle began as a red sun rose over the plain. As Roderic eased into the saddle, the first of the scouts from the front lines galloped up to him. "Lord Prince."

Roderic wrapped the reins in one hand. "Tell Lewis to hold his men in reserve on our left flank. Are the Harleys ready to ride?" he asked, although he knew the answer.

"Yes, Lord Prince. The Kahn is leading his men in the first assault on the other side of the ridge."

"Good." Roderic nodded. He spurred the horse on and galloped down the ridge. He caught Deirdre's eye. "Well?" he asked as he reined in beside her.

"Well, Lord Prince?"

He could see the gleam of battle in her eyes. Her stallion danced beneath her, and the wind whipped at her battle-plaid. "Ready to win the battle?"

"Ready to win the war," she returned. "Lead on."

He raised his hand and shouted the order to advance.

The battle raged as the sun ascended, and the heavy heat was like molten lead poured from the sky onto the backs of the men. In the middle of the morning, another messenger, holding a bloody side, lurched up the rise. "Lord Prince," he gasped, "their first line has broken, and the second is breaking down—the road is open. It looks as though they're retreating."

Roderic glanced at Deirdre. "Follow with caution. I don't trust Amanander."

Like a flood, the troops swept over the plain, down the wide road bed, following the black-garbed soldiers to the very base of Amanander's fortress. On another hill overlooking the fortress, Roderic gave the orders to halt. "We'll make camp here for the night," he said. "Make sure the men who cannot fight are sent back. We don't want the wounded in our way tomorrow." He gazed grimly at the wooden walls rising before them. "Nothing will get in our way tomorrow." With a feeling of satisfaction, he went to rest.

It was close to dawn when something roused him. He came awake with a start, reached for his sword, and sat up. Something niggled at the back of his awareness, some detail he seemed to have forgotten or overlooked. The element of surprise had worked well to their advantage; Phineas had been correct with his assessment of Amanander's troops. Although they fought with deadly precision, the greater numbers easily overwhelmed them, especially when coupled with surprise or unexpected counter-maneuvers. But hadn't it been almost too easy?

He rose and paced, wishing Brand or Phineas or even old Garrick was there. Or even Vere, for that matter. A dark figure approached. Evan Lewis nodded a greeting. "Restless?"

Roderic nodded. "Hard not to be, I suppose." The gray light intensified. Before Evan could reply, a high-pitched scream rose over the camp. Roderic jerked his head in the direction of the sound. From his vantage point on the higher ground, he could see the whole camp, the sleeping forms of the soldiers spread out, the few who stirred at that early hour.

"By the One," gasped Evan.

Roderic squinted. Along the perimeter of the camp, a long line of dark figures were shambling into position. What light there was gleamed on the edges of their weapons, and even in the dim twilit dawn, he could see that some wore the uniforms of the King's Guard.

"What in the name—" Evan breathed.

The missing information clicked into place. "The dead," murmured Roderic. "The dead walk in his service."

Without another moment's hesitation, he was off, shouting for his sword, calling to the men. They bolted awake, reaching for weapons, gathering in tight formation, as the dead advanced upon some unseen signal. Deirdre grasped his arm.

"We won't win this way," she hissed between clenched teeth. All around them the air was thick with bodies, the weapons flashing in the growing light. "Our men cannot hold up under the onslaught—there're too many—too many who do not die."

He wiped the back of his sleeve across his forehead. "What are you suggesting?"

She gestured with her sword. "We've got to get in there—into the garrison. Amanander is the key to this. We're just food for him out here."

Roderic wrapped the reins of his horse more tightly

around his hand. "Think we can get through?"

Deirdre stood in her stirrups. "Darmot—Donner—to me!" She looked back at him with a grin. "Or die trying, Lord Prince." She pointed with her sword. "The walls aren't guarded. He's not balanced his offense. If we can just drive a wedge through, enough to get us in the gates, we can let the ranks close behind us. I have a feeling all it's going to take is one stroke of a broadsword through Amanander's neck."

A spear, thrown across some great distance, landed in the chest of a soldier near Roderic. His stallion reared beneath him and he brought the animal under control. "All right, Deirdre," he said as her men formed a tight group around them both, "let's go."

The tide of soldiers which swept across the plain was a like a river at spring thaw. Roderic dug his spurs into his horse's sides, and the animal leapt forward, into the thick of the melee. The enemy bore their weapons in rotting hands. He hacked on either side, right and left, with an eerie, steady rhythm. The dead made no noise as they fell, and all the world seemed to filter down into that one horrible time and place, where the dull thunk of his blade biting bone and the soft slump of the dead falling to the ground, the weird whisper of their strides surging inexorably forward were the only sounds that came to his ears. Beneath his horse's hooves, the ground cracked in long fissures, and steam seeped in a low hiss.

The horse reared and screamed, and Roderic wrapped the reins around his hand again, desperate to maintain control. Clouds roiled in the sky, blotting out the sun, and the sky grew green and purple with a weird, unnatural light. Lightning forked beneath the clouds, arcing in jagged spikes. It struck the earth, lashing the ground with tongues of blue-white flame.

Pressing on and on, Deirdre's soldiers forced an ever widening wedge, which closed behind them as they moved forward. It was then Roderic realized the advantage they had: the dead didn't turn and follow. Amanander couldn't think of every contingency at once.

Finally they rode through the open gates of the garrison. Deirdre's face and arms were slick with blood, and all the Islanders were covered in gore. Roderic wiped his blade against his thigh. Their horses trotted into the wide inner courtyard. Nothing moved.

The silence which greeted them was even eerier than that on the battlefield. Slowly Deirdre urged her horse to the very steps of the keep. She tossed her reins to Donner and dismounted.

Roderic handed his horse over to another soldier. He gestured in the direction of the keep and she nodded. She looked back and put her finger to her lips. Donner saluted.

With drawn swords, they crept inside. Silence hung thick as the dust on the furniture. How odd, thought Roderic. Amanander had always been so fastidious. Long wooden benches were strewn haphazardly on the floor. Deirdre gestured to a flight of steps. The floorboards creaked beneath their feet, and halfway up they heard a gasping sob.

"No!"

Roderic froze. "That's Annandale."

He took the rest of the steps two at a time, Deirdre

hard at his heels. Down the long corridor, he followed the sound of Annandale's sobs. He cursed beneath his breath, and without warning, the earth shifted beneath their feet with a sound like lightning striking wood.

The floor lurched underneath him. Roderic staggered, fell against Deirdre, and recovered. Annandale screamed.

Together, they ran down the rest of the hallway and burst through the last door. On a narrow pile of blankets, Alexander lay prone—claw-like hands gripping at his covers, staring with terror-wide eyes.

Annandale crouched by his side. She looked up in disbelief as Roderic and Deirdre burst into the room. "Roderic, stay back," she cried.

"Come here," he shouted.

At the foot of the bed, Amanander stood, his hand on Vere's throat.

"Let him go, Aman," Roderic said, sidling toward Annandale. "Let him go. I'm the one you want. Let Vere go."

"In turn, Roderic." His voice was like the purr a lycat made as its fangs found its prey.

"You can kill him," put in Deirdre as she moved to the edge of the room, "but you won't get away with it."

Amanander turned his head. "Such a brave little girl." With a swift motion, he threw Vere into her. He bent down, reached for Alexander, and Roderic shouted, "Annandale, get away from him."

But Annandale threw herself on Alexander's chest and wrapped her arms around him.

Amanander's face contorted, and any resemblance he had to a human being melted away like hot wax under a flame. "You will not defy me!" His voice echoed like thunder in a summer night.

Alexander found the strength to cling to her like a drowning man to a rope.

Amanander grabbed Alexander's legs. "Get away from them, Annandale," Roderic cried.

Amanander threw him a triumphant smile. "Oh yes, little changeling Prince. Save your bride. Be a hero." The air thickened, as though the oppressive breath of some hideous beast was exhaled. The shadows flowed and swirled like black water, and the floor gave a warning tremor.

Annandale looked up, over her shoulder. Her face was wet with tears. "Beloved, this is the only way."

Where Annandale clutched Alexander, the healing light glimmered, a mere flicker at first, gradually intensifying, changing from a soft shimmer of gossamer flame into a beacon of a light, radiant and clear. Roderic stared, unable to look away, as it grew brighter, until he was forced to turn his head and cover his face with his hands or be blinded by its brilliance. As though a thousand suns had come to earth, the light shone, encompassing them all, dispersing the darkness, chasing the shadows from every corner, and though his eyes were shut against it, he felt its terrible, glowing blaze. The tower shook, bucking like a beast in its death throes, and the land rocked on its foundations. He heard the roar and the rushing of a mighty wind. Horses screamed, and the cries of the soldiers outside were like children lost in nightmares.

He fell to his knees, blindly groping for some steady anchor, and the floor collapsed beneath his hands. They crashed in a heap of splintered wood to the ground below. The light faded, and the wind died. The land heaved once more and was still. On knees that shook, he struggled through the debris to his feet. Annandale and Alexander lay entangled a few feet away. He picked his way through the wreckage and gently lifted her. She opened her eyes. "Roderic." Her skin was red and peeling, blood oozed from her mouth. "My love."

Roderic cradled her in his arms, rocking her as though she were a baby. "What have we done to you?" He smoothed the dark curls back from her blistered face.

Alexander shook himself free from the ruins. His hair was like the new-fallen snow: white, with not one strand of gray. He walked with firm steps to kneel by Roderic's side. "She saved us all. If Amanander had taken me, all would have been lost. She's broken him, once and for-ever."

"My love—" Her voice was labored, and in her throat Roderic heard a chilling rattle. "Bury me beneath the tree where the empaths lie. Don't put me in cold stone—give me warm wood in the living land."

"Use me, beloved, use me, like when Rhodri was born. Take me, take my strength—"

"Too late. Tell the children—love them always. And Deirdre—tell her—"

"I'm here, lady." Deirdre spoke over his shoulder, splinters in her hair.

Annandale gasped and writhed a little in his embrace. "Love is worth all costs. All costs—"

Roderic soothed her hair off her face. "All right, all right. My love—"

"Roderic." Her palm found his cheek. "Tell—" In a long sigh she went limp against his chest. He made a little sound of protest and tightened his hold.

Alexander touched his shoulder. Roderic looked up. From the ruins of the tower, a dark figure rose to its feet. Amanander stepped across the wreckage, sword in hand. Deirdre's men, who had crept closer, drew back as he advanced. His face was a cratered ruin. Black, burnt flesh clung to his cheeks. One eye was gone, a jellied mass which oozed down his face. His skull was red and blistered, covered in tufts of scorched hair.

Roderic placed Annandale gently in Alexander's outstretched arms and fumbled in the ruins for the King's broadsword. The hilt was warm and smooth in the palm of his hand. They faced each other silently, and the only sound was the hollow clang of the metal as their blades rang together.

They circled, wary. Amanander lunged with a fierce intensity, picking a moment when Roderic kicked a piece of wood out of his way.

Roderic parried and riposted, faster than he ever had before. Amanander blocked the attack and lunged again. Roderic could hear the other men breathing around him, Deirdre helping Vere out of the ruins, all eyes fixed. Roderic met Amanander's blade and, sliding the point along his own, flicked his arm.

Amanander did not react to the wound. With a sure, graceful move, the edge of his sword whipped over Roderic's in a feint, then under, and dealt Roderic a glancing blow to the chest. Roderic did not take his eyes off his opponent, despite the sound burst of pain.

He fell back and felt the blood begin to seep through his tunic.

Amanander attacked again, sword swinging in a high wicked arc, and Roderic needed the strength of both arms to block the blow. Without pausing, he swung again and again and again, and Roderic fell back, circling as the strokes fell like punishing rain. "Now you have no woman's skirts to hide behind," His voice gurgled in his throat. "Put the sword down, Roderic. It never belonged to your father—you have no right to wield it."

Roderic faltered. Amanander's attacks were insistent, methodical, and his arms and chest ached.

"Meriga is mine, Roderic. I am the heir. I am the blood son of Abelard Ridenau."

Roderic stumbled backward, made a halfhearted lunge toward him, and Amanander turned his blade and wounded him across the shoulder.

He laughed. "Surrender now and I'll kill you quickly. I'll give you a cleaner death than you deserve. You—the get of a stablehand's son. You're no prince."

Out of his peripheral vision, Roderic saw Annandale's head loll lifelessly against Alexander's shoulder, her eyes, so like the King's, shut forever. And in that moment he remembered Rhodri, whose were like both hers and Abelard's, the child who was his son.

Some rage, some fury born of anguish, ignited in him, and Roderic threw himself at Amanander like an animal defending its lair and its young with its last strength. Sparks flew as he dealt Amanander a series of blows so quickly, Roderic saw his shoulders shudder at the force. "You're right, Amanander." Roderic spat the words as his blade connected with his neck. "I'm not a prince. I'm the King." With one last, mighty stroke, Amanander's head rolled off his shoulders to lie in the dust.

Roderic looked up to see Deirdre standing over Alexander, Vere leaning against two of her men. The courtyard was full of soldiers, all standing silent and still.

Roderic straightened, though his chest still heaved with his final effort and the sweat ran down his face like tears. Miles and Evan were there, too, the officers and the soldiers all pressing close. Had they heard Amanander's words? he wondered wearily.

He stared them in the eyes, thinking that he might simply give the sword to Alexander and be done with this burden which had been his for so long, rightfully or not. He drew a deep breath and took a single step forward.

And then, as one man, Miles and Evan and Deirdre and even Vere fell to their knees and, with Alexander, began to recite the ancient words of the Pledge of Allegiance, swearing themselves into his service, until death. One by one, the other men followed suit, captains, foot soldiers, archers, horseman, the sons of Senadors, until all that company knelt before him in the dust, and he alone remained standing.

The undead horde fell with Amanander. Reginald and Harland were found among the enemy host, corpses which clung even in death to the hilts of broken swords. But Roderic was mourning his lady; there was no victory for him.

Chapter Thirty-two

$\mathscr{T}$hey placed Annandale in a rough-hewn coffin, scarcely worthy of her. The man who made it had tears in his eyes and on his face, so Roderic smiled and thanked him for her sake. They wrapped her body in clean, white linen. The only ornament she had worn had been the sapphire ring Roderic had placed on her finger such a short time ago. The women brought it to him. He placed it in the coffin with her.

The messengers had been sent on ahead, with word to prepare the King's body, and the people lined the roads. Some wept, some threw evergreen branches in their path, some only stared.

On the border of Missiluse, Roderic turned toward Arkan. He would see her buried as she had requested, beneath the tree where the empaths were buried. Vere rode beside him, silent, pale; Alexander so fully restored to health he looked ten years younger.

Roderic watched numbly as they dug the grave and placed Annandale's coffin in it. A few of the soldiers offered to stay and guard the grave. He accepted their gift with a shrug.

News reached him as he neared Ithan of the great

changes which had been wrought upon the land. On the day of that last battle, a great earthshake had once more rocked the length of Meriga. What had been blocked was opened, and a mighty river had roared out of the southern mountains of the Northern Plains all the way to Missiluse. The Misspy Gorge was again the Misspy River.

At the gates of Ithan, the flags flew at half staff, and the towers were draped in black. The street was lined with silent people who watched Roderic ride with shoulders straight and back upright. The burden of his loss weighed like lead upon his heart.

At the steps of the keep, he dismounted and walked up to where the household waited. Norah stood in the center, the welcome cup in her hand, steaming with spices. She raised her face to his, and in her eyes, he saw only the greatest of sorrow. He glanced past her to Tavia's tear-stained face.

Then a small figure detached itself from the haven of Tavia's skirts and launched itself into his arms. "Dada!" Melisande cried.

He hugged her tightly, unable to speak, as the little arms wound themselves fiercely around his neck. She gave him a loud smack of a kiss on one cheek. "Pooh! Dada, you smell like a horse."

Roderic smiled through the haze of tears and patted her back. He shifted her weight to one arm and looked back at Tavia.

Norah offered the cup once more, and as he took it, she sank in a deep curtsy. "Welcome to Ithan." She hesitated the fraction of an instant and then looked him full in the eyes. "Lord King."

He drank deeply of the hot wine and passed it on to Vere. "Thank you. Tavia, I would see my son."

"He's well, Roderic. He's in the nursery."

"I'll take you there, Dada." Melisande wriggled in his arms. "Come on."

As Roderic stepped past the women, he came to Phineas' litter. He looked old, older than he had ever seemed. His shoulders were stooped, and the lines in his face were deep crevices. "Lord King." He bowed his head.

"I'm glad to see you, Phineas."

"And I, you, Lord King." He raised his head, and Roderic was so startled he nearly dropped Melisande. Phineas' eyes were clear, as clear as his, the deep rings of scar tissue gone.

"Phineas?"

"We'll talk about it later, Lord King."

He clapped one hand on the old man's shoulder and went on. As he passed, the household bowed and curtsied, like willows bending before a great wind. Melisande led him to the nursery, where Rhodri slept, uncaring, in his cradle.

"I must talk to you, Meli," Roderic said when he finally put her down. "About Nanny."

She clasped her small hands in front of her. "Oh, yes, Dada. I know you're very sad."

"Did Tavvy tell you that? That I'd be sad?"

"No. Not Tavvy. Nanny did. She said you'd be very sad for a while, and that I would be sad, too, because she would not be with us for a while, but that—"

"Wait, Meli. What do you mean, Nanny told you?"

"She told me last night, when she came to say good-bye."

"Last night? Meli, sweet, that's not possible."

"She said you'd say that. But that's all right, Dada."

"What else did she say?"

"She said she loved me very much, and that I would grow up to be very beautiful . . . Dada, do you think that's right? Am I going to be very beautiful?"

"You're very beautiful now, little one. What else did Nanny tell you?"

"She said you'd be sad, and that we must be very kind to each other and take good care of Rhodri, because he was to grow up to be King someday after you went to her."

"Melisande." Roderic knelt in front of her, looking in her deep gray eyes. "Nanny can't be with us anymore. It isn't possible to talk to her—when you are older, I'll take you to see the place where she is."

"She said you wouldn't listen. She isn't under that tree. She's with us. She said so, and I believe her." Tears of frustration were forming in the wide eyes, and he saw a miniature version of his own frown spread across the little face. "Besides, last night wasn't the only time I saw her."

"When else did you see her?"

Melisande's frown grew deeper. "It was the day of the big earthshake. The sky was dark, and the wind blew so hard, I thought it would blow us all away. And then we saw a great flash of lightning, and then came the earth-shake, and Tavvy fell down the steps and landed in the hall."

"Tavvy was hurt?"

"Yes, and I thought she must be very hurt, because her neck was twisted wrong, and the next thing, I saw Nanny standing over her, and she touched her, and looked at me, and went 'Sshh,' you know, like I wasn't supposed to tell, and Tavvy's neck was straight, and she sat up and asked what happened and was I all right. And I said I was, but I didn't say anything about Nanny."

Roderic picked Melisande up again and looked down at the sleeping baby. Soft, dark curls covered his head. "Come, sweet, we don't want to wake your brother."

"Dada, you do believe me, don't you?"

"I want to believe you, sweet. I hope someday I can."

He went, then, to his rooms, the ones which he had shared with her. He could not look at the bed. The coverlet drawn over the pillows reminded him of the sheet drawn over the face of the dead. He leaned against the hearth, and his eyes fell on the basket which contained her needlework. He pulled a silk square from the top, shook it out, touching the careful stitches her hands had wrought. It was a design of the shield of the Ridenaus, mostly unfinished, except for the lettering at the bottom. "Faith shall finish what hope begins." The "s" was missing. He held the square to his face, and the silk reminded him of the touch of her hand. And finally, for the first time, he wept.

Epilogue

❧

Six months he mourned his lady, and one year they mourned the King. How can I tell you of his grief? I have never heard the like before. He could not even conjure her in dreams. But slowly the land healed, and his children grew, and life became once more the bits and pieces of ordinary things in an ordinary time.

He remembered the bargain he had with me, but he couldn't bear the thought. It rubbed against the memory of his love like a burr on a wound. But as the anniversary day of her death drew closer, he decided to ride down into Arkan and visit her grave, taking only a few of his most trusted guards with him.

They traveled quickly, easily, and he told me how much the land had changed in the course of that one year. With the elimination of most of the Harleyriders, Arkan was changing from a wasteland into a wide plain where crops could once more be cultivated.

At last, they reached the little town which had sprung up around the tree. He found the beginnings of farms, fields newly under cultivation, and stands selling what looked like jewelry made from pearls. "Where did they get all the pearls?" he wondered as they guided their horses to the one inn, which was so small it seemed hardly worthy of the name.

But the innkeeper was so overwhelmed by his appearance, babbled greetings and bowed so earnestly, Roderic was amused. He asked him, when they were seated in the common room with food and drink, where the people were getting all the pearls.

"They grow, Lord King."

"Grow? Where do pearls grow here?" The men listened and guffawed amongst themselves.

A hurt look spread over the innkeeper's honest face. "It's the flowers, Lord King."

"What flowers?"

"They grow, Lord King, near the grave of your lady. Some people call them Annandale's roses, but they aren't roses, not really. But they are very pretty, I'll say that."

"But where are the pearls?"

"Inside, Lord King. They aren't really pearls, I guess, though they look as good as any I've ever heard about. It's the seeds, you know, the seeds of the flowers. In every flower, there're always exactly nine."

Roderic drained his mug and rose. "I think I'll go see this marvel for myself."

The captain of the guards stood up. "Shall we accompany you, Lord King?"

"No. No, I want to go alone."

He bowed. "As you say, Lord King."

And so, he told me, he rode out past the winding streets of the village to find if what the innkeeper said was true. On the grassy knoll beneath the spreading branches of the tree, where they had buried Annandale, was a thick carpet of leaves, dark green with a fine tracing of veins like a delicate silver overlay. No flowers bloomed, but he fancied something of their scent clung, sweet, but not cloying, in the chilly air.

He sat down upon the ground beside her grave and leaned against the great trunk of the tree. He was tired from the journey. He looked at the clear blue sky through the branches. It was very still.

A wave of longing came over him, then, and he bent his head while slow tears dripped through his fingers. He says he slept then, but I am not so sure.

For suddenly, she stood before him, fairer than ever, he said, smiling down with eyes like the summer sea under a cloudless sky. About her was an incandescent quality, as though a brilliant light shone through her, from within. Her garments were so pure and white they almost looked blue. "Annandale!" He bolted upright against the trunk.

"My dearest love." She settled next to him on the ground and picked up his hand, and her flesh seemed as firm and substantial as his own.

"Are you real?"

"Those who are part of the Pattern are the realest of all."

"I've missed you so much." He wrapped his arms around her and drew her against his chest. She touched his cheek in that old, familiar way, and he pressed a kiss into her palm. "Will you come back with me?"

She shook her head sadly. "I have no place here, now."

"Annandale, how can I bear it without you?"

She smiled. "We'll be together again. Your task is just beginning. There are many who need you."

"I miss you."

"We will never be apart." She took his hands in hers, and his sorrow ebbed at her touch.

"Rhodri is so like you—"

She took his face in her hands and kissed his lips. "You need a woman worthy to sit by your side," she said.

"There is no one who can take your place."

"There is one who loves you with her life. Go to her, Roderic, and give her the son she longs for."

"How can I let anyone take your place? I wear the crown of Meriga, but it is nothing to me without you. What is any of this for, if I cannot have you with me?"

"Do you remember the words on the shield of the Ridenaus?"

"Faith? Hope? What of our love?" Tears ran down his face.

"Oh, my one beloved. Remember this: hope begins, faith finishes, but it is love that sustains."

"I cannot go on without you."

He said, then, that she cupped his wet face in her hands and kissed away his tears. Her mouth on his was warm and real, nothing like the stuff of dreams. "I shall be with you always, until Time itself has ended."

"Will I ever see you again?"

"I await you when your part in the Pattern is complete."

He woke from the dream clutching a crushed flower. In the palm of his hand were nine perfect pearls.

And in the morning, when the first rays of the rising sun pinkened the sky and the last clouds of night gathered in purple masses on the horizon, they saddled, and mounted, and rode at last, to me.

THE MISBEGOTTEN KING is Anne Kelleher Bush's third novel, the sequel to *Daughter of Prophecy* and *Children of Enchantment*. She is now writing a new novel to be published by Warner Aspect in early 1998. Anne Bush holds a degree in medieval studies from Johns Hopkins University, and lives with her children in Farmington, Connecticut.